Pythagorean Crimes

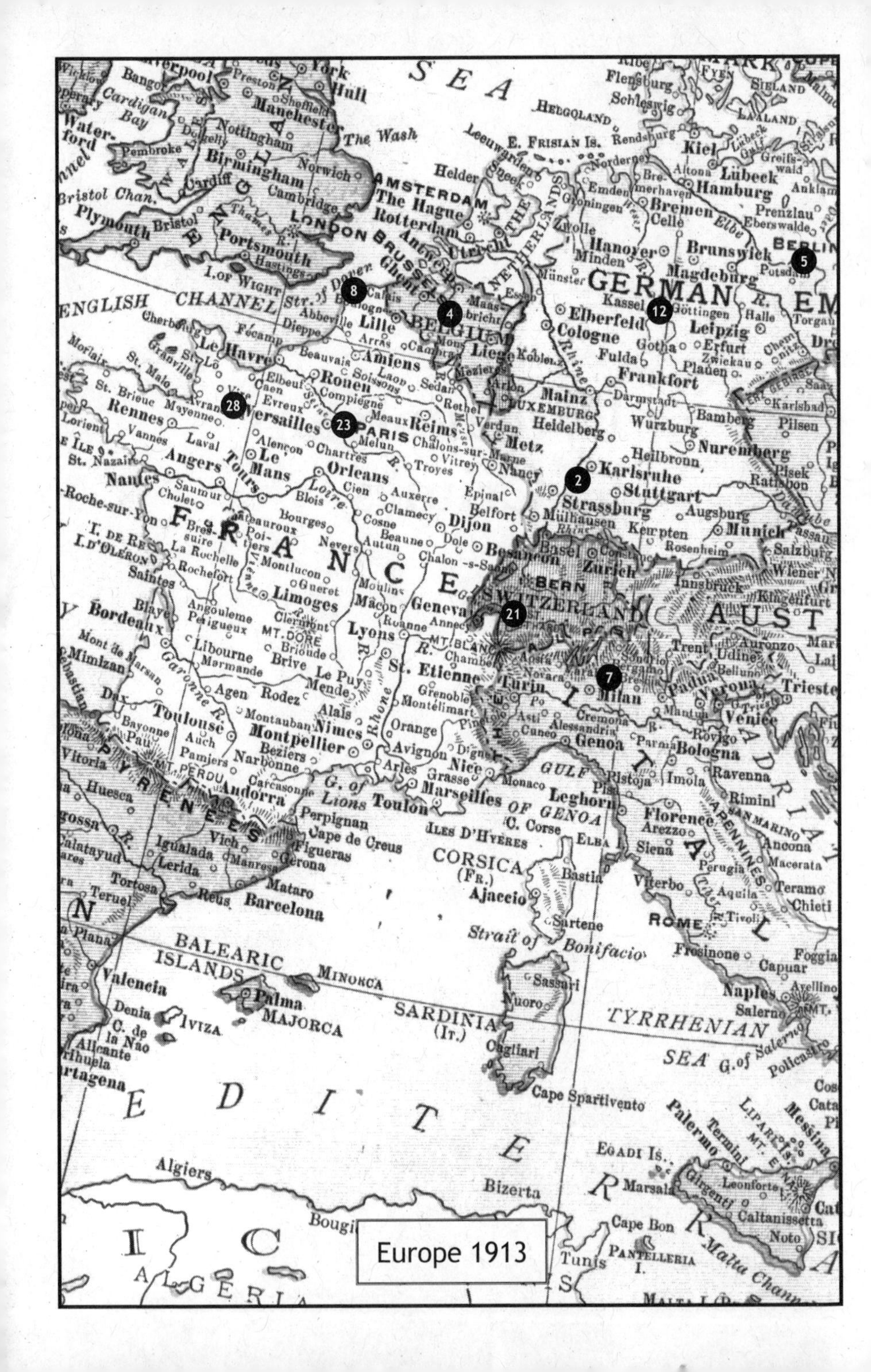
SEA
Hull
Manchester
Nottingham
Birmingham
Cardigan Bay
Pembroke
Bristol Chan.
Plymouth
Bristol
Portsmouth
LONDON
Cambridge
Norwich
The Wash
I. OF WIGHT
ENGLISH CHANNEL
Str. of Dover
Calais
HELGOLAND
E. FRISIAN IS.
AMSTERDAM
The Hague
Rotterdam
Utrecht
Antwerp
BRUSSELS
Ghent
Lille
Abbeville
Dieppe
Amiens
Arras
BELGIUM
Liege
Cherbourg
Le Havre
Fécamp
Rouen
Beauvais
Soissons
Laon
Sedan
Compiegne
Reims
Rethel
Verdun
Metz
Nancy
Caen
Evreux
Versailles
PARIS
Meaux
Melun
Chalons-sur-Marne
Troyes
Chartres
Alençon
Le Mans
Laval
Rennes
St. Brieuc
St. Malo
Vannes
Lorient
St. Nazaire
Nantes
Angers
Tours
Saumur
Orleans
Blois
Bourges
FRANCE
Nevers
Auxerre
Dijon
Besançon
Belfort
Epinal
Poitiers
La Rochelle
Rochefort
Saintes
Angoulême
Limoges
Montluçon
Gueret
Moulins
Mâcon
Clermont
Lyons
Geneva
Annecy
MT. BLANC
Bordeaux
Blaye
Libourne
Marmande
Agen
Rodez
Brive
Le Puy
St. Etienne
Grenoble
Montelimart
Mende
Alais
Nimes
Orange
Avignon
Arles
Montpellier
Beziers
Narbonne
Carcassonne
Toulouse
Montauban
Auch
Pau
Bayonne
Dax
Perpignan
Toulon
Marseilles
Nice
Grasse
Monaco
G. of Lions
PYRENEES
Andorra
ILES D'HYERES
CORSICA (FR.)
Ajaccio
Bastia
Sartene
Strait of Bonifacio
Flensburg
Schleswig
Kiel
Lübeck
Hamburg
Altona
Bremen
Emden
Groningen
Zwolle
Hanover
Minden
Münster
Celle
Brunswick
Magdeburg
BERLIN
Potsdam
GERMAN EM
Kassel
Göttingen
Halle
Elberfeld
Cologne
Leipzig
Gotha
Erfurt
Fulda
Frankfort
Mainz
Darmstadt
LUXEMBURG
Heidelberg
Wurzburg
Bamberg
Nuremberg
Heilbronn
Karlsruhe
Stuttgart
Strassburg
Mülhausen
Augsburg
Munich
Kempten
Rosenheim
Salzburg
Innsbruck
Pilsen
Basel
Zurich
BERN
SWITZERLAND
AUST
Turin
Novara
Milan
Bergamo
Brescia
Verona
Padua
Venice
Trieste
Udine
Belluno
Trent
Mantua
Cremona
Alessandria
Asti
Cuneo
Genoa
Parma
Bologna
Rovigo
Ravenna
Rimini
GULF OF GENOA
Leghorn
Pisa
Pistoja
Imola
Florence
Arezzo
Siena
ELBA
C. Corse
APENNINES
SAN MARINO
Ancona
Macerata
Perugia
Teramo
Aquila
Chieti
Viterbo
ROME
Tivoli
Frosinone
Foggia
Capua
Naples
Salerno
G. of Salerno
Policastro
TYRRHENIAN SEA
Sassari
Nuoro
SARDINIA (IT.)
Cagliari
Cape Spartivento
LIPARI IS.
Messina
Palermo
Termini
EGADI IS.
Marsala
Girgenti
Leonforte
Caltanissetta
Noto
Malta Channel
PANTELLERIA I.
Cape Bon
Tunis
Bizerta
Algiers
Bougie
ALGERIA
MEDITERRANEAN
Huesca
Vitoria
Lerida
Igualada
Vich
Manresa
Gerona
Figueras
Mataro
Barcelona
Reus
Tortosa
Teruel
Calatayud
Valencia
Denia
C. de la Nao
Alicante
Orihuela
Cartagena
BALEARIC ISLANDS
MINORCA
Palma
MAJORCA
IVIZA
2
4
5
7
8
12
21
23
28
Europe 1913

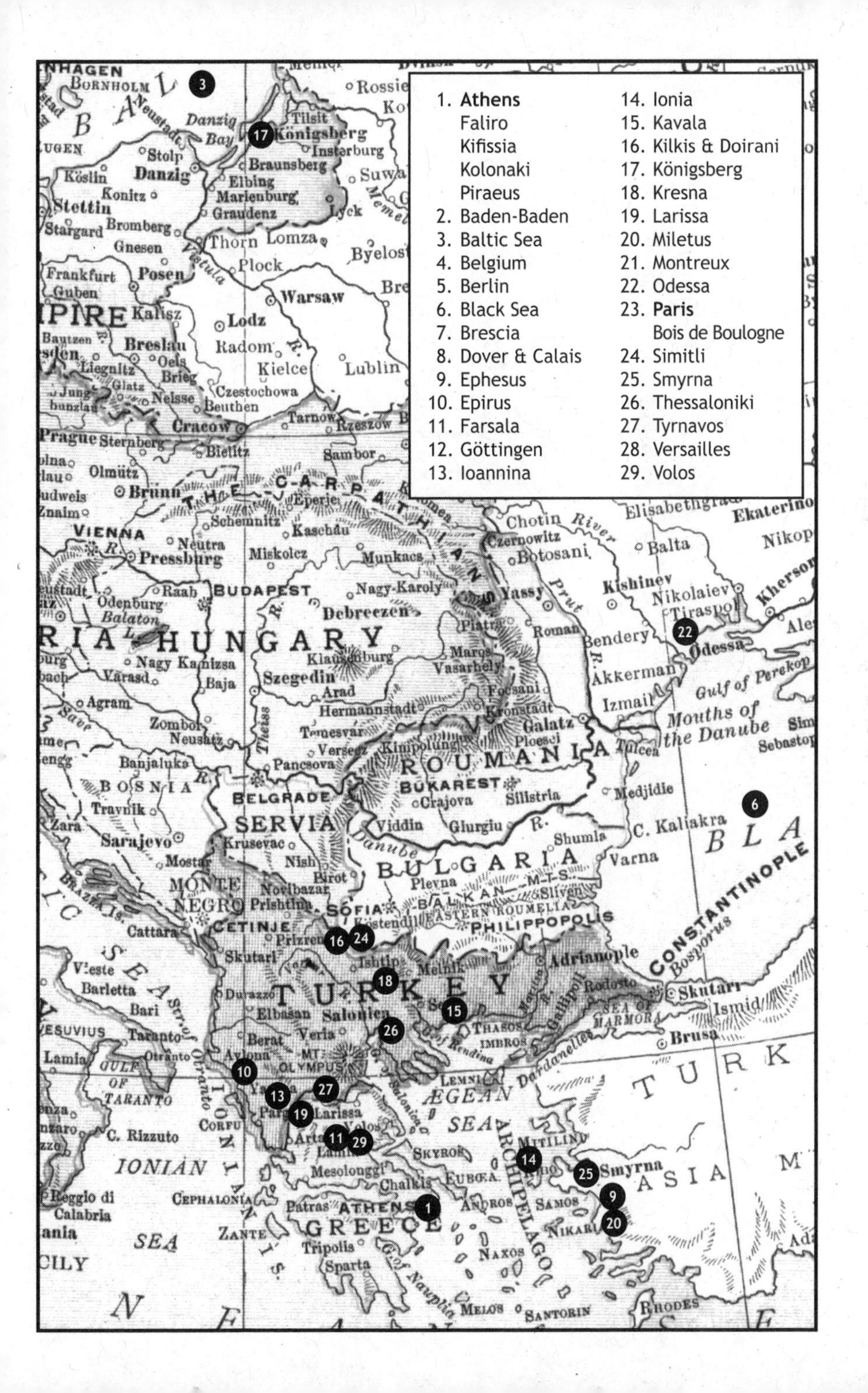

1. Athens
Faliro
Kifissia
Kolonaki
Piraeus
2. Baden-Baden
3. Baltic Sea
4. Belgium
5. Berlin
6. Black Sea
7. Brescia
8. Dover & Calais
9. Ephesus
10. Epirus
11. Farsala
12. Göttingen
13. Ioannina
14. Ionia
15. Kavala
16. Kilkis & Doirani
17. Königsberg
18. Kresna
19. Larissa
20. Miletus
21. Montreux
22. Odessa
23. Paris
Bois de Boulogne
24. Simitli
25. Smyrna
26. Thessaloniki
27. Tyrnavos
28. Versailles
29. Volos
Königsberg
Danzig
Warsaw
Posen
Lodz
Breslau
Cracow
Budapest
Vienna
Pressburg
Hungary
Roumania
Bukarest
Belgrade
Servia
Bulgaria
Sofia
Philippopolis
Adrianople
Constantinople
Turkey
Salonica
Smyrna
Athens
Greece
Odessa
Mouths of the Danube
Ægean Sea
Archipelago

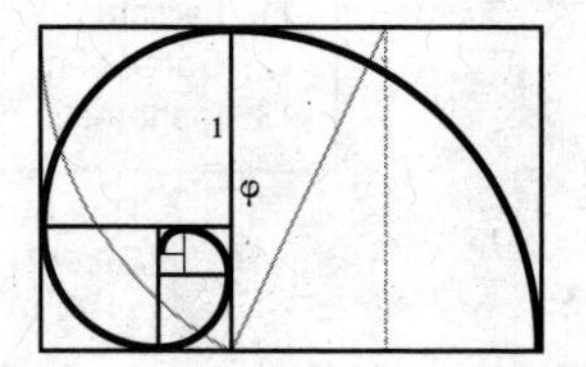
1
φ

Pythagorean Crimes

Tefcros Michaelides

PARMENIDES
FICTION

Las Vegas • Zurich • Athens

PARMENIDES FICTION™
Las Vegas | Athens | Zurich

Translated from the Greek by Lena Cavanagh
Edited by Jennifer Morgan

ISBN hard cover: 978-1-930972-26-1
ISBN soft cover: 978-1-930972-27-8

Library of Congress Cataloging-in-Publication Data
Michaelides, Teukros, 1954-
[Pythagoreia enklemata. English]
Pythagorean crimes / Tefcros Michaelides ;
translated from the Greek by Lena Cavanagh.
p. cm.
"*Pythagoreia Enklemata* © 2006 by POLIS Publishers and Tefcros Michaelides"
ISBN 978-1-930972-26-1 (hard cover : alk. paper) —
ISBN 978-1-930972-27-8 (pbk. : alk. paper)
I. Cavanagh, Lena. II. Title.
PA5638.23.I24P9813 2008
889'.34--dc22

2008027047

Typeset in Adobe Garamond Pro and OdysseaUBSU (Greek) by 1106 Design
Printed by McNaughton & Gunn in the United States of America
World Atlas 1913 Europe courtesy of Historic Map Works™

1-888-PARMENIDES
www.parmenidesfiction.com

Note to the Reader

This book was originally written in Greek and published by POLIS Publications in Athens, Greece in 2006. The people, places, and events are based in the late 19th and early 20th century within the rich tapestry of European culture. The characters are deeply involved in the social, political, scientific, and intellectual circles of the time, in France, Greece, and Germany.

The story begins in August of 1900, when the Olympic Games, the World's Fair *(Exposition Universelle),* and the Second International Congress of Mathematics were being held in Paris. Throughout the book you will find numerous references to famous and lesser-known but important mathematicians, artists, and philosophers, to the various problems and solutions that dominated their discussions, and to the colorful and vibrant settings of Montmartre, the Moulin Rouge, and the infamous "Zut," among many others.

The publisher has provided an extensive glossary of terms with descriptions and explanations of names, locations, expressions and historic events that occur. This glossary was not part of the original Greek novel and is an exclusive feature of this English edition. Its purpose is to make the book both enjoyable and educational, with the hope of inspiring further interest in the many themes and subjects it explores.

We would like to thank Lena Cavanagh for her superb translation from the Greek, and also the editor, Jennifer Morgan, for her valuable insight and suggestions. Finally, we'd like to extend a special note of appreciation to Mark Ryan, whose mathematical expertise and devout attention to detail contributed substantially during the final stages of the book. If any errors remain, he is certainly not at fault.

Prelude

Violet vine, pink and purple wisteria, honeysuckle, and trailing ivy—all were preparing to greet her. Anemones, daisies, chamomile, and poppies laid a thick colorful carpet for her to tread on. Flies, bees, butterflies, and ladybugs wove her ethereal robe. All nature wore its finery to welcome Persephone back to Earth.

Down by the sea, Hippasus celebrated too. His long term of study at the school of Pythagoras had come to an end. He had passed all the tests—even the unbearable trial of silence, the most demanding—and he had been found worthy to be accepted as an equal member in the brotherhood of initiates. Sitting on the sand with a stick in his hand, he now attempted out in the open to do what had been forbidden to him for all those years while he was still an acousmatic: he tried to solve a geometrical problem of his own.

It had troubled his thoughts for a long time, haunting his dreams, keeping him awake at night. He had tried many times, in secret, to scratch some diagrams in the ground to make his problem more tangible. But he always panicked and erased them as soon as he heard footsteps. The rule was clear: No student was allowed to practice geometry by himself. Punishment for those breaking the rule was unconditional—permanent exclusion.

But now everything was different. He was a mathematician, and he had a duty to search for and reveal truths for submission to the judgment of the brotherhood. If his discoveries were approved by the members, they would be added to the great corpus of Pythagorean knowledge that was ascribed collectively to the Master and kept secret under seven seals, for the exclusive use of the initiates.

Hippasus had often asked himself silently whether it was right that knowledge should be kept secret. He had heard that in Ionia, at the other end of the Greek world, things were done differently. There, anyone who thought he had discovered some truth could go down to the marketplace of Ephesus or Miletus and proclaim it out loud to the world. The philosopher defended his truth in front of the crowd, heard their objections and criticisms, and responded, and through such dialogue, knowledge and truth became the possession of anyone who was willing to learn. But whenever Hippasus considered this other method of obtaining knowledge, he became frightened by his own blasphemous thoughts and tried to turn his mind to other things.

Indeed, today his mind was occupied elsewhere. He drew a square in the sand and tried to join together various lines—connecting verticals to the diagonal, connecting them to other verticals. Every now and then he gave up and erased everything, smoothing the sand with his foot and starting anew. Something was not quite right.

As the sun set, Hippasus was still at work. Deep in thought, he didn't hear Hermolaus approaching.

"Where were you? We missed you. I thought you would want to talk to me, now you've passed the trial of silence."

Hermolaus was just above Hippasus in the Pythagorean hierarchy. He, too, had passed the tests only a few months ago and moved from the students' quarters to the mathematicians lodgings. During the probation period, the two youths had formed a close friendship, but Hermolaus' promotion had temporarily separated them. Now that they were equal again, Hermolaus was eager to renew their friendship.

Hippasus looked at him in a daze. "All is number," he murmured. Hermolaus wasn't sure if Hippasus was addressing him or the empty space. "All is number," Hippasus repeated, looking at the other man imploringly.

"So? I know that. Thus spoke the Master!" replied Hermolaos with a touch of irony in his voice, using the customary phrase with which the Pythagoreans attributed every knowledge to their teacher.

"Therefore ... ?" asked Hippasus in exasperation. He pointed to the shape he had traced in the sand.

Puzzled, Hermolaus bent down to look. Hippasus explained his drawing, while his companion listened attentively. Finally, Hermolaus understood what Hippasus was saying.

"You are right," Hermolaus acknowledged, with fear in his voice. "But do you realize what this means? I suggest you do nothing for the time being. You must consider carefully whether or not you're going to speak out and what you will say. Above all, don't do anything hasty. We'll be late for dinner."

"Do you know what we're having?" asked Hippasos, more to say something than because he really cared.

"No beans, at any rate," replied Hermolaos. They both laughed a little too forcefully.

One

I was woken up by a persistent knocking on the front door. I heard Martha's steps as she went to open it, followed by the creaking of the door, an unfamiliar voice, then silence. Next came Martha's quick footsteps approaching my room. Although she was more than eighty years old, she still bustled about the house full of energy, taking care of everything, controlling everything.

At the age of ten, Martha had been taken into the service of my grandfather, Konstandinos Mavroleon. When my mother was born four years later, Martha was charged with the care of the newborn child. She worshiped the baby from the very beginning and gave it all the tenderness she herself had never had, filling in the best possible way the void left in my mother's life by my busy, distant, socialite grandmother and the lack of any siblings. My mother was the only child the couple ever wished to have, or were able to.

Mother married Alexis Igerinos, an engineer, at eighteen, and Martha followed her to her new home; after I was born she became my nanny, too. There are times I think she still maintains the role, although I'm now over fifty years old and, strictly speaking, she holds the position of housekeeper.

"Michael, are you asleep?" she asked through the door.

"No, my dear, I'm awake. What's the matter?"

"There is a policeman downstairs. He's asking for you."

"For me? Did he say why?"

"No. He says it's something urgent. He apologizes, but says he must see you."

"Tell him I'll be down in five minutes."

I dressed quickly and went downstairs. A young police officer was sitting on the sofa in the drawing room. He jumped up as I came in.

"Mr. Michael Igerinos? I'm Officer Antoniou. I'm sorry to trouble you at such an early hour, but we need your help. Did you know someone named Stefanos Kandartzis?"

My heart gave a jump, and I felt the blood drain from my face. I latched onto the use of the past tense. "*Did* I know? Why do you use the word '*did*'? Stefanos Kandartzis is a very good friend of mine. We were together only yesterday afternoon."

"I'm very sorry, Mr. Igerinos," he replied. "Early this morning, Stefanos Kandartzis was found dead. The inspector asks if you would come with me to his apartment."

I swallowed with difficulty, thinking of Stefanos. "But how? I mean … he was fine yesterday. What happened to him?"

"I don't know any details, myself. Apparently his landlady found him. She was the person who told us that you had met yesterday afternoon. As you know, he had no relatives. That's why the inspector would like you to come over."

"I'll be with you straight away. Just give me a few minutes to get ready. In the meantime, can the maid get you something? Tea, coffee?"

"Thank you, there is no need. I'll wait for you, Mr. Igerinos."

Stefanos' lodgings were in Neapolis, at the foot of Mt. Lycabettus. They consisted of only one room, with a communal toilet in the yard—all he could afford on his small salary as a mathematics teacher at a school in Athens. His academic achievements and qualifications should have secured him a post in the university, but Venizelos' party didn't consider him loyal enough, and the royalists had him down as too much of a democrat. This position meant that not only did he have to content himself with a teaching post at a secondary school, but also that he lived in constant fear that a political upheaval or the emergence of some new favorite would exile him to the provinces or make him (on a well-contrived pretext, naturally) redundant.

Aside from his work at the school, Stefanos was completely engrossed in his studies. I was his only link with the outside world. We met once a week to play chess, a passion we shared from our student days. Less often, we talked about mathematics, another mutual passion of ours, although I had confined the subject to a small, airtight compartment of my own life, rather than letting it take over my existence, as Stefanos had.

We took turns meeting at each other's house for our matches. Visits to his damp, moldy room were a trial for me, especially in the winter, but I didn't have the courage to upset the balance of our relationship by proposing he come to my place every time. He seemed to be unaware of any difference between his room and the warm, thick-carpeted parlor of my house, and his friendship was too precious for me to risk losing it by making an insensitive suggestion.

So every other Thursday we shared his watery, lukewarm herbal tea, while I dreamed of the fine blends and silver samovar at my house that Martha made sure was always steaming hot. We played chess and talked from five until nine in the evening, and then I would make my way home. And now Officer Antoniou was telling me that yesterday was the last of our Thursdays.

I was rather grateful to feel the slap of the morning wind on my face as I walked with the policeman to Stefanos' home. It took us twenty minutes to get there from my house in Stadiou Street. The entrance to the yard was blocked by curious onlookers, and the policeman signaled to his men to let us through. As we entered the familiar room, the doctor who was bending over the bed stepped aside, and I saw Stefanos. He was lying on his back with his eyes shut, his cheeks blue and his lips nearly black. I felt my legs tremble. Before me lay not just the only true friend I had ever had, but my whole youth, an entire chapter of my life, a chapter that was now closed. Instinctively, I caught hold of Antoniou's arm so I wouldn't fall down.

Two

Paris
International Congress of Mathematicians
Wednesday, August 8, 1900

The lecture hall at the Sorbonne was filled to capacity.

I had been warned. "It will be packed for Hilbert's lecture," they said. "Go early if you want to get a seat." Mathematics played an important role in my life at the time, but I had no intention of wasting a single night in Paris. I wasn't going to forgo the nightlife just so I could get up early for a lecture, even if this was my first conference; the lecturer was the famous David Hilbert, professor at the university where I was studying; and the lecture had an enticing title: "On the Future Problems in Mathematics."

The title made it clear that this was not going to be a standard talk aimed at specialists, presenting the proof of a theorem or developments toward the solution of a problem. Such lectures are often heard at conferences on mathematics and are, of course, necessary, as each contributes a small piece to the construction of a future grand theory. Naturally, as with all sciences, these lectures are the primary path by which the field of mathematics advances. And yet, with the exception of those who are deeply immersed in mathematical research, very few people enjoy such lectures, and even fewer understand the technical details mastered only by those specializing in a particular field. In contrast, Hilbert's lecture would be a panoramic overview, a global presentation of the science of mathematics—a summing up that very few mathematicians would have been able to present at the dawn of the twentieth century.

Hilbert's forthcoming lecture had been the main topic of conversation in Göttingen for a whole year. From the moment that he had received Poincaré's invitation to speak, the normally calm and carefree Hilbert had been riddled with anxiety. He had begun a regular correspondence with his close friend Hermann Minkowski, then a professor in Zurich, trying to decide the subject and content of his lecture. It was probably Minkowski who had first suggested a panoramic vision of the mathematics of the future, a kind of reply to Poincaré's address at the first International Congress of Mathematicians in Zurich three years earlier. Minkowski had described Poincaré's talk as "boring and banal," suggesting that his friend respond with a dynamic, powerful lecture comprising a sort of challenge to the French mathematical establishment.

Hilbert probably didn't share his friend's readiness for "warfare." He had lived in Paris in the past and knew most French mathematicians personally. In any case, he preferred to direct whatever appetite he may have had for controversy to his fellow countrymen, or at least to the frame of mind and attitude to life that they represented. At the end of the nineteenth century, the scientific circles of Europe were dominated by the theories of the German physiologist Emile du Bois-Reymond, who was carrying out pioneering research in the field of electrophysiology (he was one of the first to associate muscle contractions with electricity). At the end of his career, du Bois-Reymond had turned to philosophy; his central thesis was summed up by the phrase *"Ignoramus et ignorabimus"* ("We know nothing and we shall continue to know nothing"). He believed that there was a limit to the knowledge of nature that can be achieved, beyond which man could never reach. Du Bois-Reymond claimed that no matter how far science might advance, there will always be questions it won't be able to answer.

The younger generation of researchers categorically refused to subscribe to such a pessimistic approach. Hilbert himself asserted repeatedly that every problem had a solution, provided one worked methodically and systematically to find it. The idea of giving a lecture that would look to the future and set out in order of priority the problems that ought to engage the mathematical community seemed to him a great opportunity to make public his opposition to du Bois-Reymond's fatalistic thesis. He wrote countless drafts and organized a large number of "rehearsal lectures" in front of his colleagues at the university. Even up to the last minute, Hilbert was adding and removing paragraphs, changing the order of sections, and reconsidering and reappraising his arguments. In the end, he had missed the deadline for submitting his paper, so the lecture didn't appear anywhere in the conference's program.

Only the echo of these discussions had reached my own ears. In Germany in 1900, the distance between professors and students was institutionalized. Hilbert himself didn't take such hierarchy too seriously and didn't hesitate to break the rules in his private life. It was not unusual for him to be seen playing billiards or drinking beer with his students in the coffeehouses of the town, but such behavior provoked hostile, if whispered, criticism from the small, conservative community of Göttingen. Therefore, even if Hilbert had wanted to hear the opinion of certain students he respected (among whom, I flattered myself, I was included), he would not have risked affronting his colleagues by having discussions with us similar to those he was having with them.

The only occasions when this hierarchical structure was put aside were the traditional excursions organized by almost all German universities in those days. Very often on a Wednesday afternoon or during the vacations, large mixed groups would leave town and head for a long walk along the bank of the Leine River or for a climb in the surrounding wooded hills. Dressed in their outdoor jackets, baggy trousers tied with laces below the knee, thick woolen socks, and hiking boots, the normally reserved and distant professors would relax and allow themselves to indulge in hearty and open discussions with their students. The sweet-smelling green countryside of Lower Saxony made it easier for teachers and pupils to step outside their strict Prussian discipline and develop warmer, closer human relationships. Of course, order was restored on their return to the walls of the university, as if the famous medieval fortifications of Göttingen dictated not only the boundaries of the town and its buildings but also the behavior of its inhabitants.

It was on such an excursion that I first heard Hilbert talk to Felix Klein about his invitation to be the main speaker in Paris the following August. I walked a few steps behind the president of the university and the rising star of the mathematics department, enjoying the privilege of being able to listen to their conversation. Klein expressed strong reservations as to the wisdom of his younger colleague's decision to present open-ended problems rather than complete solutions. He himself inclined toward a more conventional lecture.

"All you have to do is present the recent achievements of German mathematicians," he said. "After all, a large part of their success is owed to you. You could say a few words about the research of your colleagues and devote the main part of your speech to your own work. People want facts, not visions!"

"No! I don't want to make a self-indulgent presentation of the past," retorted Hilbert. "The proud look a magpie gives her young, believing them to be the prettiest birds in the world, is not for me. I want to look forward. In fact, I'm hoping that, in talking about the future of mathematics, I will to some degree be able to influence it."

Klein didn't insist, but I saw in his face the trace of a skeptical and slightly deprecating smile.

A few months later, I had the opportunity to hear in person a second discussion regarding Hilbert's plans for his talk. Otto Eschenberg, a young university lecturer and a member of a rich Göttingen family, had organized a "musical soirée" at his house, similar to those held by Rebecca Mendelssohn, the wife of Lejeune Dirichlet and sister of the famous composer. When they left Berlin in 1855 to replace Gauss as professor at Göttingen, Rebecca found it difficult to adjust to the ways of this small, provincial town, having been used to the busy, cosmopolitan life of the Prussian capital. Her need to socialize and her passion for music led her to establish a series of musical soirées. She persuaded the professors at the university, many of whom played an instrument, to form a small amateur chamber orchestra. Soon their concerts became one of the few cultural events in town. When I arrived in Göttingen, half a century after Dirichlet's death, the tradition was still being observed.

I had started learning the flute at a very early age, thanks to my grandmother's insistence that I acquire a rounded, upper-class education. I must have been just seven years old when the dynamic and ambitious Fevronia Mavroleon announced, full of pride, to her daughter and son-in-law that the Master of Music at the palace had agreed to take my musical instruction in hand. I have happy memories of endless hours alone in my room giving voice to my dubious artistic talents and executing (both literally and metaphorically) pieces by the great German composers. I also recall with horror the occasions when I was dressed in a ludicrous little sailor suit and made to perform the same pieces in front of my grandmother's friends. By the time I went to university at the age of eighteen, I could play the flute reasonably well. Although I was not aware of the privileges that my limited musical abilities would make available to me, I had no reason to hide them; thus my talent was revealed, and I was invited to take part in the rehearsals of the orchestra, in which I was offered the place of reserve flutist. From the beginning, the position, despite its low place in the hierarchy, gave me free entrance to the musical gatherings in Göttingen.

In April 1900, the town was visited by Heinrich Weber, professor at the University of Strasburg (which belonged to Germany after the war of 1870), and the chamber orchestra of the University of Göttingen organized a concert in his honor. Hilbert, who was an old student of Weber's from his Königsberg years, had sent him the manuscript of the lecture he was preparing for Paris. Naturally, the conversation turned to it again during the concert's intermission. Weber congratulated Hilbert on his paper, advising him only to keep his introductory words short. The host then seized the opportunity to make a particularly flattering toast to Hilbert. "By publishing the *Foundations of Geometry,* you became a modern Euclid. Now, with this paper, you can claim the role of a modern Archimedes as well," he said, raising his glass.

This promotion from the role of Euclid (who first standardized and recorded the whole mathematical system of the ancient Greeks, through his axiomatic deductive method) to that of Archimedes (who used pioneering methods to make strides into the future, daring to challenge even concepts, such as that of the infinite, that were taboo for the Greeks) was especially apt and was applauded warmly by the audience. Even though I agreed with it, I couldn't help thinking that if our host had half the skill in mathematics as he was displaying in public relations, he would already be a famous name.

In this way, Hilbert's lecture had grown into a matter that concerned the whole university, or perhaps I should say the entire German mathematical community. The fact that I was fortunate enough to have twice witnessed a discussion about the proposed lecture made me want to be there at its presentation, even though attendance was not expected of first-year postgraduate students. The idea of finding myself among the elite of the mathematical world for a few days—as well as the chance to visit Paris, of course—led me to decide to attend the conference, and my father generously agreed to finance the trip.

That summer, Paris justified more than ever its title as capital of the world. The *Exposition Universelle* of 1900 had drawn huge crowds. More than fifty million visitors from all corners of the earth had walked along the banks of the Seine and on the adjacent streets, where the pavilions of over eighty thousand exhibitors had been set up. At the same time, the events of the second Olympic Games took place in the city from May to October. The theaters, bistros, cabarets, the racing course—all were teeming with life.

Sarah Bernhardt, at the zenith of her career, was staging Sardou's *Tosca* in her own theater; the poster by Alfonse Mussat was one of the first things I had seen when walking out of the railway station. Naturally, I hastened to buy a ticket for the play, and so found myself on Tuesday night sitting comfortably in the sixth row of the *Théâtre de la Renaissance*. During the intermission I joined a group of Germans in the foyer; they were in Paris for the exhibition and I knew one of them, a young businessman I had met in Berlin. This man got us an invitation to a soirée after the show organized by his French business partner. This was particularly tempting because it was rumored that the great actress might make an appearance there. Indeed, Sarah Bernhardt not only came, she was in great form—so much so that she agreed to sing for the guests, filling the salon with her silvery tones. We didn't leave until the early hours of the morning.

Now, at the conference, I found myself standing in the middle of the aisle, bleary-eyed and with a head still heavy from the champagne of the night before, to which I was unaccustomed. I was desperately looking for a tiny corner in which I could collapse and stay for as long as it took me to regain my strength.

The crowd around me was noisy and disparate. Voices, gestures, and movements created a buzz of confusion. One could hear words in every language. Of course the French were in the majority, but next to them the Germans exchanged compliments and jokes in Teutonic French with the locals. The memories of the Franco-Prussian War were thirty years in the distance, and nothing was signaling the mathematical community (which in any case led a life outside the sphere of politics) of the bloodbath that would follow fourteen years later.

"*Gamoto!*" I cursed under my breath.

If my aristocratic Grandmother Mavroleon had heard me express myself in such "language of the lowest order, wholly inappropriate for the son of an Igerinos, scion of the Mavroleon family," there would have been mayhem. But in the packed auditorium of the Sorbonne this magic word was enough to solve my immediate problem—and open a whole new chapter in my life.

"Are you Greek?"

Puzzled, I turned around. The man who had spoken was around my age—slim, rather tall, with an open, friendly face. At first glance, nothing about him betrayed his Greek origin, apart perhaps from his nose. He was poorly dressed in obviously second-hand clothes which only barely fit him, and so had no resemblance to the picture I had formed in my head of "Parisian Greeks." He squeezed to one side to make room for me.

"Would you like to sit here?" he asked.

I accepted his offer with gratitude. "Thank you. It's a great relief to meet a fellow countryman in this Tower of Babel." I offered my hand: "Michael Igerinos."

"Glad to meet you. Stefanos Kandartzis. Do you live in Paris? How come we haven't met before?"

"No. I am studying in Göttingen. This is the first time I've been to Paris—I'm here only for the conference."

"I wondered." He made a wide gesture toward the audience. "All the best people are here."

I smiled encouragingly. It was obvious that he, too, felt a bit out of place in the crowd. Finding a compatriot put him at ease, and he felt the need to talk.

"Look down there on the left, at those two talking ..."

He indicated an amazing duo who reminded me at once of characters from the novel *The Prince and the Pauper*. One was thin and dark, with small, bright eyes and a pitch-black, rather unkempt moustache—he had a typical Jewish countenance. He wore a fedora, a worn jacket that was too large for him, and a kind of cravat instead of a tie. Despite the season, he was holding a coat made of a material woven in the common herringbone design. The appearance of the other man left no doubt as to his aristocratic background: he wore an expensive black suit, pure white shirt, and silk tie. He sported spectacles with a gold frame and his silver hair was combed to perfection. His upper lip displayed a thick, well-shaped moustache. Neither of them seemed to be aware of the striking contrast they made, and none of the others in the auditorium seemed to find them a curiosity. They were talking cordially, the first man occasionally making big gestures with his hands, the second using subtle movements of his lips and eyebrows.

"They are Hadamard and de la Vallée-Poussain," Stefanos informed me. "One is a Frenchman, the other Belgian. Four years ago they proved the prime number theorem. They did it separately, neither knowing what the other was doing. Fortunately, they published their work simultaneously. Otherwise, we would have had a repetition of the Newton-Leibniz controversy."

Although number theory was not my strong point, I knew that prime numbers were those that cannot be divided except by themselves and the number one. I also knew that early on in the number system, we come across many prime numbers—2, 3, 5, 7, 11, 13—but that as we progress they become fewer and fewer. There are 25 prime numbers between 1 and 100 (one in four), 168 from 1 to 1,000 (around one in six) and 1,229 from 1 to 10,000 (around one in eight). Euclid had already proved that the number of primes is infinite; however, as we move higher and higher, their frequency decreases dramatically. The question naturally arose as to how they space themselves out in the total series of numbers. Mathematicians had formed various conjectures but, apparently, those two characters had made an important step forward in this field.

Wanting to hear more about this, I asked: "Isn't that Gauss' conjecture? If I'm not mistaken, he worked out, but was unable to prove, how many prime numbers are smaller than a given number."

Stefanos laughed mischievously. "If I were French and not simply a student living in France, I would have challenged you to a duel. Here everyone believes fanatically that the idea was Legendre's, not Gauss'."

"I am not surprised in the least. That happened to Gauss a lot. Because of his perfectionism he took too long to publish his ideas. No matter how far ahead of everybody else he was, someone would always beat him to it. And then a quarrel would break out. Gauss would write somewhere, 'I discovered such and such a theorem years ago,' and the other would object, 'No, I found it first,' and the whole thing would just explode. Nevertheless, he stubbornly refused to publish anything except fully formed conclusions. He would never publish a supposition before he could also prove it. '*Pauca sed matura*' ('Few words, but ripe ones') was his personal motto. My reply to him would be, if you will insist on hesitating and allow someone else to publish ahead of you, then, my dear sir, you may as well shut up."

"He also took great pains to destroy evidence after deducing the proof of his theories," added my compatriot. "A deduction is like a building. When its construction is finished, one doesn't leave the scaffolding in place," he said, paraphrasing a favorite saying of the prince of mathematics.

"Whether it was Gauss or Legendre," I replied, "what does it matter who formulated the question first? You're telling me that these two discovered the answer independently. I'm amazed they haven't yet come to blows." I made this last comment in jest, of course, wishing to keep the conversation at the level of simple gossip. I didn't feel like entering into a deep mathematical discussion, particularly in a field where I felt lacking in knowledge. With a whole bottle of champagne still running through my veins and a lot of unfamiliar, fascinating faces around me, I was happy to continue our light mathematical chitchat, rather than engage in a serious discussion on mathematics itself.

My friend swallowed the bait. "If they were to come to blows, they would have a thousand and one reasons for doing so, quite apart from the disputed theorem. Can't you see? Hadamard is a Jew, de la Vallée-Poussain a Catholic—and a graduate of a Jesuit college, to boot; Belgian, but of French extraction. And observe what each is wearing: one a fedora, the other a silk tie and pince-nez. If you ask the latter who Dreyfus is, he may not even know. As for the other, he's passionately committed to the campaign for a retrial. A follower of Zola and all that. In fact, I think Hadamard and Dreyfus are related."

French society in 1900 was being torn apart by a scandal revolving around Alfred Dreyfus, a young lieutenant convicted six years earlier of being a spy. After a farcical court-martial, the military had sentenced him to hard labor for life and sent him to Devil's Island, a penal colony off the coast of French Guiana. The royalists, backed by the Catholic Church, seized the opportunity of the conviction to attack the Republican constitution. The fact that Dreyfus was a Jew contributed to the rekindling of anti-Semitic feeling among certain sections of French society. However, evidence that Dreyfus was innocent had begun to surface gradually. The liberal voices of the public had come together and demanded a retrial. The whole of France was divided into two camps: those who supported Dreyfus and those who opposed him.

On January 13, 1898, Émile Zola had published his famous "J'accuse" letter in the newspaper *L'Aurore,* which that day sold over three hundred thousand copies. He openly accused the military and political leadership of knowingly suppressing the truth that Dreyfus had been wrongly convicted. Zola was himself prosecuted for writing his article, but his text became a banner for the Republicans behind the calls for retrial.

In 1899, President Félix Faure expired in the arms of his mistress (letting loose all sorts of salacious gossip), and he was succeeded by Émile Loubet. One of Loubet's first acts was to grant a pardon for Dreyfus. Dreyfus didn't let the matter rest there, but continued to demand a new, fair trial. In 1906, when I was back in Greece, I heard that after more than eleven years of persecution and struggle, he had at last been vindicated.

So to all appearances, the two people talking together belonged to opposite camps socially, politically, and culturally. However, they went on talking, unconcerned and seemingly oblivious to the gulf that separated them.

Behind Hadamard, a man in his forties with a thick beard was chatting with a young man whose dress and demeanor loudly broadcast his British origin. Stefanos continued his observations: "The older man is an Italian," he informed me. "Giuseppe Peano, professor in Turin."

"The one who proposed the axioms of arithmetic?"

"The very man. These axioms are part of a larger program that works toward the development of a symbolic language, free from any intuitive or subjective implication. He envisages the expression of all mathematics in this language—something which, inevitably, makes his lectures extremely difficult to understand. His students complain that rather than split hairs over linguistic expression, he should provide them with practical knowledge to help them in their professional careers. I myself believe that correct definition and fully developed deduction are basic prerequisites for the development of mathematical theories, rendering them safe from contradiction and vicious circles."

"I have no objection to that. But it's surprising coming from you. Didn't your own D'Alembert say 'Go forth and faith will come and find you' to those who doubted the foundations of mathematics?"

Stefanos laughed.

"Don't forget that I am Greek. Like Pythagoras, I too am worried that any imperfection in the harmony of numbers reflects a corresponding imperfection in the harmony of the universe."

It was my turn to laugh. I turned again to Peano and his young companion. "I know the other man from somewhere," I mused.

"His name is Bertrand Russell. He's a Cambridge graduate. He and Peano met eight days ago at the International Conference for Philosophy. Since then they've been inseparable. Every time you look, they're together talking about mathematical logic."

I remembered that I, too, had met the young English aristocrat. He had visited Germany the year before and had given lectures on non-Euclidean geometry, while at the same time studying economics and frequenting events organized by the Social Democratic Party. He was a grandson of Lord John Russell, the former prime minister of Great Britain, and had been brought up by his grandfather and grandmother after both his parents died. However, the conservative environment in which he had grown up didn't prevent him from adopting extreme radical views—rather the opposite, one might say.

Just then, a rather plump man in his fifties approached the duo. He greeted Peano cordially, and Russell stood up respectfully to offer him his seat. It was my turn to enlighten my new friend.

"That's Gottlob Frege. Half philosopher, half mathematician. He has written a strange book called *Theory of Concepts,* or something like that. Like Peano, he has also published a book called *The Foundations of Arithmetic.* It seems that this group puts mathematics above politics. Otherwise, as Frege is ultraconservative and Russell a socialist, they would not even be on speaking terms. In fact, Russell admires him. It is said that he's one of very few people who have read all of Frege's works."

We didn't then know that two years later the young socialist would unintentionally deliver a fatal blow to his idol. While the second volume of *The Foundations of Arithmetic* was still in press, a letter reached Frege in which Russell proved that his axiomatic system led to contradictions. After that, Frege never published anything relating to mathematics. A friend from Germany wrote to me recently that shortly before he died, Frege had embraced fully the burgeoning National Socialist Party and had published articles full of fanaticism and prejudice, supporting racial purity and blaming liberals, communists, and Jews everywhere in the world for all the evils on earth. I confess that, although Frege was not the only such example, my friend's letter had shocked me. Of course, none of all this was on our minds as we watched the three founders of mathematical logic chatting away genially.

We now turned toward the other side of the auditorium, where the "analysts" had gathered round the Nestor of French mathematics, the elderly Charles Hermite—Hadamard's teacher, among others—who was talking amiably to Lindemann.

"*There* is a true Franco-German friendship," I commented.

"Not just friendship; it's a close, creative collaboration," Kandartzis responded. "My man, Hermite (I can call him 'mine' since you have labelled me as French) first devised a method of proof. Then your man, Lindemann, seized the opportunity and proved that pi, the ratio of circumference to diameter, is a transcendent number."

"So your man and my man managed to answer a question posed two and a half thousand years ago by … our men," I added with a smile.

Indeed, the proof of pi's transcendence had definitively resolved the oldest and most notorious problem in the history of mathematics, the squaring of the circle. The problem had been formulated by Greek mathematicians of the fifth century B.C. and had tantalized, in the most creative way, whole generations of mathematicians. And lo and behold, two and a half thousand years later, a Franco-German collaboration had solved it, albeit in negative terms, that is, by proving that it's impossible. What a splendid example for those who argued that in mathematics there are no questions without an answer! Sooner or later, systematic study would produce an answer. It may be positive or negative, but nevertheless, there is a clear, definitive answer.

"My man has another reason for feeling proud today," I said to my compatriot. "The star of the day used to be his pupil."

Behind Hermite's circle sat a dignified-looking man in his sixties, with a large beard and thick white hair. Beside him, a tall man in his mid-thirties was talking to him respectfully. He had a handlebar mustache and wore glasses fixed on his nose and tied to a leather cord hanging from his breast pocket.

"The younger man is Minkowski," I informed Stefanos. "So I suppose the other one must be Jordan."

"Yes, it is—but how did you guess?"

"Well, Minkowski had not even finished his doctoral thesis when he won his first great distinction, the first prize of the French Academy of Sciences. Jordan was the one who had backed Minkowski's candidacy. Indeed, he had written a wonderful letter to him, saying, 'I beg you, work hard, and you will become a great mathematician.'"

I knew Minkowski and his work very well, so I was about to give my new friend all the details when our mathematical gossip came to an abrupt end. A loud murmur near the entrance announced the arrival of the speaker. He rushed in, dispensing smiles and greetings all around. He looked barely forty and was of medium height, slim but well-built, with an impressively wide forehead. He was wearing his characteristic Panama hat with a drooping brim (from which he was never parted); small, round glasses, behind which shone a pair of bright blue eyes; and a suit that resembled that of a dandy on the Champs Élysées more than that of a respectable professor at Göttingen. All the Germans in the audience, and I, were used to seeing him dressed like this, but the others, particularly the English and the few Americans there, looked surprised. Hilbert had an honorary escort made up of Poincaré, the host of the conference, and Klein, the president of the mathematics department at Göttingen. The delegates stood up and remained standing until Hilbert and Klein took their seats and Poincaré climbed up to the podium. Poincaré introduced the speaker briefly, emphasizing the importance of his contribution to mathematics but not forgetting to stress, very politely, the French influence on his work: "Fourteen years ago, we had the pleasure of Herr Professor's brief visit to our town," he remarked innocently, but everyone, even I, understood the insinuation. Then Hilbert took the stage.

"Who of us would not be glad to lift the veil behind which the future lies hidden; to cast a glance at the next advances of our science and at the secrets of its development during future centuries?" he began. "What particular goals will there be toward which the leading mathematical spirits of coming generations will strive? What new methods and new facts in the wide and rich field of mathematical thought will the new centuries disclose?"

His speech continued amid deathly silence. He emphasized the defining role that problems play in the development of any science. He even claimed that a science is alive only as long as it contains certain unsolved problems. "A lack of problems foreshadows extinction or the cessation of independent development," he said. Even an extremely esoteric and unimportant problem can have tremendous effect on the science itself, he explained.

Hilbert gave as an example Fermat's problem. It's very easy to find triads of whole numbers that comply with the Pythagorean Theorem, $x^2 + y^2 = z^2$. The numbers 3, 4, and 5, for example: $3^2 + 4^2 = 5^2$; there is also 5, 12, and 13. But if we replace the exponent 2 with 3 or 4 or any other power, we cannot find any numbers that will comply with the equation, whole numbers for x, y, and z, such that $x^3 + y^3 = z^3$ or $x^4 + y^4 = z^4$—at least, no one has found such numbers yet.

In 1637, French mathematician Pierre Fermat claimed he could prove that "we cannot break up a cube into two cubes or a number to the fourth power into two numbers to the fourth power or any other power higher than two into two identical powers." He meant that the equation $x^n + y^n = z^n$ has no integral solution for any n power higher than 2, except of course, the simple solution $x = y = z = 0$. He even wrote a note in the margin of a book, claiming that he had found the proof, but that he could not fit it in the margin! Had he really found the proof? Or did he mistakenly think that he had? Or did his isolated, boring life as a civil servant in Toulouse lead him to play a trick on future readers? Whatever the truth, the fact remains that, to this day, that famous proof hasn't been found. From a purely mathematical point of view, the only interest that this problem poses is the fact that it was formulated by a mathematician of Fermat's calibre.

And here we were today, listening to another famous mathematician, Hilbert, explain to us how, in their efforts to resolve Fermat's last theorem, mathematicians such as Kummer, Dedekind, and Kronecker had laid down the foundations of the modern algebraic theory of numbers, whose scope and importance went far beyond the humble little problem. Still, they had failed to solve the problem itself, nor was there any sign on the horizon that anyone else would.

What encourages us in our work, Hilbert insisted, is the certainty that all mathematical problems have a solution. As we labor over our papers, "we hear within us the perpetual call: There is the problem. Seek its solution. You can find it by pure reason, for in mathematics there is no *ignorabimus*."

This was a head-on attack! A man of action, Hilbert didn't confine himself to hints about his philosophical position. He chose to express it directly and clearly, publicly questioning, in the most formal way, a dogma that enjoyed almost universal acceptance. Despite my admiration for the speaker, I had the arrogance to doubt his words. When you're flirting with a beautiful woman, imagining a work of art, or designing a new machine, a large part of your pleasure arises from this concept of *ignorabimus;* it's not just the uncertainty of the outcome, but also the fear there won't be an outcome at all. In this respect, I felt more akin to the Prussian philosopher with a French name. But this was not the time for philosophical musings. I turned my attention once more to Hilbert.

The handout we had been given before the lecture began contained twenty-three problems that embraced the whole spectrum of the science of mathematics. It was not just a list of specific problems; it was a complete research guide, opening up new approaches, mapping new directions. In his lecture Hilbert concentrated on ten of these, analyzing them in detail. Although for certain problems he was bold enough to describe (in the form of a conjecture) the solution he anticipated, he devoted the greater part of his talk to what we must look for rather than what we might find. He was especially clear when describing the kind of solution he considered to be acceptable:

"It shall be possible to establish the correctness of the solution by means of a finite number of steps based upon a finite number of hypotheses which are implied in the statement of the problem and which must always be exactly formulated… . A new problem, especially when it comes from the world of outer experience, is like a young twig, which thrives and bears fruit only when it is grafted carefully and in accordance with strict horticultural rules upon the old stem, the established achievements of our mathematical science."

Hilbert was staking out the boundaries of mathematics, drawing a dividing line between it and the empirical sciences. Sitting beside him, Poincaré was unable to hide a momentary grimace despite his Gallic tact. His own lecture three years earlier at the conference in Zurich had concentrated more on the importance of intuition, the interaction of science and practical experience, the acceptance of self-evident principles. If one compared the two lectures, one would conclude that the two colossi of mathematics disagreed fundamentally as to the understanding of what mathematics is and how it develops. The Frenchman was closer to the traditional idea of a natural philosopher. He saw the natural sciences as a unified body of knowledge with mathematics as an integral part, drawing experience from and testing itself against them. The German, on the other hand, was more what would be termed a "pure mathematician": he treated mathematics as something separate, independent of the natural sciences, with its own rigidly strict logic and following its own independent course.

The lecture was a magical experience. At the turn of the century, the leading mathematicians of the world were gathered under one roof, listening to a colleague who referred to the work and methods of the rest and revealed the future prospects of their discipline in the new century. You could see vividly the reactions of those immediately concerned as their faces showed agreement, reservation, or hostility.

When the speaker mentioned the problem of the foundation of mathematics and the need for a mechanism that would ensure that its axioms are complete and devoid of contradiction, all eyes turned to Peano, Frege, and Russell. They, in turn, began to look around with self-conscious satisfaction. But in Peano's face I could see clear signs of annoyance. Beside me, Stefanos was taking it all in, wide-eyed.

Then Hilbert made reference to the problems of prime numbers. Bowing slightly toward Hadamard and de la Vallée-Poussain, the speaker said that, thanks to their work, the theory for the distribution of prime numbers had made significant progress. However, he added, there remained the proof of Riemann's Hypothesis regarding the roots of the zeta function. The audience turned their attention to the two mathematicians honored by this reference, sending them bright smiles of approval.

Hilbert continued to talk for about an hour, listing problems of geometry, analysis, theoretical physics, and proving to be a real expert in each of these topics.

He finished his lecture by stressing, "The organic unity of mathematics is inherent in the nature of this science, for mathematics is the foundation of all exact knowledge of natural phenomena. That it may completely fulfill this high mission, may the new century bring it gifted masters and many zealous and enthusiastic disciples!"

The audience erupted in prolonged applause. Hilbert had taken a big risk in choosing to speak about unsolved problems rather than give a conventional type of presentation—even more so, because for every problem he mentioned, there were people in the audience with clear and explicit positions vis-à-vis that particular topic. His success was equal to the risk. The standing ovation continued for about five minutes.

When the applause died down, Poincaré asked if there were any questions or comments. Peano got up and observed that the second problem presented by his honorable colleague regarding the consistency of the axioms of arithmetic had virtually been solved by himself and his team. "In fact," he added, "Signore Alessandro Padoa will have the chance to present our recent results in his lecture tomorrow." The singsong French of the Italian professor could not hide his obvious displeasure. He believed that Hilbert had deliberately undervalued his work.

The latter's response was very diplomatic. "I'm sorry I didn't have the chance to study the work of my distinguished colleague's team," Hilbert responded. "I'm afraid my Italian is not good enough for me to read scientific articles in your language. I will pay particular attention to our colleague Pantoa's lecture tomorrow. However the basic proposition I made regarding the second problem remains. How can we establish *a priori* the completeness and consistency of an axiomatic system? How can we, in a finite number of steps, establish that any problem which comes within the framework of a specific axiomatic system can be solved, either positively or negatively, based on these same axioms? A theory can only be considered complete when we are certain that it doesn't require any more axioms. On the other hand, how can we establish whether a set of axioms can lead to a consistent theory, a theory which doesn't contain contradictions? Even if our Italian colleagues have solved this problem for arithmetic, the question remains open for dozens of other areas of mathematics: to find an algorithm which will test their consistency and completeness."

There followed some more questions before Poincaré declared the morning session closed. People began to exit the auditorium, but Stefanos and I stayed in our seats waiting for the room to clear. Watching the leading mathematicians of the world leave the room in groups talking, laughing, and gossiping was as interesting as the content of the lecture we had just heard.

"Fantastic," I declared, when the last person had left the room. "Shall we go and have something to eat? We have two hours until the afternoon session."

Three

We sat down at a bistro on the Boulevard Saint-Michel. It was a gloriously sunny day. A sweet, moist warmth enveloped us, intensely reminiscent of home. We ordered crepes and a small carafe of *cidre,* the famous Normandy cider. I spoke first.

"Have you lived in Paris for long?" I asked.

"I came here after the war. Mr. Avgerios Manousakas was kind enough to pay for my studies." He blushed. "On my own I would not have been able to afford to study, not even in Athens."

Manousakas was an important financier and a family friend. In fact, my crafty grandmother had tried to arrange a marriage between me and his elder daughter Dorothea, who was two years older than I and rather ugly. Although I was then only eighteen, I had put up strong resistance and, with my father's help, managed to evade the engagement. My family sent me off on a "golden exile" to study at Göttingen, while Dorothea Manousaka ended up marrying some distant cousin of Crown Prince Constantine, who had lost all his money at the roulette table.

The mention of the name Manousakas rousing my curiosity, I encouraged Stefanos to continue.

"When the war of '97 was declared, I was doing my national service," he said. "We had moved up to the border already in February. I was in the same company as Mr. Manousakas' second son, Theodoros. He had just graduated from the military academy at Athens and held the rank of second lieutenant in the infantry. The retreat began on the night of April 11. Although we learned afterward that it was a planned withdrawal, there was panic nevertheless. On the 12th, the Turks took Tyrnavos and began the push toward Larissa. The Deligiannis government gave *carte blanche* to the chief of staff, Prince Constantine, to take whatever action he thought was best. He gave orders that we should abandon Larissa and regroup at Farsala. Seeing the army retreat, the locals were seized with terror and began to flee alongside us, in total disorder. The road to Farsala filled with refugees—old people, women, and children, who were trying to save themselves from the Turks. Time and again the enemy managed to isolate a group of civilians and cut them all down. The retreat was hampered even more by the flocks of sheep and herds of cattle that had escaped from their pens and poured onto the main road.

"Suddenly we found ourselves cut off from the rest—Theodoros Manousakas, three other soldiers, and I. At a distance, we could see some Turks approaching on horseback, probably a reconnaissance detachment. The moment they saw us, they opened fire. My three companions were killed, and Theodoros was shot in the leg. His wound was not serious, but he couldn't walk. For a brief moment a bluff hid us from view and the Turks lost sight of us. I seized the chance and pulled Theodoros into a wooded thicket. We hid among the undergrowth and waited. The scouts looked over the dead soldiers and then continued on their way without searching for us. After a while, I came out of hiding to look around and take stock. A bit farther down I came across an abandoned farm. As luck would have it, there was a donkey in the stable. I hauled Theodoros onto its back and, following a footpath, we managed to reach Farsala. I handed him over to the military hospital that had been set up in town and left in search of my company.

"As you know, the armistice was signed in May. Just before I was discharged, one of Mr. Manousakas' clerks sought me out at the camp. Theodoros, God bless him, had exaggerated the part I had played in his rescue, and his father had sent his man to find me and take me to his office as soon as I was out of uniform.

"To cut a long story short, Mr. Manousakas showed his gratitude for the rescue of his son by offering me the chance to study whatever and wherever I wanted. Last month I graduated, and I am now searching for a subject for my doctorate. I'm perhaps the only Greek to have benefited from that pointless and tragic war of 1897."

He finished his story with a timid smile. I was stunned. As a family friend, I knew well the story of how second lieutenant Theodoros Manousakas had been saved. In fact, I had reason to believe that the role played by the man I had just met had been much more crucial than he had described. The man who had very nearly become my brother-in-law had told us how Stefanos had fought heroically to keep the horsemen at a distance until they found a chance to hide. After that, they had wandered through the countryside for three days before they reached Farsala. All that time, Stefanos had nursed Theodoros, whose wound, though not serious, was at risk of turning septic; he had fed them both somehow, and had managed to avoid crossing the enemy's path again. Theodoros owed him his life in every sense of the word. As for old Manousakas, a self-effacing man despite his great wealth, he had never told us how he had rewarded his son's savior.

It was then my turn to tell him my own, much less interesting story. I avoided any mention of the events connected with the Manousakas family that had precipitated my departure from Athens. I merely said that when I had finished school, I had followed the family tradition and gone to study at Göttingen. My family's wishes had been that I should acquire the necessary technical and financial knowledge to one day take over the family business. As a matter of fact, I had taken many courses to serve this purpose, but my interest in mathematics had prevailed in the end. This was not surprising, since my university was where Hilbert and Klein were teachers, a place haunted by the ghosts of Gauss and Riemann. I, too, was now looking for a subject for my doctoral thesis.

Stefanos asked if I had chosen any particular area, and was surprised when I told him I had been thinking of working on the foundations of Euclidean geometry.

"I didn't think there were any unresolved topics left in Euclidean geometry," he said. "The French don't think much of it. I was surprised that Hilbert included the foundations of geometry among the serious problems of the future. But I must admit, I'm not very well acquainted with the subject."

I, on the other hand, had counted geometry as a favorite subject since my high school days. Apart from reading the official school textbook by Ioannis Hatzidakis, I had found in my father's library his own school textbook, *Principles of Geometry by Legendros,* which was a translation of one of Legendre's geometry books. One of the first books I had bought when I arrived in Göttingen was a German translation of the *Elements,* and I had devoted a substantial amount of my time to studying it. Like all first-year students, I too had attempted at some point to construct my own system of axioms to replace Euclid's and had given up halfway through, as was to be expected. Hilbert's particular interest in the foundations of geometry, which had culminated in the publication of his *Foundations of Geometry,* was incentive enough for a young mathematician like me, especially because, being Greek, I considered myself a born geometrician.

The best gift I had received the previous summer, on the occasion of my completing the first cycle of my studies, had been a rare, leather-bound edition of Euclid's *Elements* in the original Greek, dating from the beginning of the last century. It had been a gift from my father, who was the only one who was sympathetic to my change of course to pure mathematics, from the practical studies that everyone else in the family felt I ought to pursue. One can imagine with what pride I showed it off to my fellow students, often succumbing to the temptation to read excerpts from it, translating from Greek to German and thus winning their admiration.

It was therefore natural that the part of Hilbert's lecture that drew my attention more than any other was his reference to the various geometries that exist, his comparison of them, and his list of matters that remain unresolved. My friend's admission that he had not given much thought to Euclidean geometry and his mention of the indifference, if not disdain, of the French towards the topic, gave me the opportunity to talk about my favorite subject.

"At the beginning of his first book of *Elements,* Euclid makes five propositions, or 'postulates'—five statements that he asks the reader to accept at face value, and on which he then bases the whole edifice of his plane geometry. The first four postulates, being short and clear, seem to contain self-evident truths, and mathematicians have for centuries accepted them unquestioningly. Never during antiquity, nor during the middle ages or the period of the great scientific inquiries and reevaluations undertaken by Galileo, Descartes, and Newton, was there any difficulty with the first postulate—a straight line can always pass through two points—nor the fourth—all right angles are equal. However, the fifth one caused great upheaval right from the start. Both its content and Euclid's complicated wording created the initial impression that the fifth postulate could be proven on the basis of the other four. Yet, despite great efforts made not only by the ancient Greeks (such as Posidonius, Geminus, and Heron) but also by the Arabs (such as Ibn al-Haytham, the poet Omar Khayyám and Nasīr al-Dīn) no-one has been able to prove the fifth postulate. Partly as a consequence of this, the fifth postulate has been replaced by others with the same meaning, but expressed more simply. For example, Hilbert and Klein like to use the parallel postulate: "Through a point *p* not on a line *l* there can be drawn exactly one line parallel to *l*."

Stefanos interrupted with a smile: "And has no one thought, during all these years, that the fifth postulate may be truly independent of the other four?"

"No one, not up to the beginning of our century. Or at least, no one with influence enough and arguments persuasive enough to be heard."

"Strange! When you try to prove something and keep failing, isn't it sensible to think that this something may be wrong?"

"I agree. However the fifth postulate, especially if you use Hilbert's version, seems so self-evident that it's hard to imagine a world where the other four axioms apply but not the fifth. So it took right up to the beginning of the nineteenth century before someone dared to suppose that something so unreal was a possibility. When this finally happened, it was not just one man who got there, but two: a Russian and a Hungarian, Lobachevsky and Bolyai. They determined that the fifth postulate is indeed independent of the other four, and proved that if we replaced the axiom of parallel lines, its negation would create a logical system without contradictions. This gave birth to the idea of 'alternative' geometries. The Bolyai-Lobachevskian geometry was named 'hyperbolic geometry.'"

Stefanos' eyes grew wider. It was obvious he had never heard of this term before. "You mean that, in order to prove something in Euclid's geometry, they invented one that is ... not Euclidean?"

"There was no other way. Either the fifth postulate is a consequence of the other four (as so many mathematicians had tried to prove in the past), or, if it is independent, there must be a geometry that can reject it and exist without contradictions."

"What does this geometry say? Where can it be applied?"

"Let's make things simpler, and say that in hyperbolic geometry we retain Euclid's first four axioms and replace the fifth by its opposition: Through a point *p* not on a line *l* there can be drawn infinitely many different lines parallel to *l*. If we take all five new axioms together, we end up with a new geometry whose theorems are, naturally, completely different from the theorems of Euclidean geometry—which is why they sound so strange at first. For example, in Bolyai-Lobachevskian geometry, the sum of the angles of a triangle is always less than 180 degrees. And the bigger the surface covered by the triangle, the smaller the sum of its angles."

Stefanos was listening with mounting interest. When the waiter interrupted to serve us, he looked at him almost angrily. I took a mouthful of crepe and a sip of *cidre* and continued.

"In Euclidean geometry, homothecy is a very simple process. If we take a plane figure, we can, using any scale, create another identical one, albeit enlarged or decreased in size. We can, for example, double the sides of a triangle without disturbing its angles, and thus we will have created a similar triangle with a similitude ratio of 2. (An architect or surveyor would call it a scale of 2:1.)

"A typical example of homothecy is a map, or a photograph—this comparatively modern invention of Niépce and Daguerre, who combined the *camera obscura* of Renaissance painters with the chemical discoveries of the German anatomist Schulze.

"Getting back to our triangles, the area of the new triangle will be four times as great as the previous one, but its angles will continue to give a sum of 180 degrees."

"Okay, I'm not that ignorant," laughed Stefanos good-naturedly. "I may not have read Euclid, but I know what similitude is."

"Well, in fact, similitude makes no sense in the new geometry," I said, almost triumphantly. I was rewarded by my friend's astonished look. I sipped my drink slowly, sadistically savoring his impatience. Wanting to torment him more, I pretended to change the subject. "This cider is excellent. I wonder why they don't make it in Greece. We have plenty of apple trees—"

"You said that there is no similitude in this new geometry?" Stefanos brought me back to the conversation.

"Think about it. It's the immediate consequence of the relationship between the total of the angles of the triangle and its area." I saw doubt creeping over his face and hastened to explain.

"What I'm saying may sound strange, but there is absolutely no contradiction. As a matter of fact, an Italian mathematician, Eugenio Beltrami (who died a few months ago) established that no matter how many propositions we prove within the framework of the new geometry, we will never arrive at a contradiction. The Bolyai-Lobachevskian system of axioms is as consistent and non-contradictory as Euclid's."

"So it seems we have two opposing geometries, which you say are both equally valid," commented Stefanos. "Isn't that too many to describe the one, unique universe in which we live?"

"Who said there are only two?" I replied playfully. "Once someone begins, nothing can stop others from following suit! A few years later, Riemann questioned the postulate that guaranteed that 'from three given points on a line, one and only one is between the other two.' He envisioned a straight line as a huge circle. Within such a geometrical system, parallelism makes no sense or, if you prefer, no parallel straight line can be drawn from a point outside a straight line. His geometry also proved to be non-contradictory, and it was given the name 'elliptical geometry.'"

"Come on!" Stefanos laughed. "How many geometries are you going to burden this poor universe with?"

"That's exactly what Hilbert asked in his lecture," I continued, undaunted. "You may have noticed that he referred to a book published by Minkowski recently. I've got it, and I will send it to you as soon as I get back to Göttingen."

A few years later we were to learn that Hilbert's foresight had triumphed. Using Minkowski's geometry, a young German, who at the time didn't even hold a university post, had laid the foundations of a theory that expanded Newton's mechanics and gave them more general application. Ultimately, Einstein would become a famous Nobel prize winner and the word "relativity" would become a widely known scientific term, even though very few understand its meaning. At the time, however, Stefanos and I had to agree that alternative geometries were simply theoretical devices.

"What puzzles me," said Stefanos, "is how one can establish *a priori* that a theory which is built on an arbitrary selection of axioms will never be contradictory. I realize that none of the theorems that have been proven using, say, Riemann's system of axioms has been shown to be contradictory in relation to the others, but how can I be sure that such a thing won't happen in the future?"

"Choosing a set of axioms is not enough by itself," I replied. "Mathematics is not the result of crazy ideas being tossed up in the air. In order for a mathematical system to stand on its own feet, it must correspond to a model. The consistency of a system cannot be tested within the context of the system itself. In order to verify it, we have to stand outside it and try it out in practice."

Stefanos made a face. "You mean geometry is an experimental science? Like mechanics or astronomy? A system is only valid if it 'agrees with the natural phenomena,' as Aristotle's friends used to say? As long as we can observe the movement of the planets and stars only with the naked eye, we accept Ptolemy's geometric model, but as soon as Galileo discovers through his telescope something that doesn't quite fit—Jupiter's moons, for example, or the phases of Venus, or whatever—do we then take refuge in Copernicus? That doesn't sound right!"

"No!" I objected. "Granted, experience plays an important role in the birth of geometry—not just important, but vital, I would say. But I never said that geometry is an experimental science, not even partly so. An experiment involves approximation, sometimes violent approximation. But contact only applies to natural solid bodies. The bodies of geometry are different. They exist in our thoughts; they are creations of our mind. They're indestructible, ethereal, ideal. Experience does nothing more than help bring out such constructs of the imagination and make them conceivable through our senses. All I said was that, in order to test whether a particular geometry is non-contradictory, one must bring it within a certain model that is established as non-contradictory. And this can only be done if we step outside the system."

A provocative smile lighted Stefanos' eyes. He was obviously skeptical.

"Let me give you an example," I continued. "Let's imagine a world that is completely flat, inhabited by creatures who also have no thickness. These beings live *within* the world's surface and can't get out. Let's also suppose that this is a world quite remote from any other, so that there is no communication with other worlds or any influence from them. If these beings are intelligent, sooner or later they will devise some geometry, which will, of course, be a geometry of two dimensions."

"I have no objection to that," said Stefanos, with a slightly ironic look. "In fact, I've read a book by some English priest describing just such a world."

I, too, had read Edwin Abbott's *Flatland,* a novel which had appeared about fifteen years earlier. It described a two-dimensional country whose inhabitants were polygonal shapes: triangles, squares, pentagons. The higher a shape stood in the social hierarchy, the more sides it had. Naturally, highest of all were the clergy—the circles. It was a clever little book that aspired to satirize the morals of Victorian England by means of geometry. At the same time, it was a first attempt to make a strange mathematical idea accessible to the wider public through a text that was not addressed to the experts.

"The difference between the world I'm talking about and Abbott's," I went on, "is that my world is isolated, whereas his was visited by a three-dimensional being."

"But such a world is still Euclidean," protested Stefanos. "I can't see how it can be used to establish a non-Euclidean geometry."

"All right, let's now imagine that these hypothetical intelligent beings, still without any thickness, inhabit the surface of a sphere, from which they cannot detach themselves. What sort of geometry will they devise? I think you will agree that they will still believe their space to be two-dimensional and flat, as far as they're concerned. Do you remember how our teachers used to define a straight line?"

"A straight line is the shortest distance between two points," recited my friend.

"Exactly!" I said with fervor. "They would define a straight line as the shortest route between two points, that is, an arc of a circle that goes through the two points and has its center at the center of the sphere. Let's not forget that our friends are unaware that the place they inhabit is a sphere. The very notion of a sphere doesn't exist. For them, the third dimension is as mysterious and incomprehensible as the fourth is for us. What they call a straight line is to us a segment of a circle around the sphere. Those beings would call 'space' the surface of the sphere. That space would define their universe, since their nature would prevent them from leaving it or being aware of anything outside it."

"But that's spherical geometry," said Stefanos. "It's what Menelaus, Theodosius, and Hipparchus describe. We're still within a Euclidean framework!"

"*We* are, yes!" I answered. "We, who live in the world of three dimensions, observe those beings from afar and watch how they live and move around the surface of their three-dimensional sphere. And we know that they behave according to the rules of Euclidean geometry. They, however, think they're living in a two-dimensional world, a boundless universe, since they can never reach its 'edge,' but one which is finite. Their universe has no limits, but if they start from one point and follow a straight line, sooner or later they will come back to the point where they started from."

Stefanos' face lit up. For the first time since our conversation on the foundations of geometry began, the expression of doubt on his face was replaced with one of agreement and acceptance. "Those beings," he mused, following his own thought, "will never grasp the meaning of the parallel, since two of their straight lines—being two great circles—will always cross. Without the concept of the parallel, the fifth postulate will have no meaning for them. No parallel can start from a point outside the straight line. In their world, there are no parallels!"

I smiled at his enthusiasm. "At how many points do their straight lines cross?" I asked, with irony in my voice.

"Two! All the meridians of the Earth, which for our creatures are straight lines, cross at the North and South Poles. There goes the axiom 'from two points passes one and only one straight line.' Moreover, if we consider three points on one of these "straight lines" each one of them is between the other two, since we can always go from the first to the second, passing from the third".

"Careful," I warned. "We could equally validly say that, if we take three points on one of their 'straight lines,' none of them is situated between the other two, because we can always go from the first to the second following the opposite direction, that is, without going through the third. In other words, the word 'between' has absolutely no meaning for those beings. Riemann's geometry, which to us seems irrational, arbitrary and incomprehensible, is for them a natural, obvious geometry. So what have we achieved? We've created a two-dimensional model of Riemann's geometry within our three-dimensional Euclidean world. Therefore, if Euclidean geometry has no contradictions, then neither does Riemann's. That's what I meant when I said that the only way to prove the consistency of a mathematical system is to create a model of itself inside another space, another system. Have I made myself clear?"

"No doubt, oh blessed one, as Crito would have said to Socrates." He was clearly impressed. However, he had not yet made his final point. "I accept that you have provided masterly proof of the non-contradictory nature of Riemann's theory, as well as of its right to coexist as a theoretical structure with classic Euclidean geometry. I imagine that the application of this proof in Riemann's three-dimensional geometry is now a simple technical matter."

I nodded.

"And I assume that Beltrami did something similar to prove the non-contradictory nature of the Bolyai-Lobachevskian geometry," he continued.

"In general terms, yes," I replied. I promised him that I would send him the notes I had taken from various classes relating to the subject as soon as I was back in Göttingen.

"Hilbert, however, posed a problem of his own," Stefanos pointed out. "What other geometries can there be in addition to the three we know about? For every axiomatic system that we could establish, we will need corresponding proof of noncontradiction. Today we have already heard demands for proof of the consistency of the axioms on which Peano's arithmetic is based, proof of the non-contradictory character of the continuum hypothesis, and who knows what else might be demanded in the future? It's this same problem that will have to be faced by all branches of mathematics sooner or later, if not by mathematics as a whole. I think the time has come for us to try to work out some sort of mechanism by which it can be shown whether a set of axioms is both non-contradictory and complete; that is, whether it's capable of answering positively or negatively all the problems that can arise within it. In that respect, although the individual problems demonstrated by Hilbert are all very important, I believe the crucial point is found in the second of his problems: how to find a direct method of proving the consistency and completeness of an axiomatic system."

I could not agree with that. The idea of a mechanism that would test a theory *a priori,* before being tried in practice, and before allowing any actually creative work, annoyed me intensely. It shattered the romance of mathematical adventure for me, the magic of the mystery that accompanies every problem in mathematics, urging you to try to solve it. Such a mechanism would equate mathematicians with industrial workers who, in accordance with some predetermined program, play a small (maybe important, but limited) role in the whole production process; they can neither visualize the work as a whole, nor experience the grandeur and beauty of creativity. I viewed mathematics as a journey akin to the travels of the great explorers like Columbus, Vasco da Gama, and Magellan. They each set off on their voyages with a vague idea of what it was they were looking for, but without knowing whether they would find it or even if it really existed at all. If the testing method envisaged by Hilbert that had so excited my new friend were feasible, and if someone did manage to discover it, mathematical adventure would be downgraded to the level of a routine journey, like that of today's ocean liners traveling between Liverpool and New York or, worse still, a ferry between Dover and Calais.

"I think you misunderstood Hilbert's words," I answered. "Or rather, you misjudged them. The way you describe the solution to his second problem, it would soon reduce mathematics to something resembling Jacquard's looms."

Exactly a century ago, in 1800, Joseph Jacquard, an engineer from Lyon, had introduced a new type of mechanical loom to the market. He had devised a method of "translating" the design of the textile he wanted to reproduce into a row of punched cards. The cards, placed in the loom, guided the weaving without further intervention from humans. Despite the angry and occasionally violent reactions from weavers' guilds, Jacquard's machines had flooded not just France but the whole of Europe. My grandmother was very proud of the jacquard cloth bought direct from Paris for herself and her daughter.

Charles Babbage, an English mathematician, had tried to make a similar machine to do mathematical calculations, in collaboration with Ada Lovelace (Lord Byron's daughter). The British government had initially funded the project, but when no practical result came of it after a few years, they abandoned it. And yet, both Jacquard's successful loom and Babbage's failed Analytical Machine were aiming to produce a predetermined result. Jacquard wanted to cheaply and quickly produce thousands of bales of cloth based on prepared designs. Babbage wanted to quickly calculate, on the basis of a prearranged process, logarithmic, trigonometric, astronomic, and every other kind of mathematical tables. But what Hilbert was looking for, as Stefanos described it, was an ecumenical machine—a loom that would not only weave all strands of mathematics at once but also automatically test their correctness.

"I don't think it can be done," I said, feeling profoundly disturbed at the prospect. "But even if I had the misfortune of discovering such a diabolical mechanism, I would keep it secret; I might even have to cut out my tongue and amputate my hands, lest they betray me and speak of it accidentally or write it down somewhere!"

Stefanos was sticking to his guns and so was I. By now, many Parisians were walking down the Boulevard Saint-Michel for their afternoon stroll. We sat on the veranda of the bistro, sipping our cider, taking in the August sunshine, and pursuing our lively, heated discussion.

"If Toulouse-Lautrec were to walk past, he would stop to paint us," remarked Stefanos. "*Deux mathématiciens grecs se disputant dans un bistrot du Boulevard Saint-Michel.* We would become famous."

We burst out laughing—Two Greek Mathematicians Arguing in a Bistro of the Boulevard Saint-Michel! The tension evaporated. It was getting late, and we had to go back to the conference.

"Do you have any plans for tonight?" I asked Stefanos.

"Nothing special. I will probably stay in to put my conference notes in order and do some reading."

"Listen. Apart from being a delegate, I'm also a tourist. This trip gives us an opportunity not only for getting to know the scientific life of Paris, but also its famous nightlife. I've booked a table at the Moulin Rouge. It's not very original," I explained," rather ashamed of my extremely banal choice of venue after such a high-level discussion. The Moulin Rouge was a place where people went just to be seen. "But, you know, if it didn't have the university, Göttingen would be just a village. Will you do me the honor of accompanying me?"

He hesitated, and I could tell he was thinking that he wouldn't be able to reciprocate financially, but in the end he accepted.

The afternoon lectures of the conference commanded a noticeably smaller audience. The topics were more specialized, and the speakers had been overshadowed by the morning lecture and the brilliance of the one who had delivered it. Nevertheless, Stefanos and I attended them all with the zeal and fanaticism of new converts. Afterward, we parted, arranging to meet again that evening.

Interlude

Lysippos, the fourth principal of the Pythagorean school, was a venerable old man with a snow-white beard and almost no hair. He admitted Hippasus to the room he used whenever he wanted to think alone or work in total silence.

"You asked to see me. I'm listening."

A private audience with the principal of the school was a privilege that new members very rarely exercised, being aware that they must not abuse it. Pythagoreans disliked too many words anyway. Gathering up courage, Hippasus went straight to the point: "All is number."

"Aftos efa. Thus spoke the Master,*" consented Lysippos, uttering the ritual phrase with great respect.*

"I am thinking of a square with sides of a certain unit."

Lysippos prompted him to continue with a nod of the head.

"According to our principles, the measure of the diagonal has to be a number."

The old man looked disconcerted, but kept calm."Go on."

"In order to find this number, that is, the ratio between the diagonal and the side of the square, I need to use a common unit for measuring the diagonal and the side."

"And?"

"I have found proof that such a common unit does not exist. The side and the diagonal of the square are incommensurable quantities. There is no number that can represent the ratio between the diagonal and the side of the square. In other words, the diagonal is … irrational."

Hippasus spoke hesitantly, shyly, as if aware of the seriousness of what he was saying. His last sentence was almost a whisper. To his astonishment, the old man showed no surprise, having recovered from his initial shock. He remained silent for a while, and then began to speak slowly, looking the young man in the eye.

"You will show me your proof later. I want to see if it's the same as mine. But first, we have more important things to discuss."

He paused, savoring the surprise in the eyes of the young initiate, then smiled and continued: "Yes! For two years now I've known that the side and the diagonal of a square are incommensurable quantities. Deep down I was hoping that my deduction might hold some hidden error, but now you have come to me and confirmed my fears. In any case, I suppose you realize the gravity of such a discovery and the consequences of making it public, whether it's wrong or (as seems unfortunately to be the case) correct. The Master used to say that the meaning of numbers is the meaning of all things. It was he who discovered that numbers govern the harmony of sounds. He left us a command that we should discover how they also govern the harmony of the universe. If we lose our trust in numbers, we lose our trust in the harmony of the universe. Every moral and intellectual principle collapses. If a system of knowledge creates shapes but cannot measure them, if it conceives of numbers that are incapable of counting, how can it ever convey the vision of a universal harmony? If our faith in the power of numbers is weakened, the foundations of the Pythagorean system weaken, threatening to undermine peace, prosperity, and life itself. The dream of an elite society will fade, just as the wind destroyed the blasphemous shapes we made in the sand when you and I were each finding proof that the diagonal of a square is irrational. I can't let something like that happen. You must immediately forget your proof. You are not to mention it to anyone, not even the other initiates. Our generation cannot cope with such a discovery. Let us leave the burden to those who come after us."

Hippasus had not said a word until now. "But if the proof is correct," he protested, "if the diagonal and the sides of the square are indeed incommensurable ..."

Lysippos interrupted him. "If the foundation of a building is rotten, it can last for centuries, until a way is found to replace it. But if the foundation is removed altogether, the building will collapse at once."

"But if the problem is kept a secret, how can anyone solve it?"

"Let me remind you of the oath of silence you have taken. I am from this moment extending it to the initiates and all members of the school. I forbid you to utter a single word to anyone on the subject. I forbid you to go on with your research. And don't forget that obedience is a condition of belonging to the brotherhood. Go."

Devastated, Hippasus rose. As he was leaving the room, he gathered up courage and whispered: "Are there no mathematicians, then? Are we to remain acousmatics forever?"

Lysippos did not reply. He buried his elderly head in his hands and sat thinking for a long while. He was awoken from his trance by the footsteps of his trusted assistant, Chirocles.

"You can see, there is no other solution," said Chirocles without beating about the bush.

"Do what has to be done," replied the old man in a trembling voice.

Four

Stefanos was staying in Montmartre; he had an attic room in an apartment block that housed penniless artists and students. We had arranged to meet at the Place Pigale. On leaving my hotel, I felt the sweetness of the warm August evening wrap itself around me. At first I thought of treating myself to a night ride in a hackney carriage. But in the end I chose the horse-drawn municipal tram to avoid an uncalled-for display of wealth to my new friend.

When Montmartre was still a village, it had thirty working windmills. It was ironic that it had become famous mainly on account of the only mill that was unable to harness the wind in its sails to turn a millstone. On the centennial of the French Revolution, in the same year the Eiffel Tower was erected, the Moulin Rouge opened its doors to the public. The building, a mixture of Norman and Spanish architecture, contained a huge dance hall and an open-air theater; its façade was dominated by the image of a red mill. It was to this temple of entertainment that I led my new friend.

Despite being well-traveled, I was impressed by the great dance hall, with its bare wooden beams. Huge candelabras filled the room with light. Velvet upholsteries shone brightly, luxurious tables glittered, and our shoes sank into thick carpets. The wall at the other end of the hall was entirely covered by a gigantic mirror. In a gallery above it sat the orchestra. A door led to the theater out in the garden.

Slipping an appropriate bank note in the maitre d'hôtel's pocket, I secured us a good table near the stage. I ordered a bottle of Veuve Clicquot and some of Fauchon's renowned champagne biscuits. Stefanos was looking around him with curiosity. Although it was obvious that this was the first time he had found himself in such surroundings, he didn't look particularly impressed.

Opposite us sat a short man with small, stumpy legs and a chest out of proportion to the rest of his body. Though he was fairly young, his face was pale and haggard. One after another, *artistes* circulating in the hall would run up to him and give him the typical French triple kiss.

Stefanos nodded in his direction. "Toulouse-Lautrec," he said "'Our' painter. It seems he would rather draw cabaret girls than us. And they're wild about him. Do you see them? I've heard he has spent time in the sanatorium recently. You know ..." he laughed awkwardly. "They call it the French disease ... but drink contributes to it. It's a shame, because he has great talent. He has a way of capturing movement in the air—it's as if he's painting not dancers but dance itself. The circular movement of their bodies contrasts with the motionless audience and lends the ritual of dance an existence distinct from the individuals. Not that bodies leave him cold, of course. He does paint them, sometimes with particular cruelty, emphasizing their imperfections—especially those that are due to overindulgence. Those same vices have destroyed him, as well.

"If you ever go to the Mirliton cabaret, the walls are covered in his paintings. The man who first appreciated his work was the poet Aristide Bruant, and when Bruant was hired to appear at the Ambassadeur, he insisted that his show be advertised through Toulouse-Lautrec's posters. Later, Bruant opened his own place, Mirliton, which became infamous for the maltreatment of its guests. Dozens of Parisians flocked to his cabaret in the 1890s to be entertained by the poet's rhyming abuse and drink cheap alcohol at exorbitant prices. At the same time, they had the opportunity to marvel at Toulouse-Lautrec's paintings, and he later undertook to illustrate Bruant's newspaper. When Paris was flooded with posters ordered from Toulouse-Lautrec by the Moulin Rouge, he became famous. It's a shame that his excesses bring him closer to his end by the day."

I looked at Stefanos with surprise. I had no idea he was so well-informed about the artistic world. He laughed. "How come I know so much? Well, there are three young painters staying in the same house as me. They arrived a month ago from Spain. One of them is in fact displaying a painting in the Spanish Pavilion at the International Exhibition. We go out together every now and then. It's they who keep me up to date with the arts scene. I will introduce you to them. Tomorrow night we've arranged to meet at the Zut, a bistro near our house. The venue is nothing special, but the owner is nice and the company interesting. If you like—"

His sentence was cut short by a sudden commotion at the door. A large group of noisy people appeared; the most boisterous of all was the hero of the day: David Hilbert himself! He walked in briskly, gesturing and shouting, but not forgetting to bow and smile at the pretty ladies, handing out compliments and kissing their hands.

It was Stefanos' turn to stare open-mouthed. In his mind, the *monstres sacrés* of our science lived only for mathematics. But I knew this was not so. Hilbert was well-known as a *bon viveur* in Göttingen. Social life in the medieval university town was restricted to a few top-quality restaurants and the musical soirées organized at the houses of the professors, but Hilbert was the star of these rare social events, taking part with gusto and a sense of fun, and sometimes overstepping the boundaries set for an otherwise respectable academic. At one gathering, he had insisted on putting on a lady's plumed hat and singing *a cappella* a rather risqué ditty of the time. The incident caused a scandal that was talked about for months. Hilbert himself didn't seem to care at all. He continued to carry out his passion for cultivating roses in his garden and offering them to the ladies of the town, often causing offense to their husbands. So I was not at all surprised to see that he had abandoned the company of Klein and Poincaré to lead a group of more high-spirited friends into the temple of Parisian nightlife.

"Is this how he always behaves?" asked an astonished Stefanos.

"Almost. And it's not so surprising considering his unorthodox behavior in the way he works. Don't you remember what happened with Gordan's problem?"

Stefanos looked at me inquiringly. He didn't speak German, so his only means of keeping informed was via lectures and articles published in French. He said he had read about Gordan's problem in the *Comptes Rendus,* the minutes of the French Academy of Sciences. There were no details (as the minutes were always in summary form), but he had learned that Herr Hilbert of Göttingen had given a "non-constructible solution" to it.

"Have you heard nothing about the storm that broke out regarding this 'non-constructible solution'?" I asked.

"I must admit I haven't. To be honest, I don't really understand the term 'non-constructible.'"

"Well then, listen. Whenever I want to solve an equation, I describe my actions step by step, leading to the solution. I raise this to the second power, I subtract that, I divide the other, and so on. If I've managed to complete all the necessary steps, I will have the solution in front of me. But if I stumble at any point—if, for example, it turns out that I have to divide something by zero, then I realize that there is no solution to the problem. Gordan tried to solve his problem step by step as I described, and in certain simple parts of it he managed to do it, after painstaking calculations. But solving the overall problem seemed to be out of reach.

"Hilbert was then a young man who had just received his doctorate (we're talking about 1888) when he decided to take on the challenge. The shock that the upper classes of Göttingen received when they heard that he had sung in public wearing a woman's hat was nothing compared with the shock of the mathematical community when they saw the solution he had given to Gordan's problem. Leaving aside computational methods, he chose not to construct a solution; instead he simply proved that *it is impossible that a solution doesn't exsist.*"

This was the first time in the history of mathematics that someone had been bold enough to prove the existence of a mathematical solution without illustrating how it was to be constructed. The article Hilbert published in 1888 created an uproar. The ultraconservative Kronecker, who doubted even the existence of irrational numbers such as the square root of 2, dismissed the solution without further argument. Gordan himself, who was known for his geniality and his generosity toward young, talented mathematicians, responded angrily to Hilbert's paper, saying, "This is not mathematics, but theology." As for Lindemann, he described his former pupil's method as *unheimlich*—profane. Others, however, such as Arthur Cayley in Cambridge and Klein studied the proof in detail and, having initially believed it to be impossible, ended up congratulating Hilbert warmly. Hilbert became a fanatical proponent of proofs of existence. "Inside this hall," he would often say in his lectures, "there is at least one student who has more hair on his head than any other. We don't know who that person is, nor is there any practical way of finding out. But this doesn't mean that he doesn't exist!"

As we conversed, I became aware that Stefanos and I had begun to address each other in the familiar singular form, used by Greeks only after long acquaintance. Although we had met only a few hours earlier, I felt as if I was talking to an old friend. Our conversation turned again to that morning's lecture.

Fortunately, no one in the hall understood Greek. Otherwise the sight of two young men sitting in Europe's most famous cabaret surrounded by dozens of half-naked women, drinking champagne, and talking about ... mathematics ... would have seemed very odd.

After a while, music announced the beginning of the evening's program, putting a halt to our philosophical-mathematical exchanges. I, for one, concentrated on the spectacular show. Shapely legs kicked the air gracefully, performing amazing moves and incredible leaps; ruffled petticoats, fishnet stockings, and laced lingerie all swept equations, roots, and consistent axiomatic systems completely from my mind.

Jane Avril was a brilliant successor to the famous Louise Weber, who a few years before had been the undisputed queen of the Moulin Rouge and Parisian nightlife. Louise's greediness had earned her the nickname "La Goulue" (the Glutton), by which she had become famous. After she left the Moulin Rouge and suffered a failed attempt to open her own cabaret, she ended up as part of a circus act in a stall at the Foire du Trône, the world-famous Parisian fairground. Toulouse-Lautrec's familiar painting bearing her nickname is the only thing that remains of her former glory.

Every now and then during the show I would glance at Stefanos, and his attention seemed equally divided between the can-can and Hilbert. As for the hero of the day, he was having a great time. That morning he had asked us to raise the veil that was hiding the future of mathematics. I could now see that he was just as enthusiastic about the raising of petticoats covering the dancers' legs. Champagne bottles were being opened one after another at his table, and when two girls insisted on dragging him on to the dance floor, he happily followed them, raising a storm of applause from the public.

After the show was over, two girls came over to our table. We introduced ourselves and laughed at the inevitable "ooh-la-la" and the faces they made when they heard that we were mathematicians. We danced, became tipsy, and the evening proceeded as expected. We ended up at the girls' hotel, from which we went straight to the conference the next morning.

"Your friend is very shy," said Charlotte as I was discreetly giving the girls their "tip." "But he's very affectionate. From now on, as far as I'm concerned, mathematicians—especially Greek ones—are the best clients ..."

Padoa's lecture relating to definitions in Euclidean geometry monopolized the morning's session, and I made every effort to follow it as well as I could. After the clashes between Hilbert and Peano the previous day, everyone was expecting the Italians to respond. Padoa delivered, underlining with particular malice a number of mistakes contained in the *Foundations* Hilbert had published the previous year. At the end of his talk, Padoa referred to Hilbert's lecture of the day before. I believe this section had been added the previous night during an emergency meeting of Peano's team.

"Our distinguished colleague," Padoa said, "asked for proof of the consistency of the axioms of arithmetic. He presumably means that we need to present a model, a group of entities that will satisfy those axioms. But just such a group can be found in the natural numbers themselves! Or does he envisage a proof of consistency without a model—for me, such a thing seems to be impossible. Can't our colleague see the risk of falling into a vicious circle?"

Hilbert, who was present and sitting in the front row, didn't reply. I'm sure he must have recognized that the Italian was right in his criticism of the *Foundations* (as demonstrated by the number of new editions that he published in the thirty years following the first one.) As for the criticism of his lecture concerning the way he framed his second problem, neither he nor his critic could have possibly imagined the way that the issue would develop in the ensuing decades.

When the morning lectures were over, I felt as if I was going to pass out. Stefanos, on the contrary, didn't betray any signs of the previous night's celebrations. He informed me that that evening he was going out with his artistic friends and assured me that they would love to meet me; without further ado, he took the initiative and invited me as his guest. "After all, they have a particular interest in mathematics," he said. I had very little resistance left.

After two nights of the high life, I welcomed a quiet evening in a bohemian bistro, and I accepted.

I arranged our rendezvous for later, made him promise that he would lend me his notes on the afternoon session, and went straight to bed.

Five

The distance between the Moulin Rouge and the Zut was no more than five hundred meters, but that five hundred meters from the Boulevard de Clichy to the Rue Ravignan separated two worlds that could easily have been a few light years apart. You left the big boulevards of the city, and in a few minutes found yourself in the narrow lanes of a small village. You left the horse-drawn carriages and cabs with their well-dressed passengers, and suddenly found you were walking along empty streets where it was rare to come across anyone—and if you did, you weren't sure whether it would be for good or ill.

Instead of the velvet armchairs of the Moulin Rouge, the Zut featured chairs with broken straw seats. Empty beer barrels stood together here and there under the low ceiling, serving as tables. The floor was made of stamped gravel covered with a layer of sawdust to soak up spilled drinks. Instead of the expensive French perfumes that intoxicated you at the Moulin Rouge, the pervading odors at the Zut were of rancid oil, anise, cigarette butts, and, worst of all, a strong smell of cat urine. Two gas lamps with hundreds of flies stuck on them shed a faint green light in the long hall. Little triangular paper flags hung from the ceiling by way of decoration. At one end of the room a coffee machine sat on top of a dilapidated bench, also roughly made from barrels and wooden frames. Behind it were shelves that seriously challenged the axiom of parallel lines, upon which stood rows of bottles of cheap wine, pastis, and the syrups of menthe and gooseberry used in the preparation of the renowned "diabolo."

The customers of this establishment were a real sight. There were small-time pimps sipping absinthe, a yellowed cigarette stuck to their lips, waiting lazily for the girls they managed to bring in their takes; dark-faced gangsters called *Apaches,* wearing flashy kerchiefs round their necks, bragging loudly of their adventures and boasting of their latest brawl, drinking red wine and spitting chewed tobacco on the floor. In the farthest and darkest corners, lovers found refuge. Young seamstresses, milliners, and shop assistants from the Dufayel came there after work to meet their boyfriends—laborers from nearby factories and workers from building sites who had also just finished work. Their routine was a glass of cassis, a few warm words, and a quick kiss before they fell into a deep, dreamless sleep, an inadequate rest between each twelve-hour shift. I tried to picture my grandmother in this setting and felt a sort of cruel satisfaction.

A narrow corridor led to the rooms at the back. We entered the second one, which was slightly smaller than the first. "Here," explained Stefanos, "is where the anarchists hang out." These comprised the editorial team of the *Libertin,* various "*libellistes*" who called themselves poets, as well as assorted out-of-work youths who were happy to channel their anger and disappointment into any sort of disturbance, whether they knew its cause or not.

"I bet you won't be able to tell who is the spy on duty tonight," said Stefanos. "But you can be sure there will be one. The security police have branded this place a 'nest of anarchists' and allow pimps and thieves to operate freely so long as they keep them informed of the political activities of the day."

After their expulsion from the Second International, an organization of socialist and labour parties, the anarchists of Paris had turned to violent forms of protest. Eight years earlier, in 1892, they had instigated a series of bomb attacks that had greatly alarmed the authorities. The arrest and execution of one of their leaders, Ravachol, had somewhat curtailed their activities, but the authorities had recently been extra vigilant because of the International Exhibition.

The third room was empty. "Come and see," said Stefanos. "This is the Spanish room. Frédé, the owner, has a soft spot for the Spanish artists of Montmartre and reserves this room exclusively for them in the winter. But as it's hot today, they're sure to be sitting outside. Frédé saves this room for 'his artists,' as he calls them, and they in turn do their best to decorate it beautifully."

The walls of the room were indeed elaborately decorated. One was entirely covered with a religious scene. "*The Temptation of St. Anthony,*" explained Stefanos. "My friend painted this." Facing St. Anthony was a picture of the Eiffel Tower, clearly by a different hand, showing a flying machine circling it. "Have you heard of Alberto Santos-Dumont?" Stefanos asked. "He's a wealthy Brazilian who is spending his family fortune building flying contraptions. They look like the Montgolfier hot-air balloons, but Dumont has equipped them with a gasoline-run motor so that they can be navigated. Here you see his latest achievement. He took off from Saint-Cloud, flew over Paris, circled around the Eiffel Tower, and landed where he started from. On that day no Parisian was looking straight ahead; they all had their eyes turned to the sky. I don't need to tell you how many tripped and fell on their faces."

At the end of the corridor a door led into the garden. The same "furniture" of barrels and collapsing chairs looked completely different under the acacias and chestnut trees. In a corner was tethered the owner's little donkey, Lolo. As I learned later, Frédé Gérard had been an itinerant fishmonger for many years, and Lolo used to draw his cart. He then worked for a while as a singer of sorts in Aristide Bruant's cabaret before opening the Zut. Following her master's promotion to café owner, Lolo had been upgraded to house mascot.

Stefanos' friends were indeed sitting outside. As soon as we stepped through the door, the sweet-smelling air of the countryside filled my lungs—the top of the hill of Montmartre was still very rural then. I drew a deep breath and felt the delicious evening breeze, lightly perfumed by the nearby gardens and parks.

They welcomed us—or rather Stefanos—warmly. "*Salut le Grec,*" called one in jest. Stefanos had explained to me that the name Kandartzis had been too hard for their Latinized tongues to pronounce, and since there was no other Greek in their group, they had decided to call him "le Grec."

"I find it very funny," he said, "especially when Pablo calls me 'el Greco,' when I'm not even capable of drawing a straight line without a ruler." He introduced me: "My compatriot Michael Igerinos. These are my friends—Pablo Ruiz, Manuel Pallarés, and Carles Casagemas." He gave an embarrassed laugh. "I don't know the ladies." I was impressed with how well Stefanos had acquired French tact; the girls sitting among the three Spaniards had nothing ladylike about them. One of them volunteered to finish the introductions: "My name is Germaine, that is Odette, and the little one here is Antoinette. Watch-out, she's still a virgin." Antoinette said something that is best not repeated, and everyone burst out laughing.

I looked our new acquaintances up and down. The only thing the three men had in common was their identical suits of black velvet. They were different in all other respects. Ruiz was a small man, with delicate, almost feminine features; he seemed to be the leader of the group, even though he was the youngest—less than twenty at the time. Casagemas' face was prematurely aged, with black circles around the eyes and a melancholy look, now staring longingly at Germaine, now with despair in front of him. His dilated pupils and shaking hands betrayed someone long addicted to narcotics. Pallarés, on the contrary, was a tall, well-built, athletic man, who seemed not to fit in with the rundown surroundings. As for the girls, they more than justified the legend of the "*petites dames de Paris*"—gay, cheerful, uninhibited. They were heavily made up, had taken extreme care of their hair and fingernails, and were dressed in such a way that—in view of the strict morals of the time—looking at them lead your thoughts straight through the gates of hell. Germaine was the one who set the tone: tall and slim, with big sensuous eyes and full lips. She pretended not to notice Casagemas' healthy interest in her, yet made sure she kept it alive, fluttering her eyelashes or throwing him an indifferent, supposedly accidental look or touching him in passing, which made poor Casagemas tremble all over. Odette was like a figure out of a Toulouse-Lautrec painting: she was plump, with a large bosom and pronounced curves, and she showed particular interest in Stefanos. Finally, "little" Antoinette was dark, with small, mischievous black eyes and a typically Parisian nose, and she was trying hard to disprove her friend's description of her.

"Pablo lives only for his art," Stefanos informed me. "He paints his soul onto the canvas and makes cuckolds of Parisians. Unless one of them kills him, one day he will become famous."

"You mean he's already famous," said Odette. "You forget that his picture *Last Moments* is hanging in the Spanish Pavilion of the Exhibition."

"Not only famous, but also rich," added Manuel. "Bertha Weil gave him one hundred francs last week—yes, sir, a whole gold *louis*—for three paintings. This morning she arrived at the crack of dawn, wanting to see the rest and choose some more to buy. Our compatriot Manach, the man who introduced her to us, had the crazy idea of arranging a rendezvous for her at eleven in the morning. So fat old Bertha climbs all six floors and starts banging on the door demanding to be heard. Who was there to answer? Carles had downed three liters of wine and was asleep, dreaming of Germaine as usual. That same Germaine had spent the night teaching Pablo ... French, and he was snoring to high heaven. As for me," he winked at the other two women, "I was having to look after the girls and I was exhausted. Bertha lost patience and tumbled downstairs again, swearing. She thought we had stood her up. Fortunately, Manach showed up just then. He calmed her down, persuaded her to come upstairs again, and after waking up the entire Rue Gabriel, managed to rouse Pablo from his slumber. You should have seen Bertha, drenched in sweat, huffing and puffing, mad with anger, while Pablo stood there in his nightshirt looking dazed."

Their laughter rang out in the small garden. Only Casagemas remained silent, drawing on his cigarette with fury and shooting pained glances at Germaine.

"By the way, have you been to the Exhibition?" Ruiz asked me. He spoke slowly in broken French, searching for each word.

"Not yet," I replied. "Stefanos and I hope to go tomorrow."

At that moment, Frédé appeared. He was rather short, with a thick beard and small, bright eyes set deep in their sockets. His attire—a red kerchief around his head and wooden clogs—resembled something between that of a pirate and a victim of a shipwreck. "What will my boys have?" he asked warmly. He loved the three Spaniards. We ordered, and I asked for a cognac, hoping the alcohol would disinfect the glass, the cleanliness of which was open to question.

"Eh, Frédé! What happened to your guitar today, is it broken?" shouted an old man from the next table. "Work comes first, my son," answered the bistro keeper. He served us and then sat at his own "private" barrel-table. "Babette, mind the shop," he called to his wife. Then he took up his guitar and began playing.

His voice was off-pitch and hoarse, a relic of his old profession; the guitar, which only played one or two chords, was out of tune. But the atmosphere was magical. He sang old, popular romantic songs, such as *Le Temps des Cerises* (The Time of Cherry Blossoms) or *Plaisirs d'Amour* (Joys of Love)—pieces that all modern piano teachers taught their pupils as companions to *Für Elise* and *Lindenbaum*. I had therefore heard them many times at the evening gatherings that my parents dragged me to, played by girls of my age with excessive care and lack of talent. They would purse their lips, bite their tongue, frown, and get to the end without any mistake, but without any feeling either. I, of course, at the time was more interested in the young breasts that were beginning to form underneath their silk dresses, and the occasional heaven-sent revelation of an ankle whenever their long skirts got caught in the carvings of the piano stool. Listening to such songs from the former employee of Aristide Bruant, now owner of the filthy but wonderful bistro in Paris, along with an international bohemian company, was a different matter.

"Do you live in Paris?" asked Ruiz.

"No. I am studying in Göttingen. I came to Paris for the conference."

"A mathematical conference?" piped up Antoinette coquettishly. "What do you confer about? Do you work out what makes one plus one?"

Ruiz darted her a look of annoyance.

"Joking aside, what have you heard about at the conference?" he asked seriously. "Is anything new happening in the world of mathematics? Anything exciting?"

I had always been reluctant to talk about mathematics to nonexperts. It annoyed me to see the disapproving grimaces of people when they thought a mathematical discussion was in store, just as I saw in the girls' faces now. I had already been irritated by Antoinette's "one plus one" comment—naturally, I was not to know that some years later Russell would devote more than one hundred pages in his book to this very question. In any case, my relationship with the "queen of the sciences" was one of full participation (in the Platonic sense) and worship that I didn't feel like sharing with laymen. The ball therefore passed straight into Stefanos' court. I now discovered that in addition to his keen interest in mathematics, he had a talent for teaching. Overcoming his natural shyness, he began to talk. Ruiz was hanging on his every word and would interrupt whenever he could, as far as his very poor French would allow. Pallarés listened with interest. Odette made an effort to follow what was being said, while the other girls were clearly bored. As for Casagemas, he was in his own world.

"Many lectures were excellent," my friend began. "Poincaré's, Klein's, Hadamard's—but I believe Hilbert's was the most important. In just one hour he managed to show us a panorama of the most pressing problems that remain unsolved. I believe that his paper will form the basic agenda for mathematical research in the new century."

"What sort of research are you talking about?" asked Pallarés. "I thought everything had been discovered by now, first by your fellow countrymen and then by Newton and Descartes."

Stefanos laughed. "The last century was one of the most productive in mathematical discoveries. But I predict that the one ahead of us will be even richer. There are still many problems awaiting their solution. Usually, new theories have to be devised in order to solve the great problems, and those theories give birth to their own new problems."

"I wonder what these problems are," Pallarés persisted. "Can you give me an example? Some problem that we can all understand?"

"Yes, I think I have a good example for you. And if I can understand it—having no natural sense of space—so much more will you, since the representation of space is part of your work." I admired the way Stefanos had managed to predispose in his favor an audience who had initially been hostile to mathematics. By making this innocent little compliment (which I myself would never have thought of doing), he had immediately won over the attention of the company.

"But first we must get a few things straight," he continued. "A regular polygon has equal sides and equal angles. Some examples are an equilateral triangle with angles of 60 degrees each, a square with angles of 90 degrees, a regular pentagon with angles of 108 degrees, a regular hexagon with angles of 120 degrees, and so on. First problem: Which regular polygons can we use to cover a plane surface? All the polygons must be the same and of equal size and the surface must be completely covered, leaving no gaps. Come on, gentlemen. This is an easy problem, just to whet your appetite."

"Let's see," said Pablo presently. "A number of polygons must meet at their corners, so that their angles make up a whole circle. It can be done with triangles, for example. Six triangles with 60-degree angles make up 360 degrees. There is your circle."

"Surely one can also do it with squares," joined in Pallarés. "Four squares of 90 degrees equal 360 degrees."

"Can it be done with pentagons?" Stefanos asked them.

"Four pentagons with angles of 108 degrees equal 432 degrees; this creates an overlap, so it can't be done," said Pallarés.

"Whereas three pentagons are not enough," chipped in Odette. "They add up to 324 degrees, and we need another 36 degrees in order to complete the circle. I think it can't be done with pentagons." She turned and looked at Ruiz triumphantly. It was obvious that this little display was for his benefit only.

"So what is your conclusion?" prompted Stefanos.

"It can't be done with pentagons," stated Pablo. "Three of them are too few and four are too many. But it must be feasible with three hexagons. Three times 120 makes 360."

Stefanos and I exchanged a conspiratorial smile. A painter usually has an excellent sense of space, so it was not surprising that they had found the three solutions so quickly. But would they be prepared to prove that these solutions were the only possible ones?

"And there are no other solutions." Pablo gave the answer before we could pose the question.

"Yes, but why?" asked Stefanos, unfazed.

"What do you mean, why?" said Manuel impatiently. "You show me another solution and I'll buy everyone a drink. There is no other solution; it's obvious."

Pablo was more circumspect. "That's what my father says: 'There is only one way of painting a portrait. One and no other. It's obvious.' But me, I'm not so sure."

"If we want to be sure there are no solutions other than the three you have identified, we must have proof," I interjected. "Nothing is 'obvious' in mathematics."

"So let's see," Stefanos began again. "It's absolutely necessary that the angles of the polygons add up to exactly 360 degrees. And since all the angles are equal …"

"… we need to make 360 by multiplying the number of polygons times the angle," blurted out Pablo in triumph.

"But the greater the number of sides of a polygon, the wider the angle," continued Stefanos. "Therefore, the more sides a polygon has, the fewer polygons are needed to complete the circle. We've already gotten as far as three hexagons. If we take two polygons, the angle must be …"

"… 180 degrees," said Odette.

"Yes, but then it's no longer an angle, it's a straight line," said Pablo.

"That's exactly why the solutions we found earlier are the only ones," concluded Stefanos triumphantly. "We've proven that the only regular polygons that can fill a given space are the triangle, the square, and the hexagon."

"We must consecrate the solution with alcohol," said Pablo with delight. "Frédé, wine for everyone. Praise be to Madame Bertha's francs!" He was genuinely elated.

After we had all drunk to Pablo's health, to "fat Bertha's" purse, and to mathematics, Pablo pressed Stefanos to continue.

"Now, since most shapes cannot cover the surface completely, we're faced with the problem of optimum coverage. If we can't do it perfectly, we can at least do it as well as possible. What is the ideal positioning of identical tiles with which we want to cover a flat surface, so that the least space remains uncovered? Let's suppose that we have a square of 10 centimeters by 10 centimeters, and we want to cover it using discs with a diameter of 1 centimeter. How many can we fit in?"

"I think that's easy," said Odette. "If the discs have a diameter of 1 centimeter and the square has sides of 10 centimeters, then we can fit ten discs along each side. We can fit ten such rows inside the square, so we will have used one hundred discs."

"*Eh ben dis donc,* you're a star!" exclaimed Antoinette, just to say something. She had been aware for some time that Odette was monopolizing the men's interest, and she didn't like that. Disapproving smiles spread simultaneously over the faces of Pallarés and Ruiz.

"That's not right," Pablo spoke first. He took some coins out of his pocket and laid them on the table. "Odette, you want to put your discs one below the other, which means you're leaving big gaps. I have a better way." He put two rows of ten coins each in parallel lines, and squeezed between them another row of nine more. "If you continue alternating between rows of ten and nine coins, you will be able to fit eleven rows inside the square: six of ten and five of nine. That already gives us one hundred and five discs. And I suppose that, as our friend el Greco here would say, you will still not be sure whether you have found the best solution. You will have to prove that there is no other, better solution."

The venomous yet triumphant smile that Antoinette flashed toward Odette would have led one to believe that she had solved the problem.

"I can give you a more difficult problem, if you like," continued Stefanos, "an unsolved problem, where all you need to do is transfer the same situation to three-dimensional space. What is the best way of stacking up identical spheres so that the gap between them is the smallest possible?"

"For God's sake, who would want to know all that?" complained Antoinette.

"Greengrocers," Manuel answered. "They would naturally want to know the best way of piling up their apples and oranges."

"You don't know how right you are," I said. "Mathematicians call this 'the greengrocer's problem.' Of course, greengrocers solved the problem long ago. They place a first layer of apples at the bottom so that they create a network of equilateral triangles—just like we did with the coins in the previous example. For every three apples whose centers create an equilateral triangle, there is a gap in which another apple can fit. This is how the second layer is formed, and so on."

"So where is the difficulty?" Manuel asked. "We've all seen pyramids of fruit in the market. You don't have to be a mathematician to understand how it's done. It's the way my fellow villagers back at Gorda del Ebro stack up the fruit in their stalls. And yet they've never been to school. Do you remember, Pablo?"

The previous year Spain had been embroiled in a war with the United States over Cuba's independence. Pallarés would have been conscripted, but he and Ruiz had taken refuge in the mountains around his village, where they had lived for six months in a cave like savages.

"The difficulty is always the same," I said. "How can we guarantee that this is the best solution? The greengrocer's method covers 74 percent of the space. A proportion of 26 percent remains unused. Is there another way of filling the space better? No one has yet found one, but no one has proven that there is no better way."

"I've certainly not found any greengrocer who doubts this is the best method," said Manuel stubbornly.

"I don't know of any doubting greengrocers either," I replied. "But I do know of a doubting astronomer, and a great one to boot. The problem of 'determining the optimum way of piling up identical spheres' was first stated three centuries ago by Kepler. He is the man who formulated the laws of the orbital movement of the planets. He, too, claimed that the greengrocer's solution is the best, but he expressed it as a conjecture that requires proof. That proof hasn't been discovered by anyone to this day."

"Here, then, is an unsolved mathematical problem, to which no one knows the solution yet," Stefanos exclaimed. "I think Kepler's conjecture can be easily understood by anyone. Expressed in its simplest form, it's one of the twenty-three problems presented by Hilbert in his lecture. Of course, there are others whose formulation at least is easy enough. For example—"

"No more mathematics, please," objected Germaine. "The night is so beautiful. Let's go dancing instead."

A flash of anger crossed Ruiz's face, as he was clearly enjoying the discussion. But he changed his mind when he saw Casagemas' miserable look when he feared that his love might not have her way. "All right," said Ruiz. As always, he decided without asking anyone else. "Let's go to the Moulin de la Galette."

In contrast to the Moulin Rouge, the dance hall of the Moulin de la Galette was part of an authentic old windmill. Legend had it that when the Russians entered Paris in 1814 after Napoleon's retreat, the owner of the mill, a man called Debray, had defended it to his death. When he finally succumbed to the superiority of the Cossacks, they made an example of him by dismembering him and hanging the pieces on the mill's sails. A few years later, Debray's heirs converted the building into a dance hall.

The colorful crowds, the swaying of the dancers, the costumes, the lights, and the spectacular atmosphere of the Moulin de la Galette all became a favorite subject for dozens of painters around the end of the nineteenth and the beginning of the twentieth century. Renoir and van Gogh had already recorded it in their paintings. Utrillo was to follow them a few years later. That night, instead of dancing, a young unknown painter from our multinational group never stopped sketching in his notebook. Those rough sketches would later form the material for yet another *Le Moulin de la Galette,* signed by the most famous artist of the twentieth century.

The great hall was decorated in shades of green, so that it felt like a huge garden. The orchestra, made up mainly of wind instruments, greeted us with a jovial polka. Germaine grabbed Carles, who followed her meekly to the dance floor. Pablo made it clear that he had absolutely no intention of dancing. Odette turned to Stefanos, who blushed and accepted, apologizing at once for not being very good at it. I signaled to Manuel and Antoinette that I would join them later, took up my glass, and sat next to Pablo, who had already begun to draw.

"What fascinates me is the fluidity of dance," he said. "You open your eyes and stamp the picture in your memory—a certain position of the faces, the alignment of colors, the alternation of light and shade. You close your eyes, open them again, and everything has changed. No rules! Some faces have moved, some have stayed where they were before. The same colors placed in a different order produce a different picture. If an Impressionist were here, he would envisage ten paintings within a few minutes, assuming, of course, that his memory could record each one without mixing them up. But me … I want to paint them all at once."

In the meantime, the polka had been replaced by a waltz. Carles staggered toward the bar, and Germaine insisted that I take his place on the dance floor. So much for the quiet evening I had planned for myself.

Our company broke up in the early hours of the morning. The house where the Spaniards and Stefanos lived was next door. They offered to put me up for the night, but the thought of sleeping on the floor after so much dancing and drinking didn't appeal to me. I chose to collapse on the back seat of a carriage, having barely managed to give the driver slurred directions to my hotel.

Six

As soon as the morning session finished on Friday, Stefanos and I jumped into a cab and went straight to the Spanish Pavilion of the Exhibition. When we got to the section called "New Spanish Painters," we saw it: Pablo Ruiz, *Last Moments.* I can't say I liked it very much. The dull, dark colors did suit the subject matter, a death scene, but they were in stark contrast not only to my mood, but also to the general atmosphere of celebration pervading Paris at the time.

"It was inspired by the death of his younger sister Conchita," Stefanos informed me. "She died five years ago, when Pablo was thirteen years old. Just between you and me, I gather that the artist himself doesn't particularly like this painting. He's of course proud to have had his work chosen for the Exhibition, but he doesn't feel it represents him. He says it's a work that could have been done by his father or even his grandfather. He himself is still searching for a personal style."

Despite not liking the painting, I felt a strange pride knowing that I had met the painter in person, had actually been drinking with him only the night before. Such is the vanity of youth.

We saw a bit more of the Spanish Pavilion, then walked over to the Greek one. I'm not sure if it was simply a matter of taste or pure chauvinism, but I was more impressed by the works of my fellow countrymen. The painting *The Children's Concert* by Jakobides was particularly touching. It showed four barefoot urchins playing music to a baby who is held by a woman. One of them is playing the drum, the second a trumpet, and you can just glimpse the harmonica in the hands of the third. As for the fourth, who is standing behind the others, he could be an uninvited participant, as he's blowing hard into a watering can, using it as a saxophone! The guest of honor is a baby, who is reaching out with open arms, as if he wants to embrace the whole orchestra at once.

"What do you think?" I asked Stefanos. "Isn't our fellow Greek better?" I knew Jakobides, who was then living in Germany; I had been to his studio many times. Stefanos had his own views about painting, in keeping with my recent observations of him. I asked for his opinion, with the intention of reporting back to the artist himself. "I was talking to a colleague in Paris about your work," I would say. "His opinion is … 'When you're twenty-three years old, such things are permitted.'"

"It reminds me of myself when I was little," said Stefanos. "A military band once passed through our village and played in the square. After that, I and the other boys would constantly play at being an orchestra. I myself have played the saxophone using a watering can, the trumpet using an empty bottle, the drum using … anything. This painting is a scene out of my life. That house is my house. Those urchins are my friends and the woman my mother. The baby is the little brother I could have had. You ask if I like it—I am moved by it. When I'm back in my cold room, frustrated because I can't find the solution to a problem, I will bring this painting to mind and it will raise my spirits. The work however is not … mathematical; it soothes me, it doesn't raise questions in my mind. I don't feel as if I'm going to wake up one night having discovered in it something that has eluded me up to then. I will always think of it with affection."

He laughed good-naturedly at my expression. "I've confused you! Sometimes I get carried away by armchair philosophy. Shall we go?"

Leaving the Greek Pavilion, we walked toward the Eiffel Tower. We stood on the hill of Chaillot for a while and looked at the tower, which rose up on the opposite bank of the Seine. Seen from afar, it was a pleasant view. Its curves and symmetrical lines had a charm of their own, and they seemed to push its narrow central axis toward the sky. As a geometrician, I could not help a feeling of satisfaction at the sight of such an extravaganza of triangles dominating its skeleton.

We followed the course of the river and crossed over the Pont d'Iéna. As we neared the steel monster, I realized how gigantic it was, and I was appalled when we finally stood underneath it. It felt as if seven thousand tons of steel bars were crushing me from above. It was an ugly, depressing construction, serving no function or purpose other than to satisfy human vanity. "The French flag is the only flag in the world to be hoisted up a pole three hundred meters high," Gustave Eiffel had said when he unfurled the *tricolore* from the top of the tower on the centennial of the French Revolution.

"Isn't it fantastic!" said Stefanos. "Do you know that the tower is lighter than the air which surrounds it? If we were to enclose the square at its base inside a circle, raise a cylinder up to its full height, and pump it up with … hot air, the air would weigh more than the tower itself." His eyes shone with delight. He was clearly proud of "his tower."

I looked at him sourly. "And what, pray, is the point of all these bits of metal? What aesthetic, practical, or social need do they fulfill?"

Disbelief replaced the look of delight in his eyes. "Don't you understand?" he asked. "This monument symbolizes a new era, the era of technology. What we have before us is a marvel of statics, dynamics, chemistry, electricity—they have all combined to make this the tallest construction in the world. And the foundations of all these subjects are to be found in mathematics. What you see is an apotheosis of algebra, trigonometry, infinitesimal calculus. It is the tower of wisdom! I'm surprised you don't see it that way."

"It's the tower of hubris," I said, annoyed. "The only thing it symbolizes is human arrogance. Mathematics can construct bridges, houses, trains, and ships. It doesn't need such contraptions to justify itself."

A playful smile appeared on Stefanos' face. "It's as if I'm hearing Alexandre Dumas speak," he said. "Dumas *fils,* of course. He and a number of others published an open letter at the time of the construction of the tower, with arguments similar to yours. I was not really surprised. It's natural that men of arts and letters remain attached to the past. But I was astounded that the architect of the Paris Opéra, Garnier, joined their ranks. He appeared to have forgotten the criticism he had received a few years earlier for his life's work, the opera house. 'What a horrible building!' the Empress herself said at the time—and in my opinion, she was not wrong in this particular case. 'It doesn't belong to any style; it's neither Greek nor Roman!' Although I don't like the Opéra at all, I can't help but admire his reply. He completely disarmed her by saying, 'It is in the style of Napoleon III, Madame!' I can perhaps understand those artists who saw their aesthetic principles being overturned; I can even understand Garnier, who feared losing his position as France's leading architect. But I can't understand you. What reason do you have for criticizing a work that embodies the triumph of modern science?"

"It's easy to dismiss an opinion by painting it in the colors of conservatism and reactionary beliefs," I said crossly. "But we shouldn't be talking down here. Let's go up. There is one good thing about your tower—the Eiffel Tower is the only place in Paris from which the Eiffel Tower can't be seen!"

Luckily, an elevator had been installed since the opening of the tower, and we didn't have to walk to the top, as the unfortunate officials had to on the day of the opening ceremony. According to the story, Prime Minister Pierre Tirard didn't make it to the top, so he asked one of his ministers to present Eiffel with the medal of the Legion of Honor in his stead.

My grumbles notwithstanding, the view from the top of the tower was breathtaking. The whole of the Paris basin spread out beneath us, the Seine uncoiling like a silver snake linking the various quarters of the city, but also dividing it into two. All the monuments, bars, and theaters that I had visited over the last few days took on a kind of functional identity from up here, although everything was so tiny that it looked unreal. Even the huge, 100-meter-high Ferris wheel of the Exhibition looked like a toy. At least the view is worth seeing, I conceded, annoyed at the thought that I had been wrong, to a degree, in my earlier appraisal of the tower.

We turned to look toward the hill of Montmartre, where we had spent the two previous evenings. Quite a few of its thirty-odd windmills were still standing, even though some had fallen into disrepair or were being used for a new purpose. At the top of the hill, a half-built structure of unclear character dominated the view, looking like a cake with plenty of cream on top.

"What is that?" I asked.

"It's the church of Sacré Coeur, the Sacred Heart of Jesus. It's being built by devout Catholics to thank the Lord for helping them slaughter seventeen thousand members of the Paris Commune, who dared to threaten the status quo for two whole months." His tone was ironic, but his anger showed through. "The people of Paris had been worn down by starvation as a result of the four-month-long siege by the Prussians, and they were enraged by the maladministration that led to the defeat of 1870. They rose against the government of Thiers, which immediately withdrew a discreet distance to Versailles with the part of the army that had remained loyal. Rather than succumb to an assault on all the established forms of authority, the former enemies became allies. Bismarck began to free large numbers of French prisoners of war, who came back and swelled the ranks of government forces. After a brief siege, Thiers' soldiers regained the city on May 28 and executed *en masse* the rebels and those suspected of being their collaborators. So much for devout Catholics and democratically elected politicians! Shall we descend?"

We chose to walk down in order to admire the view for a bit longer. On the first level we made a stop. This was the spot in the tower designated to honoring French science, to which it owed its existence. All around the railings were plaques with the names of seventy-two prominent French scientists. Among others, we recognized the names of the geometrician Poncelet, Lagrange (who had written the first analytical mechanics based on Newton's infinitesimal calculus), Laplace (who claimed that if we knew both the exact position and the exact velocity of a piece of matter at a given time, we would be able to calculate its path in the past and into the future), Fourier (who devised the series bearing his name, in order to solve heat equations), and Cauchy (who, with Weierstrass, founded modern analysis).

When Stefanos saw the last name, he got furious. "If the name of that latter-day St. Ignatius of Loyola is inscribed up here, I wonder what names appear on the gates of hell."

I looked at him inquiringly. My professors at Göttingen always referred to Cauchy with great respect. They included him among the founders of complex analysis, as important a mathematician as Riemann. His construction of the set of real numbers based on the sequence bearing his name was being taught in Germany in parallel with the method of cuts devised by their compatriot Dedekind. So I couldn't understand why Stefanos was branding him with the name of the bloodthirsty leader of the Holy Inquisition.

"In the first place, he too was a Jesuit," he said with a passion such as I had not seen in the three days I had known him. "However important their geometry is, it's not enough to wipe out their crimes. Still, it's not his religious or political beliefs that make me angry with him. It's the way he behaved toward other mathematicians, especially Abel and Galois. It's enough to blot out any pioneering work he may have done in mathematics."

I could not agree. I, too, am strict in my judgment of people. But I believe that an intellectual creation exists independently of its creator's character. Newton, for example, was undoubtedly a rogue, using any legitimate or illegitimate means to crush his opponents: he showed unparalleled ingratitude to those who, like Halley, had supported him when he was still unknown. He even became embroiled in a financial scandal as director of the Royal Mint. It is said that he went so far as to trade his niece's favors to gain the patronage of those in power. But none of that diminishes the value of his law of universal gravity, his inventing of the infinitesimal calculus, or his theory of white light. In the same way, I believed Cauchy's contribution to mathematics existed independently of the way he had behaved toward any other mathematicians, and I said so.

"But what would you say if I proved to you that his behavior set mathematics back a number of decades?" retorted Stefanos stubbornly. The sun was shining and the view was magnificent even from the first level, but the conversation was leading to a storm. We went inside the tower café and each ordered a glass of Beaujolais. We settled into two armchairs, and Stefanos began his attack.

"The problem of polynomial equations is as old as man," he said. "Almost every nation in antiquity knew how to solve problems in which an unknown quantity is added to or multiplied by a set of known numbers, or is multiplied by itself, that is, it's raised to the second power. If we translate the methods they were using into modern conventions, we realize that they're equivalent to our solutions of the quadratic equation. What happens, however, if the unknown is raised to the third power? In the year 1100 A.D., Omar Khayyám—whom you mentioned the other day, I think, in connection with Euclid's axioms—devised a method to solve such cubic equations using geometry. But he failed to invent a formula equivalent for cubics to our quadratic formula. This, in fact, seems to have been his great regret. His writings are full of wishes and blessings on the wise man of the future who would solve the equation in an analytical way."

I didn't know the story about Omar Khayyám's equations, but I knew who was the wise man who deserved his blessings, the man who had discovered the formula for solving a cubic equation. He was Niccolò Fontana, a self-taught Italian mathematician who had been wounded in the mouth during a French invasion of his home region of Brescia and so stammered when he spoke—hence his nickname, Tartaglia ("stammerer"). It was he who found the solution to an equation of the third degree. His solution was published in 1545, against his wishes, in the *Ars Magna,* a book by Cardano, another mathematician. It included a clever trick by which the formula could also be applied to an equation of the fourth degree. So the baton was waiting to be passed down to the one who could create a formula for an equation of the fifth degree.

"Hilbert said nothing on Wednesday about the problem of polynomial equations," I said. "As it's not possible that he left it out as insignificant, could it be that it has been solved?"

This was an area that Stefanos knew well. "Mathematicians had tried and failed to solve the fifth-degree equation for a very long time, some of them famous names. In the end, an unknown Norwegian, Abel, who was only twenty-two years old in 1824, turned everything upside down. He proved that there is no formula that can solve fifth-degree equations that uses only the four basic operations—addition, subtraction, multiplication, and division, plus the extraction of roots! In other words, although we know there is a solution to any fifth-degree equation, he proved that we can't express it with the usual means available to us."

"Well!" I remarked. "Hilbert found it hard to impose his non-constructible solution on Gordan's problem. I can just imagine what it took for Abel to get his proof of the nonexistence of a formula accepted."

"That's true. Poor Abel, who was destitute, spent his last penny on privately printing the text of his solution. He sent copies to various mathematicians, but the response was minimal. Can you believe it? Gauss didn't even open the letter. When he died, they found it, still sealed, among his papers. In despair, Abel obtained a travel loan and secured the means to come to Paris. He called on Cauchy in person and explained his work in detail, but the man completely ignored him. There was worse to come: Abel formally submitted his work to the French Academy, and they asked Cauchy to present it to them. Well, not only did he not present it, it seems that he lost it! Meanwhile Abel, who was living in dreadful conditions, fell ill. To make a long story short, after traveling all over Europe, Abel returned to Norway, where he died in 1829 at the age of just twenty-seven. Now you know why Monsieur Cauchy is responsible for holding mathematics back by decades. He was the only man who had the knowledge and the reputation to appreciate Abel's work. If he had spent just a little of his time to look at it more closely, if he had not lost the papers ..."

"I think you exaggerate," I replied. "You blame Cauchy alone, yet Gauss behaved just as badly; you said so yourself. I get the impression that most great mathematicians, as well as other scientists, have the same attitude. They look upon the work of younger men with suspicion, especially if it's of a revolutionary nature like Abel's discovery, and they don't spend any time examining it seriously unless they can get some personal gain from it.

"Speaking of Gauss, do you remember yesterday, when we were talking about Bolyai's non-Euclidean geometry? His father, who was friendly with Gauss, asked him to assess his son's work.

Well, guess how Monsieur Gauss (as you say) responded. He told Bolyai senior that his son's work was not original, as he himself had reached the same conclusions earlier. Okay, granted, this was true. But what need had Gauss to insist on his originality over that of a young mathematician for a discovery which, even if we believe he had made himself, he nevertheless had decided not to publish? I'm telling you, it's all right for great men. It's we who ought to worry ..."

"Well, I'm not worried," Stefanos laughed. "When I solve Hilbert's second problem with a general method for testing the consistency and completeness of an axiomatic system, then I'll ask my friend Michael to introduce me to the man himself."

I laughed too, remembering the argument we had begun at the café on the Boulevard Saint-Michel and continued at the Moulin Rouge. "You won't have to do that," I answered. "You will never find such a general method, simply because it doesn't exist. And in the unlikely event that you were to find it, I'm the last person who would help you publish it. I would make Cauchy and Gauss look like little angels with the obstacles I would put in your way. I won't let you reduce mathematics to a routine process with your blasted method. Why don't you think like Abel? When everyone else was trying to find a formula for solving equations of the fifth degree, he managed to prove that such a formula doesn't exist, because he was working without any pre-conceptions. You should do the same! And if you do find a negative solution to Hilbert's problem, you can rely on me. I will take you to Hilbert, to Poincaré, and even to Crown Prince Constantine."

We ordered another glass of Beaujolais and drank to our future success. Stefanos responded, "Maybe you're right. Perhaps I'm too harsh on Cauchy. But the story of Galois has got me all worked up.

His name ought to appear here, among the other French names. All right, so Cauchy was not the only one to blame. Galois was destroyed by everyone: academicians, monarchists, the clergy, women, but also by his pigheadedness."

In my isolation in Göttingen, I knew little about the political intrigues of French science. I had heard of Galois' name and knew that he was a promising mathematician who had died young, but that was all.

Stefanos filled me in: "Évariste Galois was born during the Napoleonic wars. His family was devoted to the revolution and the emperor. His father, who was mayor of Bourg-la-Reine, clashed disastrously with the church authorities. In 1829, he fell victim to a conspiracy set up by the parish priest and in his despair committed suicide. His death had a strong influence on young Évariste, who, after a stormy school career (all his teachers wanted his blood, except the mathematics teachers), twice tried to enter the École Polytechnique. He failed, however, and had to enroll in the École Normale, which didn't then have the reputation it does today.

"At that time, Galois had already solved not only the problem of the fifth-degree equation, but the whole general problem of polynomial equations. He had discovered a criterion which one can use to demonstrate whether or not any polynomial equation can be solved using the four basic functions plus the roots of numbers. He wrote a memorandum on it and submitted it to Cauchy, who proceeded to—"

"Lose it?" I interrupted.

"Exactly, Michael. He lost it! So how could I not be furious with him? Within a few years he managed to lose the evidence that would have secured the future of the two most brilliant mathematicians of his time."

"I'm beginning to think you're right. So what happened to Galois?"

"He didn't give up. He wrote a second memorandum, addressed to the Academy. In the meantime, he had learned about Abel's achievements a year after Abel died. He studied the Norwegian's work carefully and realized that what Abel had discovered could be deduced directly from his own, more general, theorems. He added these observations to a further memorandum and resubmitted it. This time, the Academy asked Fourier to assess it."

"Don't tell me that he also ignored it. As far as I know, Fourier was a close collaborator of Napoleon's, who took Fourier with him on the expedition to Egypt, before he became emperor. So Fourier couldn't have had any prejudice against Galois' political persuasions."

"No. But fate played a dirty trick on Galois. Fourier died a few days before the Academy's decisive meeting, taking to his grave both his opinion of the memorandum and the memorandum itself, which was never found.

"Shortly afterward, unrest broke out, which led to the expulsion of Charles I and his succession by Louis-Philippe. The latter was a Bourbon, but he had taken part in the revolution and declared himself an ally of the Jacobins. After the 1830 uprising, he relied on support from Thiers and Lafayette and ascended to the throne, taking the nickname of—would you believe it?—'citizen-king.' The students of the École Normale tried to join in the uprising, but their director locked the doors and shut them up inside. A huge row erupted, and Galois, wishing to carry on his father's democratic legacy, played a leading role in the confrontation between the École's students and its director. The result was that he was expelled from the school. This, coupled with the unhappy fate of his applications to the Academy, his failure twice to enter the École Polytechnique, and his depression over his father's suicide, was too much for the young Galois, who was not the mellowest of characters. He turned to politics to give vent to his anger. He enrolled himself in the National Guard, an organization which the 'citizen-king' had hastened to outlaw straight after his coronation. One evening, Galois drank a toast in a tavern that the king's spies denounced as insulting to the monarch. He was arrested, tried, and acquitted. The court deemed that a toast made by a half-drunk youth didn't constitute a threat to the state.

"Without giving up his political activities, Galois began again to apply himself to mathematics. He composed a third memorandum to the Academy, published a few articles in periodicals with a small circulation, and started giving lessons in a café, trying to explain his theories. But his capacity for explaining things was not equal to his talent for making discoveries. It's quite possible that the reluctance of academics to read his papers was due to the fact that they were difficult to understand. In any case, his lessons at the café ultimately petered out, as his students surreptitiously abandoned him, one by one.

"Meanwile, Galois continued to take part in the demonstrations until he was again arrested. This time he was sentenced and taken to Sainte-Pélagie prison. There he was informed that his third memorandum, which had been given to Poisson to review, had been rejected. Poisson had written: 'His arguments are neither clear enough nor sufficient to allow us to assess their correctness.' This could well have been the case, because, as I mentioned, Galois found it difficult to express himself. However, a better mathematician than Poisson would surely have realized the importance of the work and would not have rejected the paper because of imperfections of expression or details in the proof."

"Well, even mathematicians include bureaucrats among their number," I remarked, teasing Stefanos, who was clearly carried away by the story he was relating. He didn't seem to notice the interruption.

"The last act of this drama was played out after Galois got out of prison. The facts are not very clear, though. There is a woman involved, someone called Stéphanie du Motel, who was the daughter of the resident physician at a hospital where Galois had been treated for a while. In any case, the name Stéphanie appears frequently in the margins of the paper he was writing at the time. We don't know exactly what happened—whether Stéphanie had a relationship with another man, or whether the other man was just another admirer of hers, or even whether she was stringing them both along. But for one reason or another, one Perscheux d'Herbinville challenged him to a duel. Galois had no delusions about his abilities; he knew he was much less skillful with a pistol than d'Herbinville and that he would likely be killed. He spent his last night writing a letter to his friend Auguste Chevalier. In it he blames a 'heartless coquette' for his imminent death and for 'involving two honest citizens' in this affair. He begs his friend to try as hard as he can to draw the attention of the leading mathematicians of the time to his work.

"The duel took place under a deserted bridge over the Seine. As he had predicted, Galois was fatally wounded, and he died the next day in his brother's arms in Cochin Hospital. It took another eleven years before someone called Liouville came along and took the trouble to look seriously at Galois' manuscripts. In 1843, Liouville announced before an astonished French Academy that he had found among Galois' papers a complete answer to the problem of solving a polynomial equation of any degree with radicals and the four basic functions. Moreover, he informed them that behind this method lay hidden a profound new theory that would have even more important applications not only in algebra, but also in geometry.

"Well, can you see Galois' name anywhere?" ended Stefanos, his voice trembling with emotion. He was pointing at the plaques. "Of course not! On the contrary, Poisson's name is right there, close to Cauchy's." It was obvious that Galois was Stefanos' hero, his idol.

"You only have to flirt with Germaine," I said to him. "Casagemas will then challenge you to a duel and you will have no problem shooting him dead, so that you can avenge Galois. If, on the other hand, he doesn't challenge you but goes and cries on Ruiz's shoulder, then, my friend, you've had it. You will never be a great mathematician." This was not the right moment for such jokes. Stefanos laughed politely, but I realized I had hurt him. One shouldn't make fun of heroes.

Seven

Saturday was the last day of the conference, and Stefanos and I decided to join the other delegates in the traditional all-night celebrations. Sunday was dawning when we came out of the last bar. After a brief stop at the hotel to pick up my things, we headed toward the train station. I said farewell to my friend and we wished each other *au revoir*—something that would not come about for another ten years.

I settled into the carriage with my pockets full of little notes with the names and addresses of new acquaintances and my brain full of new ideas and experiences. Life, however, would soon make me forget both.

In Paris, I had felt that a new chapter was opening in my life. But when I got back to Göttingen, I discovered that another chapter was about to close. Two days after my return, I received a telegram telling me that my father was gravely ill and urging me to hurry back to Athens.

Upon arriving in Athens, I realized that things were much worse than I had expected. My father's condition was untreatable, and he died a week later. The family business had been flourishing, but it now needed a guiding hand. Grandfather Mavroleon was very old and had long since left the business in the hands of his son-in-law. My formidable grandmother, who had a real genius for public relations and cultivating connections, had no knowledge of commerce, freight, storage, loans, and so on. As for my mother, her activities were confined (in accord with the custom of the time) to playing the piano, embroidery, and charitable works.

So in the space of a moment I was forced to exchange my mathematics textbooks for accounting books and my easy, cosmopolitan, European life for working lunches and business appointments. As if that weren't enough, after a decent period of mourning had elapsed, my grandmother's pressure on me to "settle down" became intolerable. She had even made her choice: in her opinion, the ideal bride for me was Anna Dellaportas, offspring of an old family of ship owners that commanded a large part of the European merchant fleet. In her mind, my grandmother was uniting not Anna and me but the shipping community, which Anna's family represented, with the manufacturing and trading community, which my family belonged to. Moreover, Gerasimos Dellaportas, her father, was a man of great experience in every aspect of business and could help me greatly with advice in my first steps as a business man.

But what particularly excited my grandmother was the friendship my future mother-in-law, Elpiniki Dellaportas, enjoyed with Queen Olga. Although the Mavroleons were an old, aristocratic family frequently invited to the most important events at the palace, neither my grandmother nor my mother had managed to cultivate a close relationship with any member of the royal family. For his part, my father, who had lived in Europe for many years, was sympathetic to bourgeois democratic movements and suspicious of anything connected with the palace.

Elpiniki Dellaportas belonged to the close circle of the queen's friends. She was vice president of the Ladies' Society, the Brotherhood in Christ, and various other charities founded by the queen, and she took an active part in Olga's attempts to publish the gospels in modern, "demotic" Greek. The Dellaportas family was one of the main patrons of the first translation, which was undertaken by Ioulia Somakis, the queen's secretary. When the Holy Synod rejected that translation out of hand, the queen turned to Pallis (who had translated Homer into demotic Greek), with the unwavering support of her loyal friend Elpiniki. In November 1901, one year after my return to Athens and my father's death, the newspaper *Acropolis* began to print installments of the new translation, creating a storm of protest.

Olga was not popular in those days because of her Russian origins. The Bulgarians had been intensifying their atrocities against the Greek population of Macedonia, and the Russians, being champions of pan-Slavist policies—aimed at the unity of all the Slavic peoples—were seen as their accomplices. The publication of the translation gave rise to bloody incidents. The demonstrators turned their hostility directly against the queen, whom they held responsible, because she had openly expressed her support for the translation as early as 1897. She had said then, rather naively, that in her opinion the wounded soldiers of the unsuccessful war of that year would feel much greater comfort hearing or reading the Bible in a language that they could understand.

Hence, it was no accident that one of the most popular slogans of the demonstrators was "Down with the Slav woman." As you'd expect, the other royal couple, Constantine and Sophia, who were impatient to succeed King George, were not unconnected with the disturbances. Their supporters went to great lengths to ensure that the cry "Long live the crown prince" was heard among the other slogans. The age-old conflict between mother-in-law and daughter-in-law applied equally to the royal family, and from there the conflict was passed down to the people. The palace was split into three factions: George admired the English, Olga supported her compatriots, and the princely couple followed a line coming straight from Constantine's in-laws in Germany.

When on November 8, 1901, the army intervened in the protests and eleven demonstrators were killed, the government of Theotokis was forced to resign, even though it received a vote of confidence in Parliament. Another repercussion was the distancing of Procopius, the Bishop of Athens, who had previously taken a stance in support of Olga's campaign. During the whole of this incident, which went down in history as "the Gospels Affair," Elpiniki paid frequent, informal visits to the palace and developed such a close relationship with the queen that it made my grandmother's mouth water. Her plan was therefore to bring together her family and the Dellaportas, hoping thereby to obtain entry into the inner circle of the palace, something she considered even more important than the economic advantages of the marriage she was plotting.

I resisted her pressure until 1906. In those six years, I fought tooth and nail to prop up the family business, and Gerasimos Dellaportas helped me tremendously. So in the spring of 1906, partly out of gratitude to her father, partly because I couldn't stand my grandmother's nagging any more, and partly because I was lonely (having in the meantime lost my mother, too), I led Anna Dellaportas to the altar. Naturally, the officiating priest was the new archbishop, the gospel was read in the original archaic form, and my wedding was a great social event, important enough to satisfy my grandmother's ambitions.

If I myself was rather cautious and hesitant about our marriage, Anna had no such scruples; her feelings were 100 percent transparent. She was an only child, spoiled from her early years, and she had won, through her father's indulgence, an independence unheard of for girls at the beginning of the twentieth century. She was the apple of discord among the young officers at palace balls, she had travelled widely, and she was a member of many of Callirhoe Parren's organizations. By marrying me, she also became economically independent due to a family trust that came into her absolute ownership on her marriage. This was, in fact, her only motive for exchanging her surname for mine. She had spoken openly to me from the first moment of our engagement.

It was a beautiful autumn day in October 1905. Anna proposed we drive to Faliro. Although the train from Thesion in Athens to Piraeus had been running on electricity for a year now and travel on it was much more pleasent than before, we chose the traditional horse-drawn carriage. It was a journey lasting three quarters of an hour, with a stop at the "lean-to" halfway there, to water the horses. The surfaced road ended at Xirotagaros, a garden housing all sorts of animals. It was a small park in which a number of peacocks strode around majestically alongside a few guinea hens. There were also one or two deer and some goats inside a fenced area. Two large cages, one with monkeys, the other with a wretched lion, gave the more pretentious Athenians a pretext for calling the place a zoo.

We asked the coachman to wait for us as we walked along the waterfront. The sweet-smelling sea breeze played with Anna's hair.

If she had not been my fiancée, imposed from above, I might have been attracted by her. As soon as we had gone far enough to be beyond earshot, she began: "Let's be clear about this. It's not Anna and Michael getting married; it's the families of Dellaportas and Igerinos, or rather Mavroleon. I need a respectable husband in order to come into my settlement, and you're nice enough to play that role, as far as I'm concerned. I will never make a fool of you; on the other hand, I don't intend to change my way of life. I have no objection to our consummating our marriage—I like you—but I certainly don't intend to start having babies right now. On your part, you too have every right to live your life, as long as it's done discreetly, as I said. If this kind of agreement suits you, we can go ahead. Of course, one of us may at some stage decide they don't want to carry on. Well, then, we will find a civilized way of getting a divorce. Otherwise we might even, one day, celebrate our silver anniversary, with a reception to which all our ex-lovers would be invited." She finished her sentence bursting with laughter.

It took me a few minutes to recover from the shock. But then my mathematical education overcame my social inhibitions. I analyzed the data calmly, considered all possibilities, and concluded that Anna's honest and forthright proposition was, despite her cynicism, definitely preferable to the hypocritical stance another girl might have taken, which would have led to the same or a similar result.

So I accepted her proposal and, on top of being an offspring of Igerinos of the line of Mavroleon, I also became a son-in-law of Dellaportas. The queen herself honored the ceremony with her presence, and her gift, a Russian samovar of pure silver, took the most prominent place on the mantelpiece in our sitting room. The next time I see Anna, I must remember to give it to her. I prefer that to having to pay another visit to the ancient Elpiniki Dellaportas and face her accusing looks and her questions.

Eight

The first year of our marriage passed rather pleasantly. Having made things clear right from the start, Anna treated me more like a new lover than a husband. After our wedding, I left the business in the hands of my father-in-law while we went on a long tour of Europe for our honeymoon. I hadn't left Greece for six years, and along with the familiar European sites, I rediscovered the carefree existence of my student days.

As every devout Muslim must go to Mecca at least once in their lifetime, so every self-respecting mathematician should visit the birthplace of Hilbert and Goldbach, the town where Immanuel Kant spent all his life, where Minkowski's family found refuge when the Tsar had unleashed yet another persecution of the Jews. So I convinced Anna that we should start our tour from Königsberg, where even the town plan is a source of inspiration for mathematicians.

Upon their return from the Crusades, the Teutonic Knights settled on the shores of the Baltic Sea beside the Pregel River. The first thing they built was a fortress, and the town slowly grew around it. At that location, the river forms two islets, which are connected to the mainland by seven bridges. A walk along these bridges is one of the main tourist attractions of the town.

I told Anna about the old puzzle that the inhabitants of Königsberg set for visitors, challenging them to make a circuit of the town passing once, and only once, over each bridge. She was intrigued by it, and resolved to set off immediately to try to solve the problem. For hours she dragged me through the narrow lanes and over the bridges trying to discover the secret route. I followed after her patiently, determined not to forget myself and reveal the fact that her efforts were in vain. We circled the town five times, but each time, sooner or later, we came across a bridge that we had crossed before. Worn out, we ended up in a café. We ordered hot chocolate, and as we savored its sweet warmth, I explained to my wife with a superior smile that what we had been attempting was impossible. She wouldn't believe me, so I offered to prove it to her. She refused point blank. She insisted that I cancel our plans for the evening, bought three maps of the town, and shut herself up in our room, forbidding me to return any earlier than midnight.

I set off without any particular destination in mind, and eventually came to a beer cellar with the sign "Die Sieben Brücken"—the Seven Bridges. Amused by the name, I entered and sat at the big communal wooden table. I didn't even have to order. A plump, rosy-cheeked waitress brought me some sausages and a huge glass of beer.

The ritual of drinking a toast doesn't differ much throughout Europe. The phrases typically called out by drinkers to indicate that they wish to buy everyone a drink often have a common mathematical basis: Counting is a one-to-one equivalence. "Chalk one up!" shout the English half-drunkenly, when their pockets can afford to buy a drink for every guest in the pub. "*¡Echai chinas!*" (toss a pebble into the cap) say the Spaniards in the same circumstances. A pebble for each drink, a line drawn with chalk for every glass.

Here tradition was rather different. Whoever wanted to buy the drinks would raise his glass and call out a name, inviting the company to drink to the health of that person or, if he was dead, to his memory. The waitress would rush to serve the customers, who would empty their glasses and repeat in one voice the name that had been called out.

We drank in turn to the health of the Kaiser, his wife, his six sons, and his daughter. Bismarck followed (as the Prussians had not yet forgotten the chancellor who had led them to so many victories), the mythical hero Siegfried, the daughter of the innkeeper, and some girl called Hannelore, the object of the passionate love of a blond young man who was sporting a full, unruly moustache. When my turn came to toast, everyone was already quite drunk except me, thanks to a technique I had developed in my student years by which I would empty a good part of my glass onto the straw-covered floor without anyone noticing. So when I shouted out a name, raising my glass, no one asked me who this Leonhard Euler might be.

When I got back to the hotel, I found Anna in a state of despair. Two of the maps were shredded to pieces on the floor among dozens of other scrunched-up papers, while the third was being dragged around the table, covered in smudges and erasures.

"I give up," she announced in wretched tones. "No matter how hard I try, I can't trace a route that goes over each bridge once and only once."

I consoled her as best I could. "It took the genius of Euler to solve the problem," I said. "The fact that you haven't found a solution to the riddle is because, as I told you from the start, it simply cannot be solved. Euler developed a test to help us prove whether a two-dimensional graph, such as the one linking the bridges and streets of Königsberg, can be drawn in one line. A graph that includes all seven bridges doesn't meet with that criterion. Let me explain."

I took pencil and paper and demonstrated Euler's method for her. I knew that Anna was clever, but still I was impressed at how quickly she grasped the mechanism of the proof. Hill's Academy for Young Ladies, which she had attended, placed emphasis on the arts, as did most girls' schools throughout Europe in those days. So her knowledge of mathematics was not extensive. However, two hours of trying it out on foot and then another four hours of a "paper exercise" had brought her to the heart of the problem. She followed my impromptu lesson with enthusiasm and was almost relieved when I completed the proof. Then we went to bed, and I must admit, graph theory proved to be a first-class aphrodisiac.

We left Königsberg the next day. Anna, who hated losing, had developed a dislike for it. We continued our journey to Berlin, Vienna, and various Swiss resorts. Finally we came to Paris. I looked for Stefanos, with whom I had lost contact after my hasty departure and all that had followed, but I was told that he had probably gone back home.

Our first days in Paris were spent doing the usual things well-off couples on their honeymoon do. In the morning, we would go shopping and see the sights: The Louvre, the Eiffel Tower (which on second viewing seemed less of an eye-sore), the Arc de Triomphe, followed by the boutiques, the fashion houses, the antique shops. Needless to say, Anna wanted to visit the *Samaritaine* almost daily.

The snobs of Athenian high society, a class to which my grandmother as well as my mother-in-law belonged, used to shop by mail order from the two largest French department stores, the *Samaritaine* and its arch-rival the *Printemps*. Every Spring and Autumn the new catalogues arrived from the Parisian shops and, after endless family councils which would last for days, the orders would be sent off. Some months later trunks would arrive with the merchandise. Personally, I didn't care for the little sailor suits and the designer underwear that came for me, which often, due to delays in the post, I had already outgrown. But I did play for hours with the empty trunks and the luxurious wrappings.

The first time I visited Paris, in 1900, I hadn't gone to any store, since shopping had been the last thing on my mind. But now, thanks to Anna, who "absolutely had to" renew her wardrobe, I had the chance to visit frequently both the stores I had known by name since my childhood.

One day my wife was taking longer than usual trying things on, and I stole away unnoticed. I thought that, to kill the time, I would try to find the pump which, according to a guide to Paris I had bought the previous day, was situated on one of the bridges over the Seine and provided the Louvre with water. Apparently, its decoration, a relief depicting Christ's meeting with the Samaritan woman, had given the area, and subsequently the store, its name. But I could find nothing. I asked passers-by and shopkeepers, but no one knew. In fact, many looked at me curiously, trying to figure out what I was talking about. As happens often, the tourist was better informed than the locals. In the end, an old man—a typical Parisian wearing a beret and tartan scarf carrying a baguette under his arm and with a yellowed cigarette stuck in his mouth—informed me that when he was a little boy the city authorities had removed the pump, which, incidentally, he had never seen being used.

Our families had been insistent that we must adorn the walls of our new house with some "works of high quality" by Parisian artists. Although we had been determined not to carry out a single one of our families' wishes during our trip, we both loved art so much that we did end up devoting some of our time to visiting exhibitions. The Impressionists were still dominating most of the galleries, but "art nouveau" now took its fair share of the limelight.

In the afternoon we would go to the races or boating in the Bois de Boulogne, while our evenings were spent at the opera (which I personally cannot stand), the theater, or soirées at the houses of friends, acquaintances, friends of acquaintances, and acquaintances of friends.

One day, Anna announced that she was tired of all this (Anna easily tired of everything). She wished to leave the world of the salons and breathe in new air, get to know the other side of Paris, visit places "not so respectable," talk to artists on the fringe. I had no objection, especially since I had some wonderful memories of my first contact with the avant-garde in Frédé's bistro six years earlier.

The well-informed receptionist at our hotel told me that the Zut had closed down by order of the Paris police department and that its owner, Frédé Gérard, had moved to the Lapin Agile, one of the oldest bistros of Montmartre.

At the beginning of the 1880s, someone called André Gill, a jack-of-all-trades—actor, singer, painter, and poet—had bought an inn that had in the past been used as a changing post for carriages and turned it into a "literary cabaret." Some self-taught painter had illustrated the walls of the building with the adventures of a legendary bandit of those days, giving the inn the name Le Cabaret des Assassins. Gill himself had painted the sign above the door of a rabbit holding a bottle of wine in its paws.

Later, the shop was bought by a woman called Adèle, a former dancer, who changed the name to Lapin Agile on account of the sign, but also in homage to its former owner, making a pun on his name: "Lapin à Gill." In 1903, the police shut down the Zut, which had acquired a bad reputation not only as a meeting place for anarchists but also as a battleground for various characters of the criminal world. Following the Zut's closure, Aristide Bruant bought the Lapin Agile and installed his old employee as manager. A few years later, Bruant left Paris and handed the shop over to Frédé, letting him take all the profits, and in the end he bequeathed it to him in his will. Frédé settled into his new den and set about recreating the Zut's atmosphere.

"If the lady wants to listen, enveloped in smoke, to avant-garde poets recite their incomprehensible verses, or to unknown half-drunk painters describe their indecipherable works, the Lapin Agile is the ideal place," said the receptionist with a roguish smile. "Of course, the ladies who accompany them all are not all Sunday School girls," he added knowingly.

All the old customers of the Zut had moved to this new hangout. The only people not welcome were the pimps and knife-toting ruffians who had given the police the excuse to close down the old shop.

"I should mention, though, that fights and other scenes are not uncommon there," said the receptionist confidentially. "If you'll permit me to express my opinion, the place is not suitable for a lady." If Anna had had any reservations, which I doubt, this last comment was enough to make her determined to go. So the following evening we found ourselves having a drink at the Lapin Agile.

The bistro was housed in an old, tile-roofed farmhouse, a remnant of the time when Montmartre was all farmland. The entrance led into a small hallway where there was a bar with the usual *cafetière* and bottles of wine and spirits. You then went through to the main saloon, where two big lampshades covered in red cloth spread a low, pinkish light. Frédé had not judged it necessary to paint the walls, which were black with smoke and dampness. It was enough for him to cover them with paintings that had been given to him from time to time by his artist protégés. In a prominent position hung a magnificent harlequin; this was, we learned later, a self-portrait by his favorite Spanish painter.

Thanks to Bruant, there had been enough money to buy a piano and hire a pianist, whom the innkeeper would accompany every now and then with his tone-deaf voice and out-of-tune guitar. At one end, over the fireplace, was a huge statue of Christ, who was surely wondering what he was doing in there.

Compared to the Zut, which I had last visited six years earlier, there was a marked improvement in the cleanliness department. Despite my warnings against it, Anna insisted on trying the pastis, and naturally felt sick after the first sip. I stayed faithful to my cognac, although the word "homemade" next to it in the menu caused me some concern.

A group of people, two men and a woman, sat at the table next to us. One of the men looked vaguely familiar. When I heard his voice, the mystery was solved; his broken French, which had only barely improved in the six years that had elapsed, and the soft "s" in his accent made me at once recognize one of Stefanos' three Spaniards. He, too, had recognized me, and we both made a move at the same time.

"You're el Greco's friend! The mathematician!"

"You're Stefanos' friend from Spain!"

We shook hands warmly, and he invited us to their table. Introductions followed: "Max Jacob, poet, painter, my best friend. And this is Fernande, my sweetheart. But I feel I ought to introduce myself again. When we first met, I was using my father's name, Ruiz. Now I sign in my mother's name, Picasso."

I was briefly dumbstruck, staring at the girl. She was truly stunning, with reddish-brown hair; big, green, almond-shaped eyes; and a voluptuous body, throbbing with life. For a few moments I was speechless. A discreet kick from my wife helped me recover.

"This is Anna, my wife," I said in return. "Pablo and I met the last time I came to Paris," I continued. "I had come here for the international mathematics conference, and Pablo had come to exhibit his work in the Spanish Pavilion of the Exhibition."

"Oh, don't remind me of that monstrosity," said Pablo with genuine revulsion. "That was art of the last century. Men living in caves painted better than that. I've destroyed it, you know. One day, when I didn't have enough money to buy canvas and I just had to paint, I covered it with white paint and did something else over it."

He asked about Stefanos, and I told him that we had lost touch. I then asked about his friends. His face darkened. "Carles is no longer alive," he replied. "Do you remember Germaine? She was with us when we first met. Carles had fallen madly in love with her. She, on the other hand, was playing with his feelings. One day I persuaded him to return to Spain with me. We had no money left, but I wanted to help him forget Germaine. It was in vain. After a few months, he returned to Paris on his own and found her again. He was obsessed with the idea of marrying her, but she carried on as before. She told him it was out of the question that she marry him, but at the same time she kept his flame burning. Then one day, in front of a big crowd at the Hippodrome Café—Manuel was also there, do you remember him?—he pulled out a pistol, shot her, and then blew his brains out. Germaine got away with only a scratch. But alas ... Carles is gone." He said these last words in a trembling voice.

Anna looked at me accusingly, holding me responsible for awakening such painful memories in our companion, and she hastened to make amends. "I'm sure he's much happier where he is now," she said trying to dispel the awkwardness with a cliché. But Jacob intervened much more drastically. He was short, with big ears, a hooked nose, and two small, wicked eyes, in which an ironic spark shone permanently. His broad forehead signaled approaching baldness.

"No one knows their fate," he said half-seriously, half-jokingly, "unless they come to the great astrologist Max Jacob: Palm reading, horoscopes, tarot cards, and Caster of his Excellency the President's horoscope." He made a comical bow toward Anna, producing a pack of cards from his pocket at the same time. "At your service, madame."

Anna laughed complacently, flattered at being the center of attention. "You wish to read the cards for me? Fine, but I'm warning you I am a complex person, you can't easily read my character. If you're wrong, I will expose you!"

"Careful, Jacob," joined in Picasso, looking at Anna with interest. "The lady is not Madame Anseau. Don't imagine you can fool her. After all, she comes from Greece, the home of Apollo. Perhaps the Pythia was her great-grandmother."

Madame Anseau ran a small grocery shop in the neighborhood and, like most traders of the area, she was particularly fond of the penniless artists of Montmartre. Jacob was her favorite, as he had charmed her with his fine manners and his clever, discerning compliments. A big plate of food and some special treat would always be waiting for him in her shop. Max would return this affection by casting her horoscope or reading the cards for her. Needless to say, he would always foresee, somewhere in the indeterminable future, everything that the poor woman longed for.

Contrary to what Anna thought, her personality was an open book for a man of Jacob's intelligence. He described her to herself as a mixture of what she actually was and what she liked to think she was. He told her—with a mischievous glance at me—that she was not a woman made for only one man, but one to be loved by poets and to inspire painters. With this I realized he was making an opening for his friend, as it was obvious that he himself was not interested in women. As he talked, he cast a wicked glance at Fernande, and his last sentence must have been intended to tease her. Whatever the case was, if he was trying to annoy me, he failed. He could not have been aware of the "gentlemen's agreement" that Anna and I had made, and if my wife was intending to put its terms into effect so soon (which seemed likley, judging by the hungry looks Pablo gave her and the meaningful smiles she returned), then good luck to her.

I was sitting with my back to the door, so I didn't immediately notice the couple heading toward our table. "Alice, *ma paloma!*" Picasso welcomed the girl. Without any hesitation, Alice sat on his lap and gave him a sloppy kiss on the lips. Her escort, a man more than ten years her senior, smiled awkwardly. I had the vague impression I had seen him (and his oddly trimmed red moustache) somewhere before. He, too, was looking at me questioningly.

When the girl was done demonstrating her affection, she got up, put her arm tenderly around her companion's waist, and hastened to introduce him: "Pablo, this is Maurice Princet, mathematician, insurance expert, and permanent victim of mine. He puts up with me, and I take awful advantage of him."

Picasso took it upon himself to complete the introductions in his Franco-Spanish dialect, with lots of hand gestures. When he came to me and mentioned that I was a mathematician, Princet smiled. "Have we not met before?" he asked. "Your face is familiar." Suddenly I remembered; we had met at the Congress in 1900. He had been one of the young men who, like Stefanos and me, had sat at in back rows of the lecture-hall in the "gallery of nobodies." His name and address was among the papers I had taken back home from Paris. Because of the turbulent events that unexpectedly occurred in my life shortly afterward, I had failed to follow up with any of my new acquaintances. Actually, the papers were still in the trunk where my books and notes from Göttingen were stored.

The conversation turned to our first encounter and our impressions of the conference. It had been six years since I had last given serious thought to mathematics, and I confessed that I was a bit behind in keeping abreast of new developments. "At the time of the conference I was inclined toward research in non-Euclidean geometry," I said. "After all, I was in the ideal environment for that, among Hilbert, Klein, and Minkowski. Göttingen was the best place for such work. But life decreed otherwise."

Princet replied that he, too—ever since he had started working as a clerk—no longer considered himself a mathematician. He had, however, retained some contact by reading articles that were not particularly specialized or technical. "Three years ago, Poincaré published a fantastic book. It's called *Science and Hypothesis,* and it looks at mathematics from a philosophical point of view. At the same time, it presents theories in bold terms, without getting lost in technical details. If you ever want to take up mathematics again, I think that's the best book to start with. In fact, it would suit all of you," he said, turning to the others. "Simple, clear ideas, without any of the jargon that mathematicians love and everybody else hates." He turned to Picasso. "Alice tells me you're interested in geometry."

"I'm interested in anything that can help me understand space with my mind," said Picasso. "I don't particularly trust the senses. Sight, in particular, often plays tricks. The Impressionists are trying to depict a momentary image on canvas. They paint an impression. But I want to capture reality. And it's rare that something is actually what it appears to be. That's why I want to learn mathematics. You mathematicians are not convinced by what you see; you want proof. But you also accept that there are many different realities, many different geometries. I can understand how one painter can represent a picture in a way that is different from anyone else. But mathematics seeks to find objective truth. What is the objective truth when you have many different theories of space? Gentlemen, you have to explain yourselves!" he added, mimicking the gestures that a public prosecutor would make at a trial.

This was an open challenge. Six years earlier, in a similar bistro, Pablo had insisted that Stefanos and I give him a lesson in geometry. I realized now that history was about to repeat itself.

But this time I didn't have Stefanos to help me through the rough waters. Fortunately, Princet saved the day. In the years that followed, he was to become an expert in explaining mathematics to artists. As a matter of fact, the nickname they were to label him with, "the mathematician of cubism," suited him perfectly. That evening he managed beautifully, considering that it was, in a way, his debut in artistic circles. He glanced at me, smiling, as if asking for permission to take the initiative, and began.

"It depends on what you mean by 'reality.' Mathematical reality exists only within the framework of some system or another. Each mathematical system is the sum of the theorems that can be proven within it. Each proof of a new theorem must be based on other theorems already proved. And those theorems, in turn, rest on other already proved theorems. Naturally, such a process can't go on indefinitely; it has to stop somewhere. Certain ideas, called postulates or axioms, will have to be accepted without proof. Choosing those axioms is basically what characterizes a particular mathematical system. In Euclidean geometry, for example, we say that 'through a point p not on a line l there can be drawn exactly one line parallel to l.' A different geometry could replace this specific axiom with another, which says that 'through a point p not on a line l there can be drawn infinitely many different lines parallel to l, or alternatively none at all.'"

"I don't understand," said Jacob. "There are certain things that are obvious. What is the point of talking about a geometry where many different lines passing through the same point are parallel to the same straight line, when we all know that we can only draw one such line? What do you think, Pablo, being an expert?"

Picasso didn't say anything, but simply looked expectantly at Princet, who smiled and continued: "An immediate consequence of the axiom of parallels is that the sum of the angles of a triangle is 180 degrees. If you accept the axiom, then you can prove this. Without the axiom, the theorem can't be proven in a million years."

"Yes, but whatever triangle we take," objected Jacob, "we measure its angles, add them up, and get 180 degrees. Don't all these tests reassure us that we've chosen a correct axiom?" He looked to me, searching silently for an ally, but this was in vain. In the past, I had admired the way Stefanos had explained Kepler's hypothesis to Picasso and his friends, and now I was waiting to see how Princet would fare with non-Euclidean geometries.

"An immediate consequence of the rejection of the axiom of parallels," he continued, unfazed, "and of the existence of more than one line through a point parallel to a straight line, is that the sum of the angles of a triangle is less than 180 degrees. Actually, the difference between that sum and 180 degrees increases as the area of the triangle increases. Now, if you measure the angles of some triangle, how can you be sure that the angles add up to exactly 180 degrees? Couldn't the total be slightly less—with a discrepancy so small that it's imperceptible and can't be measured with the instruments we have available today? And how do you know whether a triangle with points on Sirius, the North Star, and our own Sun, has angles that total 180 degrees, or less?"

"Or even more?" interjected Alice coquettishly. She was delighted that her friend was monopolizing the conversation and wanted to remind us that Princet was her possession.

"Or even more," agreed Princet, looking at her adoringly.

"You mean," persisted Jacob, "that we don't know yet which is the correct geometry?"

"Do we know whether white or red is the correct wine? Your question makes no sense," replied Princet. "It's like asking whether it's more correct to measure distances in meters or in yards, or if it's more correct to weigh something in kilos or stones. There are no correct or incorrect geometries. Any geometrical system that doesn't contain contradictions is 'correct.' No one geometry can be more correct than another; it can only be more convenient. Euclidean geometry is and will always be the most convenient way of building our houses, sewing our clothes, finding our way around the countryside. I don't know if it will be the most convenient when we want to send projectiles into space like those that Jules Verne imagines, or when our trains start to go faster than the speed of sound or light. But, I stress again, if we chose a different geometry for such applications, we will do so because it will be more convenient, not more correct."

Picasso appeared fascinated. "Do you mean to say that breaking the age-old tradition that endowed us with the geometry we have is not taboo? Are we allowed to contravene its laws, to imagine, understand, and represent the world differently? Are you saying that the geometry that was founded on the wisdom of thousands of years is not necessarily the most correct?"

"You are aware of Darwin's theory," replied Maurice. "Our brain has adapted over the years, through natural selection, to the conditions of its environment. Through this process, it has also adopted the most suitable geometry, the geometry that has contributed most positively to the evolution of our species."

"Does that mean that another biological species could have created a different geometry?" asked Anna, with a look that urged me to join in. But because I felt that Princet was doing a great job and because I was enjoying the way he led the discussion, I saw no reason to intervene.

"This is what Poincaré says," Princet answered. "Strange as it may sound, you have to imagine some hypothetical creatures, perhaps with a different physiology than ours, but with mental functions and senses exactly like ours. These creatures would not have come under the same influence that our own environment has on us, nor would they have learned the lessons that we've learned in school. If these beings lived in a world different from ours, which had given them different perceptions and sent them different signals, they would perhaps have created a completely different geometry, one that would have no reason to be like Euclid's.

"Now if, by some magic means, we were to find ourselves transported to that world armed with our own experiences, the direct and indirect influences on us, and our preconceptions, I believe we would have no difficulty in describing the phenomena we observed using Euclidean geometry.

"And vice versa, if one of those beings turned up suddenly in our world, it would be able to explain everything it observed here using its own geometry. I even think that if it were to teach us the laws and principles of its geometry, we too would be able to describe the phenomena of our world with this different geometry, provided we were able to study it long enough."

Princet turned to me and asked, "Which of the Greek philosophers said that the universe is enclosed within a sphere?"

"All of them," I answered. "Or at least the most important ones—Pythagoras, Plato, Aristotle. They all believed that the universe is finite and that its outer covering was the sphere of the fixed stars, the firmament. Pythagoras (or rather his pupil, Philolaus) envisaged a fire at the center of the universe. Around which, in a series of concentric spheres, travelled the Earth, the Moon, the Sun, and the five planets then known. And all of that was contained within the firmament, its outer sphere. Now these added up to only nine spheres. Because the Pythagoreans believed that the number ten most closely resembles perfection, expressing the harmony of the universe, they imagined one more sphere around the Earth's sphere, in which travelled a hypothetical planet called Antichthon, or 'Counter-Earth.' Plato and Aristotle, on the other hand, along with most philosophers of antiquity and the middle ages, placed Earth at the center of the universe, with the Sun and planets traveling around it in concentric spheres and with the outermost sphere rotating around everything. You can take your pick."

"So the idea of a finite universe, a universe enclosed within a sphere, is not new," continued Princet. "Let's imagine such a universe. Since we're experimenting with our imagination, we can make up the rules that govern this universe. These rules will sound strange and very different from ours, but I assure you that they are one possible set of valid rules; they're not illogical. So here they are: The highest temperature of this universe can be found at its center, and it decreases gradually as we travel away from the center, until we reach the boundary, the outer sphere, where the temperature becomes absolute zero. We have to further imagine that the objects in this universe all have the same contraction coefficient, so that the length of a ruler, made of any material, will be proportional to its temperature, and therefore inversely proportional to its distance from the center of the universe. This means that any object contracts as it approaches the outer sphere, and expands as it nears the center. Finally, we need to suppose that this alteration is automatic and regular, so that the object undergoing the change cannot feel it.

"According to that geometry, this universe is finite. But for its inhabitants, it's infinite. As they approach the outer sphere that marks the boundary of their world, they grow gradually smaller, so that they view the distance to the 'edge of the world' with ever-decreasing units of length. From this it follows that form their perspective it seems that they never get any closer to the edge. And it's therefore natural that they would think the 'edge of the world' is infinitely far away, or that it doesn't exist. It would be the same sensation that we feel when we're crossing the sea and there is no land around us to orient ourselves by. We are heading toward the horizon, but we don't have the sensation that we're getting any nearer to it. In such a world, Zeno's paradoxes would not seem so paradoxical."

"Whose paradoxes?" asked Jacob.

"Zeno's, Max, my love," said Fernande ironically. "Don't tell me you haven't heard of Zeno. That tall, muscular guy with the big mustache. What a shame! There is no chance of meeting him now; he died a few centuries ago. He was just the type you would have loved!"

"Forgive my ignorance, countess of the hill," replied Max, without a moment's thought. "You see, I don't have the luxury of being able to educate myself lying on my lover's divan all day, smoking Turkish cigarettes, and reading popular magazines. Yes, I confess I don't know who Zeno is, but I'm surprised that you have met him. I must say, you don't look that old."

Picasso seemed to be enjoying the spat between his mistress and his bosom friend, which, I realized, was an ongoing thing. Picasso had formed his close friendship with Jacob the previous time he was in Paris. The young poet had put him up in his shack and had even gone to the length of getting a job as a stock-keeper in a shop in order to make ends meet for both of them. They would pass endless hours discussing the paintings of the one or reading the poems of the other. The young Jew was the first who tried to help Picasso improve his French. He had to, because the Spaniard was the first to whom he read the poems he concocted. But unlike his friend, Picasso was very interested in women. And for as long as the painter's erotic activities were confined to brief, opportunistic affairs (like the one with Alice), Max had no objection. After all, he himself pursued his own eccentric love life.

But one day Fernande came into their lives. Picasso fell madly in love with her, at least to begin with. The poet, already ill-disposed toward women, didn't like this "invasion" at all. He began to fight her with the best weapons at his disposal: irony, sarcasm, and hurtful remarks. Fernande answered back in the same way, but without showing particular aggression, since she was a rather lazy type of person. She was interested only in Picasso, and so didn't consider Jacob a real threat. But this time, her having heard of Zeno (whom Jacob clearly didn't know anything about) placed her at an advantage, and she didn't let the opportunity slip by.

Unlike Picasso, I was worried that a quarrel was going to break out, and I hastened to prevent it by describing Zeno's paradoxes, which, after all, Maurice had indirectly asked me to do. "According to Aristotle," I explained, "Zeno of Elea, a student of Parmenides, invented four paradoxes against the notion of movement, that is, four examples that prove that movement is ... impossible. Of course, he wasn't crazy enough to say he didn't accept what his eyes could see. He just wanted to show the other philosophers of his time that their definitions of movement were imperfect and didn't stand up to close scrutiny.

"One of his paradoxes was that if we throw a stone toward a target, it will never get there. Before it reaches the target, the stone must travel half the distance. In order to cover the remaining distance, it must next travel half of the remaining length, that is, one-quarter of the whole. In order to cover again the rest of the distance, it has to travel another half-length, that is, one-eighth of the whole, and so on and so forth. Therefore, it will need to cover an infinite number of distances, which, according to Zeno, is impossible. In our world, despite its apparent logical validity, this idea is a paradox. But in the world that Maurice has described, such an argument would be perfectly logical."

"Your fellow countrymen never had good relations with infinity, with the exception of Archimedes, perhaps," observed Princet. "Today we all know," he said, turning to the others, "that the sum of an infinite series of numbers can itself be finite. For example, Zeno's summation, as we said just now, of a half, a quarter, an eighth, a sixteenth, and so on can easily be proven to converge to one. But in the imaginary world that I described, this would not even be considered paradoxical. If the stone we used as an example were to be thrown outward following a radius of the sphere, it would become half its original size when it covered half the distance, because, as we said, a body shrinks as it goes further and further away from the center. The same would apply to an intelligent traveler who followed the same route. When he reached the halfway point, he would see the remaining distance as double of what it looked like before, viewed from the center. Thus, from the center, he would see the remaining distance as equal to the original total distance. This wouldn't seem strange to us, as we would see someone travel a finite distance, but shrink during his movement, with the result that his ability to cover distance would constantly diminish. This is the way we would explain why, within the framework of our geometry, he would never reach his destination. But neither would he observe anything strange, using his own geometry; in his eyes, the distance would be infinite right from the start, and therefore, no matter how much of it he covered, it would always remain infinite.

"Shall we take another example? You know that when light passes from one medium to another—for example, from air into water—it is refracted and changes course. How much it's altered depends on the refraction index of the medium. Glass has a different refraction index than does water or air. Let's suppose that, in the strange world contained within the sphere, the refraction index grows in proportion to the distance from the center. The inhabitants of this world would not see light like us, dispersing in a straight line, but in a curve.

"As you can see, I'm describing what happens in that world in terms of our own geometry, even though it's certain that the intelligent beings inhabiting it would create their own, completely different geometry; they would accept their geometry as self-evident, while they would consider our geometry as some sort of theoretical game, fit only for oddball mathematicians."

"*¡Olè!*" shouted Picasso delightedly.

Anna was puzzled. "You show great enthusiasm for geometry," she remarked. "The only thing left now is for Michael to start … painting."

"A friend of ours says that geometry is to the visual arts what grammar is to the art of writing," said Alice. "By the way, where is Apollinaire? Isn't he coming tonight?"

"The erudite Guillaume is too busy today," said Jacob with mock pomposity. "He was commissioned to write a book some time ago, and he took the money and spent it, but hasn't submitted any manuscript yet. Yesterday the publisher put a knife to his throat, so the scholarly Monsieur Guillaume Apollinaire had to stay at home tonight to finish it. But he will come to the reception hosted by the Maestro and by her Highness Madame Fernande."

"No wonder, since there will be food tomorrow," joked Fernande.

Those who knew Apollinaire's habit of paying surprise visits to his friends during mealtimes laughed. The rest of us were left wondering.

"Incidentally, why don't you come as well?" suggested Picasso. "Mathematicians are always welcome in our group. And the same goes for beautiful ladies," he added, addressing my wife.

"Will you show us your paintings?" asked Anna. "Michael and I have exhausted ourselves walking around all the galleries and museums. But I've never had the chance to be given a guided tour by a painter around his own studio."

Picasso hesitated. An ironic smile appeared over Fernande's face. It was obvious that the young painter was reluctant to give in to Anna's request. But my wife kept her gaze on him, with the look of a spoiled little girl who won't take no for an answer.

"Just come along, and we'll see what we can do," he said at last.

Uncertainty, and then annoyance, took the place of irony in Fernande's face. It seems that our friend had made a concession—to Anna, that is to say—that he was not in the habit of making. Jacob confirmed this; with an extravagant gesture toward Anna, he declared, "Madame, I bow before your beauty. This is the first time in a year that the Maestro has agreed to show his works." He then turned to me with a mocking smile. "Naturally, part of the honor belongs to the husband." I think I disappointed him with my indifference to his obvious insinuation.

Taking the part of the "master and head of the family," I accepted the invitation on behalf of both of us. It was a special pleasure to think that our expensive box at the opera would remain empty tomorrow night. I would be spared a baroque spectacle, very weak in content, created to display the singers' talents and the audience's new clothes. At the same time, our empty box would still serve our standing in society, because everyone who knew us would also know that it was we who had reserved it. Furthermore, the present company was certainly far more interesting.

It was now Alice's turn to act jealous. "Since you have made your plans for tomorrow, can you tell us what we're doing tonight? I thought cinema was on the program."

It was around 450 B.C. that Zeno of Elea had questioned the possibility of movement with his paradoxes. In addition to the paradox of dichotomy, which I had described earlier, there was also the paradox of the arrow—which was in a way related to the prospect of attending the cinema. Because an arrow, as it travels through space, occupies each point along its path for a fraction of time—effectively being stationary in each point—it's a paradox how it's possible for it to ever complete a movement. A movement would have to be the sum of an infinite series of unmoving stops. Interestingly, about twenty-three hundred years later, thanks to Edison, Reynaud, and Lumière, a series of unmoving stops was used to create the impression of movement, notwithstanding the objections of our fellow Greek from Elea. By projecting images in quick succession (sixteen images per second in the early cameras) and taking advantage of the after-image effect in the eye's retina, a cinematographer could offer viewers the illusion that they were watching a scene that had actually taken place in the past. The images that form in our eye don't automatically disappear; instead, our eye "remembers" an earlier picture while viewing the next one. This succession makes us believe that what we're watching is not many pictures one after another, but a single uninterrupted moving scene.

Some ten years earlier, in December 1895, Louis Lumière had organized the first showing of a film to a paying audience. Terror-stricken, the viewers saw a train appear from the back of the screen and head straight toward them. Some women screamed in fright. Then everybody burst out in loud applause. The film was *The Arrival of a Train into Ciotat Station (L'Arrivée d'un Train en Gare de la Ciotat),* and it marked the birth of the art of cinema. The success of this new public entertainment was unprecedented. In the space of ten years, Paris had dozens of projection rooms where, for thirty or fifty *sous* (less than half my tip to the usherette at the opera), you could watch the program as many times as you wanted. All the cinemas featured live music; some had only a piano, others a whole orchestra.

Picasso and his group of friends adored the cinema and dedicated at least one night every week to this newly invented art. The young artist was searching for a way to use this new means of expression to understand space better. George Méliès, a former magician and now the most famous film director, invented cinematic special effects one after another. These were an inspiration to Picasso because they shook every kind of conventional thinking regarding the representation of truth, the use of space, and even the chronological sequence of events.

Picasso was himself an enthusiastic photographer, experimenting with various tricks of photography, trying to find ways of transferring to the canvas his own, more cerebral than optical truth. But tonight he seemed so carried away by other things that he had forgotten the cinema.

It was obvious that Fernande was jealous of Alice. Not only was she her boyfriend's ex-lover from his first stay in Paris, but their relationship had turned into a strong friendship, which didn't necessarily exclude occasional sex. By introducing the group to Princet, to whom Picasso had taken a liking, Alice seemed to have scored another point over the beautiful redhead who, as the night progressed, was pushed more and more to the sidelines. But Fernande knew how to judge situations; she realized she had every reason to side with Alice and lure the group to the cinema. Anna and I assisted in their efforts, since we had never been to one.

In a few minutes we found ourselves seated in the fifth row of the cinema on the Rue Douai. Our friends explained that the film being shown was George Méliès' *A Trip to the Moon.* Although inspired by the works of Jules Verne, the film was simplistic both in concept and plot. As for its special effects, they were superb, especially for us, who were new to them. The scene where a spaceship hits the face of the Moon in the eye is justifiably a point of reference, even today, when the technology of cinema has made such great strides.

In those days, cinema theaters in Paris were mainly places frequented by the lower classes. In Montmartre especially, cinemas had a low reputation. The permanent darkness—given that there were no breaks between shows—and the comfortable seats were not only a temptation for unmarried couples to give vent to their passion (with musical accompaniment, at that!) but also a site for the prostitutes of the hill to ply their trade. The customers smoked, shouted, and spat, and the most shameless ones used the darkest corners to pee in. Sitting there, my thoughts turned gleefully to my aristocratic grandmother. Anna seemed to be thinking of Madame Elpiniki Dellaportas, the personal friend of Her Majesty the Queen—or at least that's what I suspected when she squeezed my hand conspiratorially.

We saw the film twice and then parted from our friends, confirming our rendezvous for next day. Anna sank into my arms in the coach that took us back to the hotel. She was thrilled with our new acquaintances. Recognizing my contribution to the wonderful evening, she wasted no time once back in our room to offer me my reward, which was particularly generous, even for newlyweds.

Nine

Picasso (as Stefanos' old friend now wanted to be known) had by then moved to a three-story building on the Place Ravignan, a few blocks away from the Zut. The slope of the hill meant that what was ground floor at the front became the third floor at the back, looking out on an internal yard.

The building, erected around the middle of the nineteenth century, had originally housed a piano factory. Later it was used for various other industrial ventures. During the turbulent years that followed the events of the Commune, some anarchists had found refuge there, which led to the building's being labelled as "a den of subversive elements." Its reputation had withstood the passage of time, although its residents now were all fringe intellectuals, and the only disturbances were caused by drinking or heated fights between lovers. Around 1890, the owner had commissioned the architect Vasseur to divide it up into studios so that he could rent them out to the artists who were beginning to flock to Montmartre in droves. Making no use of his (probably nonexistent) imagination, Vasseur had simply put up wooden partitions and internal staircases, creating ten very uncomfortable apartments. A single tap provided water for all the residents, and a foul, dirty bathroom, with a door that could never be shut, served, somehow or other, the needs of all ten apartments. The whole complex was strongly reminiscent of the huts used by trappers in Alaska, which is why most of its residents called it "*la maison du trappeur.*"

Max Jacob was renting an apartment in the same building (which he preferred to call "Le Bateau Lavoir," "the laundry ship"). Indeed, the huge building, with its rows of small windows at the ground floor on one side and the third floor on the other, looked like an ocean liner, while the dozens of items of underwear hanging outside the tiny apartments to dry reminded one of a laundry. Others said that the name was due to the fact that it looked like the barges moored along the banks of the Seine, which were used as laundries.

As we were told later, the single tap of the Bateau Lavoir had begun the passionate and stormy love affair between Fernande and Pablo. When in 1904 the young Spaniard made his fourth visit to Paris, determined this time to stay and establish himself in the art world, he came to live in this house of penniless artists, together with the various animals he loved. After a difficult, troubled adolescence and an unhappy marriage, Fernande was living with a sculptor, Laurent Debienne, in the same building. Pablo first laid eyes on Fernande at the tap and fell head-over-heels in love with her at first sight. From then on, the story was predictable. An August downpour brought the two together. Running to escape from the rain, Fernande unexpectedly bumped into Picasso and he blocked her way, offering her a kitten he was holding in his arms. She followed him to his studio, and ever since they've been inseparable, despite their frequent fights and his unfaithfulness. Even though Picasso was extremely possessive of Fernande, he was not prepared to give up other women for her sake.

Anna and I climbed the shaky stairs to the third floor. A sign written in chalk said "The Poets' Rendezvous," so we knew which door to knock on. Max opened the door and led us in, making a deep theatrical bow. "Let's see," he said. "You already know Pablo, Alice, and Maurice. Also the beautiful Fernande, of course," he added, looking at her ironically. He ignored the face she made and went on, "So let me introduce you to the others." He turned to an overweight youth with a large nose, thick mustache, and square jaw, from which protruded a hint of a double chin. He presented him with arms outspread: "This is the famous poet Guillaume Apollinaire." Then he turned around to face a slim man with big eyes sunk in their sockets, a small, slightly crooked mouth, and thin lips: "And here is his equally famous colleague André Salmon. Next to him, Madeline, the most sought-after model in Montmartre. And finally, underneath the chair, her highness, the dog Frika, the artist's confidante and expert snatcher of unsupervised meatballs."

Of course, Max was joking when he called his friends famous. At the time, they were all obscure and penniless. They partly managed to survive by means of a few badly paid temporary jobs but mainly due to the sympathy of the older inhabitants of Montmartre—Madame Coudrais, for example, "a clever hunchback of uncertain age, with a sharp tongue," as Jacob described her. She was the concierge of the Bateau Lavoir and had a soft spot for the hungry artists and poets who lived under her jurisdiction. She always had some nourishing vegetable soup in her cooking pot saved for them.

Everyone recognized the young painter as the leader of the group, which was already becoming known as "*la bande à*

Picasso"—Picasso's gang. By now they've each made a name for themselves, and they frequent the best salons, where their opinion on anything to do with art is widely sought and greatly feared. The night before, at the Lapin Agile, Max had boasted of his ability to foresee the future. Today I can vouch that, at least as regards the fame of the members of Picasso's gang, his skill at prophecy has been confirmed in every respect.

The studio was lit by two candles and a hurricane lamp, as there was no question of electricity or gas being available at such a building in those days. There was a strong smell of paint, mold, and dog. Frames and canvases were stacked up everywhere along the walls and on the bed. The floor was covered with cigarette butts, squashed paint tubes, and rusty cans full of water and brushes. And yet Anna didn't seem to be the least bit perturbed. At a signal from Picasso, she immediately went and sat on the floor next to him. Fernande's face betrayed a flash of annoyance, but she recovered quickly and asked coyly if I could help her with serving the food. I followed her to the corner of the room that served as a kitchen. It was now Pablo's turn to scowl in irritation.

I knew that in such circles dinner parties relied on everyone chipping in, so I had remembered to bring two bottles of Beaujolais and a large Toulouse salami. We gathered together everything that the guests had brought—olives, sardines, cheeses (I still have nightmares about the smell of the Camembert brought by Salmon)—and we laid them out on small, cracked plates of uncertain cleanliness. The whole time we were sorting out the food, Fernande never stopped giggling and flirting with me. Picasso was shooting angry glances at her every now and then from his corner, while Madeline couldn't take her eyes off the young painter. This silent game of charades, in which Alice and Princet gradually also became involved, lasted the whole evening, providing Jacob with wonderful entertainment, as he had a merely academic interest in heterosexual relationships.

When all the plates were ready, Fernande picked up the crumbs of cheese and salami left over and motioned me to follow her into the next room, which was much smaller and better kept. In the middle was a large wooden chest, covered by a dark red cloth. On it was a portrait of Fernande, bits of bric-a-brac (booty from market fairs), and a cardboard box full of holes. When Fernande opened it, I saw to my surprise that it held a little white mouse. It was another member of Picasso's zoo, which had included at times Siamese cats, tortoises, and a monkey, in addition to little Frika. Behind the chest was a huge canvas, its face turned to the wall. I looked at Fernande inquiringly. She motioned to me not to speak and whispered confidentially, "It's a huge frustration for him—a painting he has been working on for years and can't finish. He won't show it to anyone."

When Fernande had fed the mouse, we took the plates and bottles to the table and sat down with the others. Our arrival stopped the conversation for a while, as everyone fell to eating and drinking. But Anna had not forgotten Picasso's promise, and she reminded him that he had committed himself to showing her his work. He had been very reluctant the day before, but today he appeared to have gotten used to the idea. In fact, it looked as if he and Jacob had already agreed as to how the works would be presented. At least this was the impression I got when Picasso silently began to point to his canvases, letting Max do the talking, who did so mimicking the voices of various other painters.

I came to realize that Max's impersonations were a fixed item of evening entertainment at the Bateau Lavoir. He would mimic everything from can-can dancers (by lifting his trousers to reveal his skinny, hairy legs) to Picasso's various animals. But the height of the fun came when he began to imitate other painters criticizing his friend's works. He was now showing us the *Moulin de la Galette;* Fernande explained that he was using the voice of Théodore Rousseau, imitating him to perfection.

"This should remind you of something," interrupted Pablo, speaking to me. "Do you remember the night we were taken there, against our will, to dance?"

I did remember that all the while we were at the cabaret, Pablo never stopped sketching. He explained that when he had returned to Spain, he used those sketches to compose the painting. Anna and I had only the day before seen the work that Renoir had painted twenty-five years earlier, but the only thing the two paintings had in common was the name. The plump, well-fed matrons of the Impressionist had given way, in our host's painting, to tall, lean figures. In Renoir's work, the hall was drenched in light, the colors standing out bright and varied. Pablo, on the other hand, had given a central role to the chandeliers, which shed their light selectively, leaving in the shade what the artist felt was unimportant and lighting up those features that he considered significant. Renoir's faces were jolly, kind, carefree. Picasso's were mysterious, other-worldly, devilish. They reflected in every way the immense mistrust with which the young Spaniard viewed the world.

From the few times I had met Picasso, as well as from my conversations with Stefanos, it was clear to me that he had a weakness for women. In his picture I could now see, with growing surprise, a deep contempt for the female sex as a whole, a disgust for women that was more intense and raw than the plainly advertised misogyny of Jacob, which after all came from his sexual orientation. Did it have to do with the story of Casagemas and Germaine? Certainly his friend's tragic love story must have influenced him. But was it possible that, behind the keen customer of brothels in Barcelona's Barrio Chino and in Montmartre, behind the heartthrob who boasted that he had slept with all the women he had ever met, lay hidden a second, much more repressed Max Jacob? I had often entertained similar suspicions about various other Don Juans I had encountered in the past, but as my interest in the subject was no more than simple curiosity, I had never delved deeper.

Jacob continued to present his friend's works, adopting in turn the voices of Degas, Cézanne, and Matisse, raising howls of laughter. But I could not get the *Moulin de la Galette* out of my head. Picasso showed us many paintings with Casagemas as their subject, in which dark, bleak, melancholy tones prevailed. There followed some brighter pictures of harlequins and scenes of the circus. I wondered whether perhaps his relationship with Fernande had contributed to the change in his mood. Then the display came to an end, but Anna was not satisfied. "You promised you would show us the one you're working on now," she said stubbornly.

Pablo hesitated, but then, with a gesture of resignation, he beckoned us to follow him into the next room. He approached the canvas that was facing the wall, and with one movement, turned it around to face us. The others had probably seen it before, but Anna and I were stunned. Five vaguely feminine figures were set out on the canvas in strange, unnatural poses. The painting was full of lines, straight and broken, but there were no curves. I tried to grasp the general idea of the composition, but failed. The only impression I took away from looking at this unfinished image was the strong suspicion—the fear, I might say—that Picasso held for what his work represented. I may have been influenced by the first work (I tend to be prone to fixed ideas), but I got the feeling that, through a completely different style, using entirely new techniques of expression, Picasso was basically showing the same thing: his contempt for women. Only this time the reason was obvious: fear.

"Ladies and gentlemen, the philosophers' brothel," announced Salmon, with a histrionic gesture. In ten years' time, when the work had at last been completed, he was himself to give it its final title: *Les Demoiselles d'Avignon*.

Pablo was covered in sweat. It was clear that he felt ill-at-ease. Slight panting betrayed the onslaught of a panic attack. Apollinaire stepped to his aid: "Come on, put it away now. You will show it to us when it's finished," he said. Then he turned around and ushered us back into the other room.

As soon as we had all sat on the floor again, Salmon began to roll a cigarette. From the way everyone looked at him, I realized it was not tobacco. It was my turn to feel uncomfortable. I had never smoked hashish—nor even a normal cigarette. My bourgeois upbringing as well as my practical mind was in direct opposition to the promises of a brief paradise that narcotics offered. Salmon lit up, drew deeply and passed the cigarette to Princet. It went from hand to hand until it reached Fernande, who eventually offered it to me. I declined as calmly as I could, keeping an expressionless face. For once, Fevronia Mavroleon's taboos and prohibitions triumphed. Next to me, Anna laughed ironically and stretched out her hand. She bravely drew on the cigarette, managing not to choke, and handed it to Picasso, who was sitting next to her.

I have no idea at which point Anna and Picasso managed to have a private word, nor what sort of arrangements they made. But when the following afternoon Anna announced coyly, "I'm going to leave you on your own tonight, my sweet," I understood. Feeling no guilt, I, in my turn, went to meet my old girlfriends at the Moulin Rouge.

Ten

After we returned to Athens, things began to get worse. If there was one thing Anna couldn't stand, it was routine. While we were still abroad, she treated our relationship as just another affair and, as long as I had no objection to her occasional cheating, our agreement worked very well. But in Athens, things were different.

For one thing, her mother and my grandmother, not to mention the whole high society of Athens, expected Anna to set up a "respectable home"—to spend most of her time running the household and divide the rest between charitable works, ladies' tea parties, and social events. All this would go on until she got under way the process of producing offspring, who would carry on their backs the triple burden of the legacy of the Mavroleon, Igerinos, and Dellaportas families.

When we had discussed things before we were married, Anna had explicitly excluded any possibility of having children, and I had gone along with this. But our family and social circle would countenance neither the absence of offspring nor Anna's behavior. She continued to pay no heed to what people said, to flirt as much as she did before our marriage, and to make forays outside the marriage nest whenever she pleased, some lasting for days.

On my part, I honored the terms of our private agreement, allowing Anna to live her life as she desired and enjoying the same rights myself. I split my time between the business and my books. I had started reading about mathematics again and subscribed to the more important German and French specialist periodicals, so that I could keep abreast of developments which, rather predictably, were following at least in subject matter the program set by Hilbert in Paris.

Occasionally, I would resort to paid female companionship, which in my youth had so fascinated me. In this, I was no different from my otherwise respectable peers, who, unlike me, ruled their households with an iron grip and in accordance with social conventions.

Gradually, gossip began to mount. The arguments between my wife and her mother became more and more frequent. Even my father-in-law, who adored Anna, took the step of advising me to "rein her in." Although I stood by our agreement to the letter, Anna grew impatient even with me, saying I should take her side more often.

The situation lasted three more years, but when the military coup took place at Goudi, outside Athens, Anna carried out her own revolt. On December 28, 1909, around the time when Venizelos was disembarking at Piraeus to form the new democratic government, the chambermaid handed me a letter informing me that "the mistress has gone." In her letter, Anna reminded me of our agreement and announced that she was leaving the country and that our lawyers would handle all matters connected with our divorce.

Although she was the woman in the case, I feel that Anna took the gentleman's part. By leaving the country clandestinely, accompanied no doubt by one of her lovers, she was taking all the responsibility for the divorce, shouldering the scandal, and handing me unsullied back to society. The only thing I could have been accused of was lack of discipline. Otherwise, I enjoyed the sympathy that commonly accompanies those ironic remarks made of cuckolded and abandoned husbands behind their backs; but such talk gradually died down, since the "adulteress" was not present for the gossips to feed on.

Putting aside the freedom I gained to meet freely with "*artistes*"—who, as I mentioned, had always been my preference in women—without giving rise to chatter, the divorce didn't change my life in any respect. I continued to divide my time between my business affairs, which—as I had no intention of expanding—now carried on almost automatically, providing me with a steady income and ensuring a comfortable lifestyle, and mathematics.

In March 1910, I went to hear a lecture given by Nikolaos Hatzidakis, a professor at Athens University, on the subject of differential geometry. I arrived late, as usual, and found an unexpectedly full lecture hall. I was looking around self-consciously when I heard a curiously familiar voice behind me.

"Are you by any chance Greek?"

I turned around and embraced Stefanos warmly; he moved up and we sat close together, just as we had ten years earlier, when we were listening to the lecture by Greece's leading mathematician, who committed the offense, among others, of speaking in demotic Greek. Among the body of Greek university students, the most vociferous were the ultraconservative elements, who had taken a leading role a few years earlier during "the Gospels

Affair." They disapproved strongly of Hatzidakis' initiative in giving lectures open to the public, and in demotic Greek at that! I had met Hatzidakis, the son of Ioannis (with whose book I had been introduced to geometry), when he too was studying at Göttingen. His excellent reputation at that university had been largely the reason for the professors there revising their opinion of the Greeks. So I, too, had in a way benefited from his brilliance.

Like many prominent mathematicians, Hatzidakis used to enjoy spending time away from his important work playing at simple, almost childish, games. He had, for example, devoted a large part of his free time to composing a poem in which the number of letters making up each word would correspond to each of the digits forming the number *pi*. There were already poems circulating in French and German, which were used as mnemonics for the sequence of digits in *pi*. The French, for example, would memorize them with the following poem:

Que j'aime à faire apprendre un nombre utile aux sages!
Immortel Archimède ariste ingénieur,
Qui de ton jugement peut priser la valuer?
Pour moi, ton problème eut de pareils avantages.

The Germans had this one:

Dir, O Held, o alter Philosoph, du Riesen Genie!
Wie viele Tausende bewundern Geister,
Himmlisch wie du und göttlich!
Noch reiner in Aeonen
Wird das uns strahlen,
Wie im lichten Morgenrot!

"Shame on us!" Hatzidakis used to say. "The French, the Germans, the English have conveyed the digits of *pi* in verse, while we Greeks, who first discovered the existence of *pi,* haven't composed anything similar."

One day, he strode into the University Library, radiant with pride. He came up to me and put a small piece of paper in front of me. "There!" he said, full of joy. The paper read:

> 'Αεὶ ὁ Θεὸς ὁ Μέγας γεωμετρεῖ,
> τὸ κύκλου μῆκος ἵνα ὁρίσῃ διαμέτρῳ,
> παρήγαγεν ἀριθμὸν ἀπέραντον,
> καὶ ὄν, φεῦ, οὐδέποτε ὅλον θνητοὶ θὰ εὕρωσι.

> *(God the Great is the eternal Geometrician.*
> *In order to define the perimeter of a circle using its diameter,*
> *He has produced an infinite number,*
> *The whole of which, alas, mortal men will never discover.)*

3.14159265358979323846 26 … I don't think he felt greater satisfaction when he was solving the difficult problems set for him by Hilbert or Klein.

When Hatzidakis' talk was over, I persuaded Stefanos to come back home with me. My cook was a master at making crepes, and my cellar contained several bottles of *cidre,* so we could re-create, as closely as possible, our first encounter.

In 1903, Stefanos had obtained his doctorate on number theory. The president of the examining committee was Hadamard himself. Stefanos then returned to Greece and, despite the warm letters of recommendation from Hadamard and even Poincaré, he was unable to get a position at the university. He was politically uncommitted, socially ostracized and too proud to ask Avgerios

Manousakas for his help. Consequently, the doors of the university remained hermetically sealed to him. After much effort, he managed to get a post in some high school in the provinces. He spent the last seven years being shunted from one town to another. Just a few months before we ran into each other, he had been moved to the Boys' High School in the Plaka district of Athens and had rented a room in Neapoli, at the foot of Mount Lycabettus.

I told him my story, confiding in him that my enthusiasm for mathematics was undiminished, but that I was now more interested in keeping up to date than actively trying to find solutions to unsolved problems.

"Well, I myself haven't yet given up on Hilbert's second problem. Do you remember it? 'To find a direct method of proving the consistency of an axiomatic system'—meaning, to find an algorithm that can demonstrate whether or not a given system of axioms is contradictory and whether it can give a positive or negative answer to all the problems that can arise within its framework."

I laughed. "I think your friend Ruiz will finish his *Les Demoiselles d'Avignon* before you find your algorithm. Did I tell you I met him again? It was in 1906 when I went to Paris for my honeymoon. He now wants people to call him Picasso, his mother's name. He even showed me a painting where we appear—in a manner of speaking, that is. Do you remember the dance at the Moulin de la Galette? He filled a whole notebook with sketches that night. Later, after he returned to Spain, he painted a big picture with that subject. After you first introduced him to me, he made another three trips between Barcelona and Paris, and then settled down in Montmartre in 1904. He now has a wide circle of friends, poets, and writers. And he has a permanent, if not exclusive, girlfriend—a real goddess, a figure out of a painting by Botticelli. Her name is

Fernande. When I first saw her, I was stunned—even though I was a newlywed.

"The group has its own mathematical adviser: one Maurice Princet. We met him at the conference. Well, Maurice was attached to a young girl named Alice, who had the face of an angel and the temperament of a devil. She had entirely adapted to the atmosphere of Montmartre. She was perfectly faithful to Maurice, provided there was no other man around. In other words, she was driving him crazy. For a while she was even Pablo's mistress."

"Just a minute," Stefanos interrupted. "Are you talking about a girl around eighteen years old, a type of Renaissance madonna, with big eyes and long brown hair? I must have met her. I often saw Pablo whenever he came to Paris, up until 1903, when I returned to Greece. There were many women in his life: there was Margot, there was Madéline, and also Alice. Alice Géry, if I remember correctly. She was a laborer's daughter who had run away from home and gotten involved with the artistic circles of Montmartre. For a time she was madly in love with Pablo. He did a sketch of her; she's shown as a slim figure dressed in white, sitting with her elbow resting on a table."

"That's her! When I went to his house in 1906, I saw that picture among his other works. She's the one who introduced Princet to Picasso's gang. He probably feels like a fish out of water among them. He's respectable, with a steady job with an insurance company. If you disregard the fact that he occasionally likes to indulge in hashish with them, he has nothing to do with the bohemian life the others lead. But when our friend heard that he was a mathematician, he immediately adopted him—you know how crazy he is about mathematics. Do you remember when he insisted that you give a lecture that night we went out with them?

Well, now that's what Maurice has to do all the time. In fact, he does it very well.

"Unfortunately for Maurice, while Pablo may be talented (although his latest works are not selling at all), he is certainly lacking in the morality department. The last time I was in Paris, after my divorce, I heard that in 1907, Princet was promoted at work, and they let him know that it wasn't appropriate for an important member of their staff to be living out of wedlock with a woman, especially one of uncertain morals. So after a lot of begging, he managed to persuade Alice to marry him. They even got Picasso to be best man. Best man, indeed! At that time, he had gotten to know another painter, Derain, and your Picasso decided that Derain and Alice would make a perfect couple. So he began playing the matchmaker behind Maurice's back. To cut a long story short, Alice and Princet were married in March, and by September they had separated. Wasting no time, Alice went from being Mrs. Princet to Mrs. Derain. They're together at the moment, but we'll see how long it lasts. Perhaps until she finds another husband herself—or Picasso finds one for her."

"And what about his painting? The last time I saw him, he was painting some strange things—death scenes, portraits immersed in sadness. I'm not a specialist, but I can't imagine who would want to look at those gloomy colors all day long—all the shades of blue. Even if you felt on top of the world, you would go all melancholy looking at them. It's no wonder he couldn't sell a single one of them. When I left Paris, he was starving."

"He was greatly affected by the death of his friend Casagemas. For a while, most of his paintings had to do with him and his suicide. But when I saw him in 1906, I think he had gotten over his depression. His love affair with Fernande has played a decisive role. He showed us his pierrots, circus scenes, all much more cheerful stuff. He had painted himself dressed as a harlequin back in the days of the Zut. He gave the painting to Frédé, who naturally displayed it in a place of honor in the large hall of his new cabaret, the *Lapin Agile*. But I think he's having great difficulty with the *Les Demoiselles d'Avignon*. Its subject is the prostitutes of Avignon Street in Barcelona's Barrio Chino district. Anna persuaded him to show it to us, but he generally doesn't like showing it to anyone. It's a big headache for him. When I was there last year, I heard that after working on it for almost two years, he left it unfinished."

The conversation then turned to mathematics. We reminisced about the conference, and Stefanos wondered if any of the problems listed by Hilbert had been solved. He had been out of touch with the international mathematical community ever since 1903, when he had returned to Greece. Foreign periodicals were hard to come by here, and his finances didn't allow him to subscribe to any of them. Needless to say, any trip abroad to update himself was out of the question. It was only through correspondence with some old classmates that he managed to keep informed.

"While I was in Paris, I only heard about the third problem," he said. "But that had already been solved by Max Dehn , a student of Hilbert's, through a negative proof before the proceedings of the conference were even published. To solve the problem, one had to find a way of deriving the validity of the formula for a pyramid's volume without employing the notion of infinity or using limits. Apparently, he proved that it can't be done. Of course, geometry is not my forte, as you know."

The proceedings of the International Congress of Mathematicians of 1900 had been one of the first books I bought when I first returned to mathematics. I had indeed seen a footnote in one of Hilbert's papers saying, "Since this paper was written, Herr Dehn has proven the impossibility of this." Unlike my friend, I had a passion for geometry and had researched the matter a lot more. So I was able to explain things to Stefanos.

"Do you know the method of exhaustion?" I asked.

"You mean the method used by Archimedes to calculate area and volume?"

"Exactly. You start by covering the space you wish to measure with triangles of a certain size. It's easy to calculate the area of the triangles. However when we cover a curvilinear shape, a few gaps always remain.

"So the total area of the triangles is only an approximation of the area we're looking for. We then take smaller triangles and cover the area that remained uncovered. Again, there is a shortfall, and we cover this shortfall with still smaller triangles. This process continues *ad infinitum;* the limit of those approximations is the area of the space we're looking for."

"Yes. It's the same method used by mathematicians of the Renaissance. Only instead of triangles, they used rectangles. It was on this idea that integral calculus was based. We were taught all this thoroughly at the university. But I'm not sure how it relates to Hilbert's third problem."

"Archimedes' method is essential for curvilinear shapes, that is, circles, ellipses, and parabolas, as well as for calculating the volume of solids. But it's not essential for polygons."

"What do you mean?"

"If we take any polygon, we can easily draw a rectangle with the same area without resorting to the concept of 'infinite summation of infinitesimal areas.' Take the example of a sloping parallelogram.

On one side, a right-angled triangle protrudes, while on the other side, a triangle is missing. If you cut off the one that sticks out and place it where one is missing, you end up with a rectangle. It's proven that we can more or less do this for any polygon. But it can't be done with solids. Take the pyramid. No one has yet managed to dissect it into one, two, a hundred pieces and reassemble it so that it forms a cube. The only way of working out a formula for its volume—the famous 'the area of the base times the height divided by three,'—is by resorting to the method of exhaustion."

Stefanos looked at me with interest. A glow of satisfaction shone in his eyes. Was it the joy of discussing mathematics, or his enthusiasm (which I also felt) to an overwhelming degree on discovering that, after ten years' interruption, our friendship was back on track?

"Even Gauss got stuck on this problem. He wrote to a friend of his that the situation regarding the calculation of a pyramid's volume was 'extremely displeasing.' And as you know, when Gauss expressed displeasure, there were dozens of mathematicians who would make it their life's work to restore things by finding what the prince was looking for. They all failed. No one could find a method of calculating the volume of solids like the pyramid without using integral calculus, and the concepts of infinity and the infinitesimal. On the other hand, no one had *proven* that it was absolutely impossible, although this was something that everyone gradually began to suspect. So it was this that Hilbert asked for in his lecture: that it be proven, in a finite number of steps, that it's impossible to transform solids like the pyramid into simpler shapes with a known volume. That's what Dehn proved, based on previous research by someone called Bricard. I've got his article. If you like, I can lend it to you."

"That's great! One out of twenty-three has been solved; twenty-two to go. There's no doubt they will be. Whether positively or negatively, they will be solved." He tried to imitate Hilbert's style: "Don't forget. There is no *ignorabimus* in mathematics!"

He laughed with pleasure, having brought up again our old dispute. "As you know, I myself shall solve the second problem one day. I shall create an algorithm that will test through a finite number of steps the consistency and completeness of an axiomatic system. With that algorithm, I'll be able to test the axioms of arithmetic. I've already progressed a little. As soon as there is an opportunity, I'll show you what I've done."

For the time being we had nothing more to say on the topic. I held the exact opposite view from my friend, but for the moment, neither of us had any new arguments to put forward.

We continued to talk about Hilbert's problems and exchanged information about developments on them. For his sixth problem, Hilbert had announced a rather vague target, the axiomatization of physics. Already by 1903, Hamel had published an axiomatic system for classical mechanics. And in 1909 (a year before Stefanos and I met up again), a Greek called Constantin Carathéodory, a professor at Göttingen, had published a particularly elegant system for thermodynamics.

The case of Carathéodory was intriguing. He belonged to an old family of Phanariotes from Constantinople, and he was the grandson of the Sultan's private physician and son of his ambassador to Belgium. His career had begun as an engineer, and he had worked very successfully for the company that constructed dams in Egypt. There, in the land of the pyramids, he came under the dual spell of the ancient Egyptians and the Alexandrian geometricians, and it was there that he had undergone his "road to Damascus" conversion. At the age of twenty-seven—rather late to be starting as a mathematician—he went back to college. His fellow students at first couldn't resist making sarcastic remarks about my compatriot, who "in his old age" had decided to become a mathematician. But very soon, as Carathéodory began to be appointed to higher and higher posts at German universities, the sneers turned into exclamations of admiration.

Stefanos and I talked deep into the night. As I was saying goodbye, I felt a sense of well-being run through me. It was the first time in the last ten years that I felt so fulfilled.

From that evening onward, we made a habit of meeting alternately at each other's houses every Thursday afternoon. Those Thursday meetings became the most important events in my life. They were something like a bridge, which connected to a past that was irretrievably gone, as well as to a future that would never come to be.

In the meantime, things were happening all around us and, although both Stefanos and I lived our lives largely outside the field of politics, it was inevitable that these events would have an impact on us. In 1912, Greece sided with Bulgaria and Serbia and declared war on Turkey. We were both called up. Stefanos, a veteran and hero of the 1897 war, was sent straight to the front, to an infantry unit. As for me, thanks partly to my mathematical background and partly to my political contacts, I was sent to the Army General Headquarters and assigned to the department of strategic planning for the artillery.

The military first started being interested in mathematics at the beginning of the sixteenth century, when Tartaglia (the Italian who solved the cubic equation) proved that the trajectory of a missile is a curve. Up until then, the Aristotelian tradition, which saw all movement on the earth as straight lines, had prevailed. The work of Tartaglia was completed half a century later by Galileo, who proved that such a curve is a parabola. Gradually, mathematics began to infiltrate more and more into the art of war. It was no accident that the École Polytechnique of Paris, which was founded by Napoleon for the education of French army officers, developed into the top educational institution in the country for mathematical studies.

As a consequence, the French advisers who undertook to organize the Greek army recommended that the General Command include men who had a knowledge of mathematics. I was one of them. On October 26, 1912, the Greek army marched into Thessaloniki; Stefanos' regiment was one of the first to camp inside the town. Two days later, the Crown Prince and Commander-in-Chief set up his headquarters in the Macedonian capital together with his officers, of whom I was one. The atmosphere was one of celebration rather than war. The Turkish garrison had surrendered without a shot and vacated the town. Everyone else—Greeks, Jews, Slavs, Vlachs, and a host of western Europeans—went on with their lives as normal. The market was bustling with activity; the shops were full; the hotels, theaters, and restaurants were doing a brisk business; and the only clouds on the horizon were the rumors that the Bulgarians would soon break their alliance with Greece. Control of the great cosmopolitan port of Thessaloniki had been their ancestral dream, and its capture by our troops was not easy for them to swallow.

I met up with Stefanos five days after we entered the town. It was midday, and we strolled along the front, both of us on a twenty-four-hour leave. We stopped at a little taverna near the water and ordered skewered mussels, whitebait, and red wine. Then we began to share our war stories. Stefanos, who had fought at Sarandaporos and Giannitsa, described with excitement the battles and victories of our forces. I was astonished to discover another side of his character, unknown to me until then.

Most of the people I knew considered the defeat of '97 to be a consequence of the incompetence of our politicians and the military. I had thought that Stefanos shared that view and that, having done his duty over and above what was expected of him, he had put all that behind him. However, partly because of the wine (delivered straight from one of the monasteries of Mount Athos) and partly because it was a gloriously sunny winter's day, his tongue was loosened, and I discovered yet another different Stefanos. Deep inside, he felt the defeat of the 1897 war as his personal failure, and he saw the present victories of our troops as a kind of atonement. He talked with passion, almost fanaticism—something that seemed out of place in a number theorist whose avowed purpose in life was to rebuild the foundations of mathematics in line with Hilbert's program.

Then it was my turn to relate my own "adventures," though these were much less dramatic. I showed Stefanos the mathematical method used by the French military advisers for their own artillary, and the formulas they used to calculate the trajectory of the enemy missiles and for determining which areas were relatively safe from them. The mathematics they used was very simple, but the top brass at headquarters considered me and the three other mathematicians who worked with the French to be geniuses. This didn't stop them from burdening us with all sorts of chores whenever they could, however, just so we wouldn't forget our place.

I asked Stefanos if he had any plans for the evening. In the euphoric climate of those days, most hotels in Thessaloniki organized dances every evening. That night, I had been invited to the Splendide, and I offered to take Stefanos with me. I immediately sensed his awkwardness. He blushed, twisted and untwisted his hands, straightened his mustache. "You know," he said hesitantly, "I've recently gotten to know a nurse, a volunteer who had been living abroad—in Montreux in Switzerland, I believe—but as soon as war broke out she rushed back to join one of the volunteer corps of nurses set up by the princesses. Her team has been supporting my regiment throughout its advance, and she now works in one of the army hospitals. I promised to take her to the dance tonight. What a coincidence that you're going to the same one! I hope you won't be offended, but I'm not sure that she wants to meet people and all that; she's an unusual woman. She seems to have no regard at all for social niceties, and yet ..."

He hesitated for a bit and then made up his mind: "You know ... if I don't make the first move, please don't betray the fact that you know me."

I was delighted by my friend's good fortune and laughed off his worries. I assured him of my tact, saying, with a teasing smile, that I couldn't wait to meet his conquest. I never for a moment imagined the surprise I would get that evening.

Two French officers, a senior member of the staff of the British Embassy, an Italian merchant, and I had formed a small social group. My foreign friends were in agreement that sooner or later our allies would have to sign a peace treaty with Turkey and that we would have to resolve the position at Ioannina so that we could sit at the negotiating table with the others. The Englishman was convinced that a new state would be formed in the north of Epirus, and he placed its border with Greece at Ioannina. That town, Ali Pasha's old capital, was still held by the Turks, who were defending it fiercely against the Greek onslaught. Just as the Italian was explaining that the creation of Albania was vitally important to his own country's interests, Stefanos appeared at the door. Leaning tenderly on his arm was … Anna.

I had last seen her the day before she "abandoned" me. The divorce had been carried out by our lawyers, and she had not set foot in Greece for the past three years. As I've said more than once, I've never felt any ill will towards Anna. Her flight had rather suited me and, as I've never felt any of the typical male possessiveness, her behavior had not been at all hurtful. Knowing her well, I was sure she would not be in the least put out by our encounter. But I did worry about Stefanos. He couldn't have known that his "conquest" was my former wife, but I knew that as soon as he realized it, he would feel terrible. Not surprisingly, that moment arrived in no time at all.

As soon as Anna saw me, she waved in a friendly manner and leaned toward Stefanos, whispering something in his ear and pointing toward me. Poor Stefanos changed a hundred colors. I had to step in and put him at his ease. I approached them and gave Anna a kiss on the cheek, saying half-jokingly that as she had given me up, I was so pleased that at least she had taken up with my best friend. The evening passed with light talk, but I can only imagine how long it took Stefanos to get over the shock.

A few days later, the division of strategic planning received orders to advance to the front in Epirus. Stefanos' unit stayed in Thessaloniki to secure the defense of the town, not so much from the Turks as from the Bulgarians. He was there on the day a man called Alexandros Schinas assassinated King George, precipitating Constantine's ascent to the throne. What had not been achieved through constant intrigues by the Crown Prince and his wife finally took place thanks to the actions of a man who was officially described as a lunatic, but whom most people immediately took to be a Bulgarian agent; as a matter of fact, some well-informed sources of mine told me that he was a tool of the German secret services. Prussia had at last managed to put a loyal ally of hers on the Greek throne.

Four months after the liberation of Thessaloniki, and only a few days before the assassination, the military governor of Ioannina had surrendered the town to the Greek army. The first Balkan War was effectively over. But it was obvious that sooner or later the old allies would clash. In the office of strategic planning, I had struck up a friendship with one of the French military advisers, Lieutenant Molon. He was a graduate of the École Polytechnique and very strong in mathematics. In addition, he was an excellent chess player. One evening, after a game of chess (which, for patriotic reasons, I will report that I won), the conversation turned to the fact that most mathematicians show a keen interest in that particular intellectual exercise.

"Chess is a game with clearly defined rules," I observed. "It should therefore be possible to devise a mathematical model to describe it."

"In that case, it should also be possible to formulate a mathematical theory of war or of international politics," remarked Kosta, the other mathematician in our newly formed social circle.

Molon remained thoughtful for a while, stroking his mustache absentmindedly. "I believe," he said at last, "that we don't yet possess the appropriate mathematics. The only sharp mathematical tool we have today is the infinitesimal calculus. But that was created for man to deal with the forces of nature, which have no self-interest or free will. Nature is governed by clear rules that apply each time in the same way, since there is no reason for anyone to bypass them or apply them differently. But in chess, things are very different. Each player must adjust his play in response to his opponent's moves. Thus, each player's strategy is determined by, among others, the strategy of his opponent. The same is true of a battle, in the planning of an expedition, and even more in international diplomatic bargaining. As far as I'm aware, such mathematics—mathematics that can combine the interaction between the strategies of two opponents—doesn't yet exist. This doesn't mean it will never be invented. Many of my old classmates who are now researchers would be interested in your idea."

It was a comment made offhand, so none of us pursued it further. However, it did occur to me that it would be very interesting if I suggested the idea to Stefanos as soon as we were able to resume our Thursday meetings. But for the time being that seemed to be a long way away. Because of the Greco-Bulgarian disagreements, we received orders to return to Thessaloniki, but when we got there, Stefanos' regiment had already taken up a position outside Kavala, on a line facing our former allies.

In June 1913, clashes broke out again. They lasted for almost a month and ended in victory for our troops. I was discharged in August, and Stefanos two months later. As soon as I heard that he was back, I lost no time going to see him. We talked about our war experiences, which in my case were mainly theoretical, while for my friend they were firsthand and real. His unit had taken part in almost all the military operations. He described the battles of Kilkis and Doirani, the clashes in the straits of Kresna, the operations at Simitli. As was his wont, he understated his personal contribution as much as possible. However, a shining silver medal designed by Jakobides—the only ornament in his desperately bare room—provided evidence that his contribution had not been so insignificant.

"Come on, I was just lucky. Anyone in my position would have done the same," was the only comment I managed to get out of him in that respect. We talked about Anna. Stefanos assured me, in halting tones and blushing profusely, that he had not known that she was my ex-wife, and that all initiative regarding their affair was hers. I had no doubt that both statements were true. When Stefanos was discharged, he stayed with Anna for a week in Thessaloniki. Then she disappeared one morning, leaving him a warm letter informing him that she was going back to Switzerland.

"So we're even," I said, laughing. But I realized that the topic made him uncomfortable, and I hastened to change the subject. What came to mind was the developments after the end of the war and the Treaty of Bucharest.

Stefanos' pessimism surprised me. "The Greeks have this amazing capacity to throw in the garbage what they've gained through so many sacrifices," he said. "Any damage not done by the enemy, they inflict upon themselves. I'm afraid that the 'axiomatic system' of the Greek nation is badly defined. Proving its consistency and completeness seems to me an impossible thing to do," he added, laughing. He was coming back again and again to the discussion we had begun thirteen years earlier in Paris, a topic that tended to make an appearance every time we met.

"Whereas proving the completeness and consistency of arithmetic is child's play," I remarked ironically.

He gave an aggressive laugh. "Arithmetic cannot stay in limbo forever," he countered. "Somewhere among God's papers is a written proof of its completeness and consistency. There is an algorithm that can, through a series of finite steps, determine whether a given system of axioms is complete and noncontradictory or not. This is where mathematics differs from politics. One day we will manage to devise a system of axioms that will be adequate for us to determine whether a statement expressed within the framework of that system is true or false. After that, my algorithm, the one I will invent, will also establish noncontradiction."

I didn't know then whether Stefanos' optimism about mathematics was justified. His dream of an entirely "domesticated" mathematical science was my worst nightmare. Finding a way to show completeness and noncontradiction, with which he was threatening all of us mathematicians, was in direct conflict with my own aesthetic perception of mathematics.

On the other hand, I was shortly to discover that his pessimism regarding the future of the country was entirely justified. Within a few years, the victory laurels would be buried under the ashes of civil discord. Gradually, the energy and decisiveness that had led to victory in the Balkan Wars evolved into hatred and pettiness, turning one half of Greece (the Royalists) against the other (the Liberals).

Even the barrel organs passing in the street were split into two camps, half of them continually playing "The Son of the Eagle," a royalist march glorifying the king, and the other half playing "The Son of Mount Psiloritis," a song in praise of Venizelos. Few of my fellow countrymen knew that both pieces were works by the same composer, Spyros Kaisaris, who in this scenario had managed to perfect the role of diplomat.

I had never understood my country's politics in depth, perhaps because I had never really tried. My rational way of thinking wasn't suited to making sense of the multiplicity, vagueness, and unpredictability that govern political developments. But at the time of the "National Schism," I was able to put two and two together: I realized that sooner or later I would have to forgo half of all my social contacts.

My father had been closely connected with the Delta family, with whom he also had business associations. I too had maintained friendly relations with Stefanos and Penelope Delta, although that didn't mean I shared their political views. I enjoyed talking to Penelope about her books, the Greek community in Alexandria, and the trips we had both made abroad. Delta himself was a cousin of Constantin Carathéodory, and he often brought me news and gossip about the mathematical community in Germany. So it was with particular pleasure that I would occasionally receive an invitation to visit them in the northern suburb of Kifissia. One evening in 1915, I accepted such an invitation, never suspecting the consequences.

From the time I was a student in Germany, I had maintained a friendly relationship with the painter Georgios Jakobides, who was now a professor at the Athens School of Fine Arts. A personal friend of Prince Nicholas', Jakobides didn't conceal his royalist sympathies; however, he didn't presume to impose them on anyone else. The day after my visit to Kifissia, I was invited to his studio. He received me cordially, as always, but I felt the coldness of the other guests right from the start. Most of them simply ignored me, but one of them launched into a direct attack on me, saying "You have to make up your mind, Mr. Igerinos, about whom you wish to be associated with. You cannot one day be visiting the lair of Venizelist conspirators, cavorting with the enemies of the nation, and the following day show up at a meeting of patriots such as this, as if nothing was wrong with that."

It took me a while to understand what he was getting at. Emmanuel Benakis, Penelope's father, had been a close collaborator of Venizelos'. So in the eyes of this half-witted man, whoever visited the Delta or Benakis families shouldn't contaminate a gathering where the host and his guests were all royalists. I was not prepared to take part in this madness, nor did I want to choose between the two camps. So instead of dropping half of my acquaintances by choosing one or the other, I decided to give up all of them and withdraw from social life altogether.

I spent the greater part of the war in solitude, with my books for company. My only social activity was my weekly meeting with Stefanos. We both watched in surprise and pain as Greece tore itself in two. Venizelos' "pro-Entente" army threatened to occupy Athens, while the royalist government of "the state of Athens" reacted with indifference to each loss of Greek territory. At a more personal level, those who had been comrades-in-arms only a short time before set about harassing, humiliating, arresting, and sometimes even shooting at each other.

With the end of the war, a ray of hope began to shine faintly. The joy of victory, the liberation of the rest of Macedonia and Thrace, the accession of the coast of Asia Minor—all these spread hope for a short while that the division might come to an end. But it turned out to be only a dream.

On March 20, 1920, the destroyer *Ierax,* belonging to the Hellenic Royal Navy, was anchored inside the port of Smyrna, hosting on its deck an unusual meeting for such a venue. The Greek prime minister, Eleftherios Venizelos; the chief of staff of the Greek armed forces in Asia Minor, Leonidas Paraskevopoulos;

Doctor Apostolos Psaltov, a prominent figure among the Greek community of Smyrna; and Constantin Carathéodory, former professor at the Universities of Göttingen and Berlin (known internationally for his pioneering work on the theory of functions and on the axiomatization of thermodynamics) were in discussions concerning the University of Smyrna, which was about to be established. Stefanos was one of the professor's close collaborators.

The plan for a second Greek university had been on Venizelos' mind for many years. The idea of a cosmopolitan university at Smyrna acting as a bridge between European cultural values and ancient Eastern wisdom was particularly appealing. It was, in a way, the peaceful face of the Grand Design, the ambition of some Greeks to repossess the lands of the Byzantine empire. The university aimed to establish the domination of Greece by means of its cultural influence on a multinational community; in the process, the university would become a melting pot of many diverse civilizations. Was it a chimera? Yes, it was, as was proven by the tragic events that followed. And yet, being disenchanted with the political reality of the divisions that had had such an impact on my life (even though I had not taken sides), I saw the plans for the new university as a bright source of hope.

When Carathéodory arrived in Athens in 1920, I went to see him and offered to help with funding and in any other way I could. During our conversation I took the opportunity to talk to him about Stefanos. I described his work, as well as his character and his dedication. Carathéodory asked to meet him.

Stefanos visited him the next day, and they talked for two hours. I don't know if he spoke of his plans regarding the proof of completeness, but I'm sure he must have talked about his research on the theory of numbers and shown him his papers on the subject. All this material, which had left the bureaucrats of the Greek establishment cold, grabbed the attention of the famous scientist of the Greek diaspora. Carathéodory immediately offered him a position on the faculty of the new university and assured him that a professorship would be guaranteed for him as soon as the chairs began to be created.

Apart from being a distinguished mathematician, Carathéodory was a brilliant administrator. Very quickly, the university acquired laboratory equipment, teaching rooms, a lecture theater, and an excellent library, all rivaling the facilities at the famous universities of Europe, where its vice chancellor had been nurtured. This was made easier by the thousands of contributions that poured in from the Greeks of Smyrna, and particularly by the generous gift of a Greek living in Paris, Stavros Palatzis, who offered two million French francs for building equipment and promised an annual endowment of two hundred and fifty thousand francs toward the university's running costs. The new university was scheduled to start emitting *ex oriente lux*, as its motto stipulated, in October 1922.

Fate decreed otherwise. On November 1, 1920, Venizelos quite unexpectedly lost the election. Following the "advice" of his enemies to avoid bloodshed, he boarded the ship *Narcissus,* which belonged to Empirikos, and sailed for France.

Total disaster followed. Millions of Greeks were forced to become refugees. After three thousand years of continuous presence in Asia Minor and the Black Sea, Greeks had to abandon their ancestral homes forever. At the same time, the torch that had spread "light from the Orient" was extinguished. Carathéodory embarked on the last ship, leaving Smyrna behind in flames. After teaching in Athens for two years, he returned to Germany in 1924, where he succeeded Lindemann at the University of Munich.

Stefanos also returned in a dreadful state, more psychological rather than physically. It was no consolation that he had foreseen the disaster at a time when the wind of enthusiasm and optimism had been sweeping everything in its path. Just as in 1897, he now took this new disaster, a disaster of immensely greater scale, as a personal defeat, and he identified with it as though it were his own failing. In comparison, the shattering of his dream of an academic career was the last thing on his mind. For him, mathematics was not a means of social and professional advancement; it was rather a calling and a way of life. And it was mathematics that helped him find himself again. His old teaching post at the high school was still open to him, so he didn't have the problem of supporting himself. He took up his little room again in the lane off Hippocrates Street and applied himself to research with renewed vigor.

We again began to meet every Thursday; I therefore had regular reports of the progress of his work. I used to update him on international mathematical developments that I read about in my periodicals, while he told me of his personal discoveries. I was glad to see that, first of all, he had gradually started to recover, and secondly, that he had devoted himself zealously to the theory of numbers, temporarily forgetting Hilbert's second problem of completeness and consistency.

And so things stood until Sofia came into our lives.

Eleven

The salon of Madame Polyxeni was one of the most popular "meeting places for gentlemen." It aimed to give the impression of a gentlemen's club in London, with a dash of Parisian *café chantant*. For reasons of propriety, this image deliberately masked what it really was: a high-class brothel for wealthy Athenian men.

The house, a large, two-story, neoclassical building, was set in a huge garden ringed by trees, which hid it entirely from the prying eyes of passersby. A number of discreet entrances allowed you to enter the garden unobserved and immediately melt behind the trees, enveloped in the scent of honeysuckle, angelica, four-o'clocks, and orange blossoms, which further stimulated your erotic mood. If the visitor's marital status or social standing required secrecy, he could enter by a side door to avoid any unwelcome encounter. If, on the other hand, he was unmarried, like me, he could walk up to the main entrance, where a servant dressed like a British butler with a manner to match led the visitor into an enormous reception room, tastefully furnished and decorated. The furniture was English, made from expensive wood, with matching velvet and cashmere upholstery, and there were large, comfortable sofas covered with cushions. On the low coffee tables were ashtrays and valuable crystal vases filled with the most beautiful, fresh flowers according to the season. On the walls hung select paintings with subtly erotic themes, as well as a few sketches of nudes. At the back of the room stood a grand piano, where the girls took turns entertaining the clients, sometimes accompanied by a second girl who either played the flute or, less often, sang. Occasionally, live music was replaced by a record played on the phonograph.

It was here that Madame Polyxeni, surrounded by her "protégés," received her guests. The scene on the ground floor didn't differ much from a normal social gathering, apart from the fact that the men were of all ages and the women were all young. The "gentlemen" had a drink, smoked their cigars, and talked among themselves and with the girls. If they chose to spend some time privately with a girl, they would let Madame Polyxeni know, and she would make one of the upstairs bedrooms available. Afterward she would collect the money—"for the poor girl's dowry" was the usual refrain. This nonnegotiable amount was set by Madame Polyxeni, and she shared it with the girl's "protector." The most trusted of Madame Polyxeni's visitors (she hated the word "clients") were allowed to take a girl home with them, provided they returned her the next day to her place of residence and work.

The daughter of poor countryfolk, Madame Polyxeni, an erstwhile beauty from Laconia, had left her father's house and headed for the capital city in search of a better life, narrowly avoiding her preordained destiny of becoming a provincial housewife. Armed with her looks and the uncanny capacity that some girls inherently possess for making themselves desirable, she won the favors of a middle-aged German architect who had been something of a failure in his country and had come to Greece looking for a second chance at a career, as well as for a second youth. The growing capital of the young Greek state was then bursting with opportunities for people like Otto Kroup. And so, in the ten years that his marriage to Polyxeni lasted, he managed to amass a small fortune, including the neoclassical house, a piece of land in a privileged location, and an amount of cash. He then had the good grace to depart from this world, leaving Polyxeni a widow with many ambitious plans in her head and the financial means to make them come to fruition.

She eventually settled on the idea of a "salon." Alas, there was no shortage of candidates for its staff. Girls from lower- or middle-class families whose indiscretions had brought down the wrath of a disciplinarian father, resulting in their expulsion from the family home, became the first residents of the house. Later, wave after wave of refugees brought a flood of vulnerable young girls to Athens, an easy prey for the gangs of pimps who had organized themselves in the meantime.

I first met Sofia in that house one night in 1923. She had been born in Odessa, the product of a Greek mother and a Romanian father who had lived in the Ukraine for many years. She was fourteen years old when the Russian Revolution broke out. Her father, having initially taken a neutral stance, later joined the Ukrainian independence movement and was killed in a battle outside Sevastopol. In the aftermath of the Bolshevik victory, the troops of the allies (the Greek battalion included) retreated, and the Greeks of Odessa, whose population was thought to have collaborated with the antirevolutionaries, were subjected to all sorts of hardship. In the course of the disturbances, Sofia had lost her mother as well and had been left on her own, with no protection and no income. In her despair, she responded to an offer from a gang of crooks who undertook to "save" young girls by bringing them to the motherland, where they promised to secure them living arrangements and a job.

So it was that in 1919 Sofia ended up, at age sixteen, in Madame Polyxeni's house. When I first met her, she already bore the scars of her experience with the darkest side of life. At the beginning I thought I was in love with her. I certainly felt tenderness toward her—a new, immense tenderness, engendered in me neither by Anna nor by any of the more or less ephemeral mistresses I had had. Deep in her large, brown, melancholy eyes, which had seen some of the worst sides of rich Athenians, I saw innocence intermingled with disbelief. Her speech, with faint traces of a Slavic accent, left me spellbound. When I discovered on her soles and toes the indelible marks of her "instruction," signs that she had dared to resist her fate, I decided to rescue her.

I first talked to the madame herself, saying I was willing to pay a considerable sum, from which she naturally would take her cut, in order to secure Sofia's freedom. She tried every way she could think of to make me change my mind. She explained that I could have Sofia whenever I wanted, that if I insisted she could make sure I had "exclusivity." "Please don't get me into trouble, Mr. Michael; the girl has to stay here." She tried to persuade me that Sofia was at the house of her own free will, that she was content, and that if she left the house, sooner or later she would end up somewhere worse. I stood my ground to the end.

When she realized I was not to be persuaded, and that I had both the will and the power to create problems for her if she didn't comply with my request, she changed tactics. She said that according to the unwritten laws of the trade, Sofia belonged to the man who had brought her over from Odessa and that her fate was in that man's hands. "Sofia belongs to Iordanis Hourdakoglou," she told me, unaware that she trembled from fear as she revealed his name. "It's better if you don't get mixed up with that man." I insisted that she put me in touch with the man in question, and in the end she promised to do what she could.

A week passed without any news from her. I had started to consider my next move, and how I could make my arguments more persuasive, when one evening, as I was returning home late, on foot, I was approached in a dark alleyway by a strange character. Neither his English suit with the loud silk tie, nor the pleasant aroma of expensive tobacco emanating from his person, nor the gold ring on his little finger could disguise the fact that he belonged to the criminal fraternity.

"Mr. Michael?" he asked.

I nodded in reply.

"You asked to see the boss," he said. "Mr. Iordanis is waiting for you."

I let him lead the way. We walked for about half an hour, until we came to a café somewhere near the district of Thesion. It was a cramped, narrow room with seven or eight half-rotten wooden tables surrounded by bamboo chairs. At another table, five old men were playing cards. In a still smaller room, two gloomy, unshaven types where playing backgammon. They wore their jackets loose on their shoulders to show they were tough guys, and each had a long, uncut nail on his little finger, another sign of "toughness." *The front guard,* I thought. We crossed the room, no one seeming to pay any attention to us. Behind a niche in the wall, sitting at a table hidden from prying eyes, was the infamous Iordanis Hourdakoglou. He was short, with a receding hairline, which he unsuccessfully tried to hide with a tuft of hair carefully pressed across his skull. His face was expressionless and corresponded precisely to the typical features of a gambler, as described to me by a friend when I was young. That friend had tried, without success, to initiate me into the world of gambling clubs.

"Your opponent must never know anything about you," he had told me. "He mustn't know if you're happy or sad; if you're scared or sure of yourself; if the money you're gambling with is a day's pocket-money or everything you possess. Poker is not won by having a good hand, but by clever bluffing. Don't let them even predict the fact that you are … unpredictable."

His advice had been of little value to me up until that moment, as my card-playing ventures had been limited to two losing nights at the "Club of Friends of the Countryside." There, amid extreme boredom and enveloped in smoke, I laid down the price of a night out at a seaside nightclub in Flisvos without receiving even a fraction of the equivalent entertainment. But here I was now, in a shady-looking Athenian café, standing in front of an evidently experienced gambler, getting ready for a game of poker in which the stakes were not money or jewelry, but a human life.

He looked at me from behind half-closed eyes for a long time without speaking. "All right, Dionysis," he told his sidekick, who left immediately without a word. He continued to stare at me silently. I sat down uninvited, not looking at him, and called the waiter over. I ordered a cognac and lit a large cigar, hoping I would not choke and start coughing. I had not smoked since I was a schoolboy. However, there were always expensive cigars available in my house, presents from captains who collaborated with my company. So that they would not go to waste, I used to carry a couple on me, and they were a welcome gift whenever I offered them. This was the first time I was using one myself. I smoked on, showing no concern, but was careful not to swallow the smoke. I stared at the man sardonically.

When he became convinced that silence would not get him anywhere, he changed tactics. "You asked to see me," he said. "I'm listening."

"How much?" I asked in a deep voice, trying not to burst out laughing. I was asking myself how this comic little man had managed to become the terror of the criminal world. Being unaware of the actual danger posed by him, I lost none of my cool. I played my role to perfection. Intrigued, Hourdakoglou was coming to realize that what he had in front of him was not a rich mama's boy, as I must have been described by Madame Polyxeni, who no doubt had given him a full report. There followed some tough negotiations, with hidden threats, insinuations, and tempting offers flying back and forth in quick succession. In the end we settled on a very substantial sum.

I insisted that the handover take place in Polyxeni's house. I added that, if Sofia or I came across him or one of his men in future, even if by accident, he would regret it bitterly. He reacted with a short sly laugh, but I knew I had made an impression on him.

At the beginning, I let Sofia stay in my house, for reasons of security. I wanted to be sure that the "other side" would keep our agreement. A friend on the police force, Officer Gouras (who had initially advised me on how to handle the situation), had mentioned the possibility that Hourdakoglou might come back hoping to get some more out of me. "As soon as you spot him, let me know," he had told me. Sure enough, one month later we saw him hanging around outside my house. He was walking with small, studied, steps, aimed at giving him an impressive air, but all they did was underline his vulgarity. Sofia went pale and began to tremble. I myself kept calm.

I reassured Sofia as well as I could and arranged an urgent meeting with my contact in the police. That same night, "unknown criminals" entered Hourdakoglou's house, tied him up, and gave him a good beating, after which they turned the house upside down. Dionysis was arrested in a shady bar which he frequented. They found a few grams of hashish on him (far less than he usually handled), enough to put him in jail for the night, where two of his cell mates beat him up badly. He was set free next morning, with two black eyes and bruises all over his body. Finally, Madame Polyxeni was summoned to the police station, where she was told that her house would be searched thoroughly, because information had been received that she was holding a girl there who had been abducted. It was one of the few times that the machinery of unofficial police activity turned not against union activists, strikers, or students, but concentrated on ordinary crime (albeit somewhat unconventionally, this being, after all, normal police practice). Gouras' brother, who was a clerk in one of my companies, received a generous raise, and we didn't hear of Hourdakoglou again.

Under no circumstances did I want Sofia to feel that she had merely traded one master for another. When I was sure that Iordanis' gang had decided to leave her in peace, I rented an apartment for her and encouraged her to find work. A seamstress took her on as her apprentice, and in a short while Sofia was earning her living in a respectable manner.

We spent three happy years together. The feeling of going out with a young girl half my age who owed me everything, the fact that this girl looked upon me as her god—all this held a strange appeal for my middle-aged mind. I felt like a knight in a fairy tale who had saved a young, unprotected princess. Of course, at times I would come to my senses and ask myself if I were becoming senile. We avoided dances and receptions, but often went to the theater, which Sofia adored. We took long walks in the countryside. Sometimes we went down to the sea at Faliron bay; other times we climbed to the monastery of Kaisariani or visited the Byzantine ruins of the church at Dafni. As long as we were occupied, either on our outings or making love, we were content. But gradually there came the long, unbearable silences. In the afternoons, sitting by the fire with a cup of tea, we had nothing to say to each other. We had nothing in common to keep us together. When there was no specific activity to occupy us, the awkwardness between us became unbearable.

In order to overcome this impasse, we began to ask Stefanos to join us. He was the only person whom I knew would accept our unusual relationship for what it was without spreading sneering comments and gossip as soon as my back was turned. The two people I loved most in the world took to each other instinctively.

Our *ménage à trois* worked very well, but gradually I began to be pushed to the side, even though I was the one who had been the link in the chain. Stefanos and Sofia always had something to say to each other, something to do together. It took me some time to realize what was happening. The first indication was Sofia's guilty look when I once entered the room suddenly and found them talking in low voices. I began to watch them, and in a few days I was sure of it—my friend and my mistress were madly in love.

As soon as I discovered this, I felt released. I steered my relationship with Sofia gently toward separation, taking on all responsibility. My Thursday meetings with Stefanos continued, and each time we met I made sure to tell him how I felt I could breathe again since Sofia and I had parted. I emphasized her virtues, but assured him that our liaison had been doomed in any case—something not untrue.

Stefanos began to see Sofia "in secret." Obviously, I knew most of the story and could guess the rest. I therefore tried to persuade him to tell me everything, so that he could be rid of the burden of unjustified guilt and we could resume our outings as a trio, even though he and I would have exchanged our roles. One day, he opened his heart to me. I gave him my "blessing" and offered to be best man at their wedding. We didn't talk to Sofia about all this, however, as she still felt awkward.

When the shadow of "betrayal" was dispelled between us, our Thursday meetings regained their old attraction. Unfortunately, our *ménage à trois* could not possibly be revived. After a little time had passed, I suggested we take a trip to Kifissia. The train took us as far as the station, and we were then conveyed by a one-horse carriage as far as the road went, up to the stream of Kokkinarás. We crossed the little stone bridge on foot and went into the wood. As we walked there was no need to talk, so the situation was bearable. But after a while we came to a clearing, spread out a blanket, and sat down. The day was warm, countless brooks off the Kokkinarás were bubbling around us, and a scented breeze felt cooling and rejuvenating. But nothing was enough to dispel the awkwardness between us—neither the jokes I told with forced gaiety, nor Stefanos' attempts to talk about the past, nor Sofia's ministrations in looking after us. We were each lost in our own thoughts, our personal regrets and feelings of guilt. It was one of the most uncomfortable meals of my life.

It was with relief that I found myself back in my sitting room, and in order to lift my spirits, I dove into the latest issue of *Mathematische Annalen* together with a bottle of old French cognac. In the street outside, a barrel organ was playing Attik's song: "I have seen many blue eyes in my life ..."

Twelve

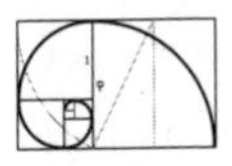

In the street outside, I heard a barrel organ playing Attik's song:

"*I have seen many blue eyes in my life.*"

Instantly all the images that had risen in my memory vanished. It couldn't have been more than three minutes, but in that short time I had seen again, as in a dream, my life with Stefanos. Suddenly I was back in the present. Clutching police chief Antoniou's arm, I looked down at my friend who was lying dead in his bed.

"Do they know ... what he ... died of?" I managed to whisper.

"Doctor?" asked the inspector.

"It looks like a heart attack. But his color makes me wonder—especially the tongue. There will, of course, have to be an autopsy. We will know more by tomorrow afternoon. What is certain is that he died in his sleep, around five in the morning. And now, if you will excuse me, I have to go. I will drop by the police station later to give a statement."

Antoniou thanked the doctor and called over the policeman who had been guarding the entrance.

"Are there any witnesses?" he asked.

"We're questioning the neighbors one by one. But some of them are not at home; they've already left for work. We will have to wait for them to come back in the afternoon."

"Fine. You stay here and get statements as soon as everybody is back. We want to know if they saw him come in or go out, or if they saw anyone else visit him. No one is to touch anything until the coroner arrives to collect the body. After that, the room is to be sealed and no one is to go inside."

He turned to me, saying, "I will need to take a statement from you. As far as I can tell, you must have been one of the last people to see him alive. Shall we walk to the station together?"

I followed him in silence. In a strange way, the depressing, yellowing walls of the police station helped me to recover. My own house was full of memories of Stefanos, so I declined Antoniou's polite offer to take my statement there.

I told him about how Stefanos and I had met in Paris, about our friendship, and about our regular Thursday meetings. I knew Stefanos' daily routine in detail and described it to Antoniou. Stefanos used to wake up at half-past six every day. Around seven he would set off for the school, stopping for a hot drink at Thanassis' café, on the corner of Asclepius and Solon Streets. He would spend the whole morning at the school. On his way back he would usually stop and have lunch in some small taverna off Hippocrates Street. Every now and then he would allow himself the luxury of a meal at a proper restaurant, like the Asti or the Europa. His afternoon was spent mainly reading, unless he was giving private lessons to some youngster in the neighborhood. Of course, our meetings on Thursdays were an exception to this rule. But every other evening he went out for a walk that lasted two or three hours. He rarely got back before one in the morning. This was, as he told me more than once, his most creative time. As he walked alone through the night, he carried out the most important part of his mathematical research. He would study in the afternoon in the usual way, seated at his desk, but during his nighttime walks he had no pencil or paper to distract him, no pressure from books and papers. He would sort out his problems in his head, put his mental notes in order, and sketch his strategy for working out the problems that interested him.

Most of the time, his attempts ended in failure. As I explained to Antoniou, a mathematician is very lucky if he manages every now and then (perhaps twice in a year at the most) to advance an unsolved problem a few steps. So Stefanos would very occasionally on a Thursday announce to me that he had finally gotten somewhere with one of his problems. Within a few days, his article would be on its way to publication in some foreign periodical. Naturally, there were difficulties at that stage, too. The referee committees of the scientific journals were particularly cautious when it came to publishing papers submitted by a nonacademic. But Stefanos had had the satisfaction of seeing three or four of his articles published: one in the *Comptes Rendus* of the French Academy of Sciences, one in the *Acta Arithmetica,* and one or two more in other periodicals.

His greatest pride was the one in the *Comptes Rendus,* "On the Conjecture Concerning Twin Primes." As Euclid had proven so spectacularly, there are an infinite number of primes (that is, numbers that cannot be divided by any other number except themselves and the number one). The question centered on whether twin primes—pairs of primes with only one number between them, such as 3 and 5, 11 and 13, or 17 and 19—are also infinite. In his talk in 1900, Hilbert had included the twin prime conjecture in his list of twenty-three problems. Stefanos himself had in 1924 devised a method by which he had proven that twin primes occur far beyond the number ten million. His method had been heralded as highly original by the French, and the echo of their praise had reached Greece. This was the only time, after the sad fate of the University of Smyrna, that Stefanos came close to finding a place at the University of Athens. But then the dictatorship of Pangalos came along, and in the general upheaval, thanks to those academics who were always suspicious of talented mathematicians with no political affiliation, Stefanos was forgotten.

Antoniou made a grimace of impatience, and I realized I had digressed into stories that had nothing to do with the case.

"Unless you believe this work of his had some connection with his death, please stick to the facts," he scolded me.

I apologized with a timid smile and continued with the matter at hand. Stefanos, as I said, used to go out every night after ten and wander around here, there, and everywhere, thinking through mathematical problems in his head. Sometimes, if his steps took him past one of the bouzouki clubs, he was not averse to going in and drinking a glass of raki while listening to a couple of songs. Afterward, he would make his way back home.

Antoniou's eyes lit up. "Do you think he visited such a place last night?"

"It's not out of the question, but I can't be sure. Stefanos never planned his visits to these clubs. If his walk led him there, he would go in for a drink, that's all. But yesterday he was particularly preoccupied with something he was trying to work out. So I would imagine his walk lasted much longer than usual. It's therefore possible that he did go as far as the bouzouki clubs."

"I suppose you're aware that many criminals frequent these places. Do you think your friend could have had any business with them? Could he have been supplied with drugs by them?"

"Stefanos had absolutely nothing to do with all that. The customers at these places liked him; they were flattered that 'the schoolmaster,' as they called him, would go and sit there. It's possible they may have offered him drugs, since they themselves use them, but I believe it's out of the question that he would have knowingly taken anything except his usual raki."

"I asked that question because some drug might well have been responsible for his death."

"It's absolutely out of the question that Stefanos was using any drugs. His 'highs' came from his mathematical problems. They were enough to lift his spirits. If he occasionally drank, it was only in very small quantities and only to enjoy the taste of the drink."

"Do you know whether he had any health problems? Did he suffer from anything?"

"As far as I know, he was perfectly healthy. His daily walks as well as the fact that he was never absent from work testify to that."

He asked if I knew anyone else who might be acquainted with Stefanos. I don't know why I didn't mention Sofia. Perhaps I was worried that her past would raise suspicions and get her into trouble, and I wished to protect her. In any case, only I knew how far their relationship had progressed. The pain of losing the man she loved was enough for her; she could do without being interrogated as well.

"All right, Mr. Igerinos," said Antoniou, when I had signed my statement. "I may have to trouble you again, but for the time being we're done." He looked at me with a worried expression. I must have looked a mess. "Would you like a policeman to escort you home? You look very tired."

I assured him I didn't need any help, and headed home. I was walking mechanically, my head in a muddle and full of dark thoughts, when suddenly I saw him. I froze. I had not seen him since that day when Sophia and I watched him creeping around my house. The lesson that Gouras' boys had taught him seemed to have put him off any wish to maintain further contact with me. So what was Iordanis Hourdakoglou doing here on this particular day—the worst day of my life—standing outside my door and looking at me with a malicious smile? For a moment I considered having a word with him, but I didn't have the strength. I stepped past him, ignoring his greeting, and went in.

Martha was anxiously waiting for me. It was three in the afternoon, and I had not eaten anything since that morning. It was in vain that my old nanny tried to persuade me to have a bite to eat. I took a bottle of cognac and went up to my room, ordering that I shouldn't be disturbed under any circumstances. After the fourth glass, I realized that the cognac alone was not going to disperse the dark thoughts that came to me in waves. *Thought is a compound periodic phenomenon,* I told myself. *Therefore it can be described by a Fourier series. In order to find its components …*

I suddenly realized I was delirious. I had to sleep. I took two sleeping pills with a fifth glass of cognac and fell asleep straight away. But before going to bed I managed to stagger to the window and, hiding behind the heavy curtain, I looked down the road. Hourdakoglou was nowhere to be seen.

I woke up late at night, and it took me a few minutes to remember where I was and what had happened. I heard Martha's footsteps in the corridor. The poor woman was obviously worried about her "baby." But I was not in a position to face her tender looks, her worries, her unspoken questions. *It's better if I stay in my room,* I thought.

And Sofia? What would happen now to Sofia? The coldness of our last encounter meant that I was excused from bringing her the bad news myself, but sooner or later she would hear. *Sofia is strong,* I told myself. *She has gone through so much, she will get over this, too.* But what about Hourdakoglou? What did he want? I approached the window and looked out again. Nothing. *He must have heard of the death of my friend and come to gloat over my grief,* I thought. Such characters don't easily forgive home defeats. But what if he was planning to interfere with Sofia again? My policeman friend, Gouras, had been sent away to the north of Greece, and as things stood, it would be difficult for me to ask for off-the-record help from the police again. *If necessary, we will pay some thugs in the private sector,* I thought. *The problem is not Hourdakoglou.*

A piercing pain shooting through my head brought me back to my situation. I looked at the clock; it was past midnight. I had slept for over eight hours, and yet sleep seemed to be the only solution for the time being. *Go on, another couple of pills, a glass of cognac. Goodnight, Stefanos ...*

The next morning I felt a bit better. I ate a hearty breakfast, something that put Martha's mind at ease. Then I went to my office. I asked one of the clerks to make arrangements for the funeral, since Stefanos had no relatives, and tried to turn my mind to my business affairs. As I was coming back home in the afternoon, I saw Hourdakoglou again. He was wearing a light-colored suit, dark shirt, and pale tie. It was clear that the style of his American counterparts, as portrayed now and then in the newspapers, had rubbed off on him.

Later on, Antoniou visited again. He came in and sat down and, refusing all offers of food or drink, came straight to the point:

"The death of Stefanos Kandartzis was not due to natural causes, such as a heart attack, as the doctor suggested yesterday. The dead man had consumed large quantities of a sleep-inducing substance, which we haven't yet identified. Was he in the habit of taking sleeping pills?"

"Not as far as I know."

"And yet, we know that the night before last he consumed a great quantity. But the fact that no wrapper or box for such pills was found in his room tells us that he could not have taken the overdose by mistake. So we're left with only two possibilities."

He stopped for a second and examined me closely. "Suicide, or murder."

I looked at him in a daze.

"Do you think he had any reason to commit suicide? Any difficulties, whether professional, personal, or financial?"

"I don't think so. Stefanos led a quiet life. He was dedicated to his work and his research."

"That's what the few people who knew him told us—his neighbors, some colleagues from the school, his landlady, the local chemist. But no one apart from you seems to have known him well. You were with him a few hours before he died. Did he seem different? Upset? Worried?"

"No. He was his usual self. And the walk he took after our meeting was, as I said before, a normal thing for him to do."

"But you said that he met people from the underworld."

"I know that policemen like to describe bouzouki players as the 'underworld'—that's one thing you have in common with communists! I don't know if you're right or not. Unlike my friend, I don't go to such places—not because I'm prejudiced in any way, but because their music doesn't appeal to me. But it was the only music that Stefanos was interested in. He had explained to me that its rhythm calmed him down, helped him to relax and to think. He especially liked the sound of the bouzouki itself. He liked its clarity and the precision of its notes."

"Even so, he must have gotten the drug that killed him from somewhere. He either took it willingly or it was given to him unawares."

I raised my hands in a gesture of complete bafflement.

It was obvious that we had nothing more to say to each other. Antoniou said goodbye and left.

Feeling unsettled, I thought I would take a walk to help myself calm down. When I escorted the policeman to the door two minutes earlier, I saw no one in the street. But now, as I left the house, I saw Hourdakoglou again. I ignored him and kept going. This charade repeated itself several times over the next few days. If I sat to have a coffee at Zacharatos' café, he would appear soon after, greet me with a nod, and then give his order to the waiter. If I came out of my office, he would be positioned outside the shop across the way, pretending to be looking in the window. If I went to the theater, there was Hourdakoglou, who seemed to have lately become an enthusiastic theatergoer.

One day I went to the bookshop Estia to find a book I wanted and to look through the latest publications. A few minutes after I arrived, Hourdakoglou turned up behind me holding a book by Dostoyevsky. The time had come to put a stop to this. I came out and waited for him. As soon as he appeared, I approached him, trying to looking as threatening as possible. "I thought we had an understanding," I said sharply. "If you need a reminder, it's easy enough for me to arrange it."

"Calm down, Mr. Igerinos," he answered, in a voice that betrayed no fear. "Listen to what I have to say first; you may change your mind. But there is no need for your acquaintances to see us together. Come and find me in an hour at the usual café."

"Look, you have three minutes to say what you have to say. After that I will do what I have to do. And you can be sure you won't like it." In some strange way, I enjoyed falling into this style of speech, with which he was clearly more at ease than I.

But Hourdakoglou was not an easy opponent.

"As you wish," he said, using, like me, a threatening, familiar form of address. "My reputation certainly won't suffer if I'm seen with you. So this is what I have to say ..."

Keeping up a blasé and indifferent front, I heard him out. I felt turmoil inside, but still kept my cool. "Very well," I answered in an expressionless voice, when he had finished. "We shall see who is right."

Thirteen

I didn't meet with Sofia after that. At the funeral we hugged each other silently and wept for the man we had both been so close to. I knew that if we were to get into a conversation, words would be difficult to find on both sides. I asked a clerk at my company to keep an eye on her and let me know if he became aware of any problems. Other than that, I left her to cope with her pain alone, just as I did with mine.

In the following days, Antoniou questioned my staff; Martha, the chambermaid, and the gardener. After that, we didn't see him for several days; he must have turned the focus of his inquiries elsewhere.

It was with great relief that I discovered that Hourdakoglou had also disappeared. It seemed that I had gotten rid of him for good. I had a young man from the office, Argyris, follow his movements from a discreet distance. The reports he brought me were reassuring: Hourdakoglou was passing his days at his usual haunts. He went around the brothels collecting his money, and the rest of his time he divided between cafés and gambling clubs. But one day, Argyris came to my house looking worried.

"Yesterday, Hourdakoglou met up with the policeman who is investigating your friend's death. I recognized him even though he was in plain clothes. They met outside the Thesion train station and walked together, talking for quite some time."

I knew, of course, that the police maintain close contact with members of the underworld, from whom they recruit their informers. Hourdakoglou's meeting with Antoniou might not have had anything to do with me. But I was naturally concerned.

Some days passed without any news. Then one day, Argyris reported that Dionysis, Hourdakoglou's right-hand man, had visited the police station and spent more than two hours there.

It was in the afternoon two days later that a puzzled Martha came up to my room to tell me that Officer Antoniou was waiting for me in the parlor.

"Can we run over your statement once again?" he asked me.

"Please do."

"You visited Stefanos Kandartzis on Thursday, January 24, 1929, at five in the afternoon and stayed with him until nine o'clock."

"Yes, I did."

"And in the four hours you were together ... ?"

"I told you. We talked about mathematics and played chess. We did the same every Thursday—taking turns—now in his house, now in mine."

"You exchanged words. Did you quarrel?"

"Stefanos and I? Of course not. Why should we?"

"His landlady, Kalliope Vourvounis, testified that she heard shouting."

"We had a strong disagreement about some mathematical matter. Perhaps we got carried away and raised our voices, but that's all."

"Mrs. Vourvounis said that she heard you shouting furiously, 'You have no right to do this. I won't let you do this!' What was it that you would not let him do, Mr. Igerinos?"

"I don't remember saying those exact words. Maybe it had something to do with the chess game. Perhaps he made an illegal move."

"Mr. Igerinos, on the afternoon of Thursday, January 24, 1929, you didn't play chess. Kandartzis had been teaching the son of a neighbor how to play chess. Their last lesson was on Wednesday, January 23, at the neighbor's house. When he went home, he left the chessboard there. No other chessboard was found in his room."

I was dumbfounded.

"I don't understand. I remember clearly that we played chess. In any case, what does that matter?"

He ignored my question and went on: "You returned home around half-past nine and didn't go out again?"

"Exactly."

"And yet your housekeeper stated that she heard you go out at half-past eleven."

"Martha thinks I'm still a child. She listens for the slightest noise. But she's getting old. She must have heard or imagined she heard something else and thought it was me. I was sound asleep by that time."

"But she also heard you come back, around half-past twelve."

"Officer, I repeat that I didn't go anywhere, and consequently I didn't come back from anywhere. If Martha imagined that I left, it makes sense that she should also have imagined that I got back in. I don't understand why you insist on this. And I don't understand what you're getting at."

He ignored my protests again.

"Who looks after your clothes, Mr. Igerinos?"

"Georgia, the chambermaid; under Martha's supervision. I have no doubt."

"I imagine she keeps an eye on her every day."

"Naturally."

"On the morning of January 25th, the chambermaid cleaned two pairs of muddy shoes. It's true that on the 24th it had been raining hard, and the roads were full of mud. But if you went out once, why were two pairs of shoes soiled?"

"I don't follow. What are you saying? Georgia may have forgotten. She may have put off cleaning them. It's not as if I have only two pairs of shoes. She knew there was no pressing need to clean them. I must say …"

I stopped talking. My eyes became misty. I felt my temples burning and my mouth became dry.

"You mean to say that … you believe that I … Stefanos …"

"On January 24 you visited your friend. You left his house at nine in the evening. He himself went out at ten."

"I told you that he used to take long walks of three or four hours every night, especially if he was thinking about a mathematical problem. After our discussion, it was natural that—"

"He returned safe and sound around one o'clock (a neighbor who has trouble sleeping confirmed this) and went straight to bed. On his table we found a jug with some water in it—Kandartzis had drunk most of it before going to sleep. We sent the water off for analysis. It contained large amounts of tranquilizer, the same kind as was found in his body during the autopsy. There is no doubt that that's what killed him."

"I understand that, but—"

"The composition of the powder doesn't correspond with any of those that are imported into Greece. The two big pharmacies that stock sleeping pills gave us samples of all such preparations they've imported over the last few years. The sleeping powder that killed Kandartzis was none of these. On the other hand …"

He looked at me coldly, with an obliging, almost apologetic smile that contained a small dose of irony.

"On the other hand, the medicine cabinet in your bathroom contains a large quantity of that very tranquilizer. As your maid explained, you obtain this yourself in Germany, where we know you often visit, and your cabinet is always well stocked. However, you rarely use. And yet, a few days after your friend's death, the maid discovered that two bottles were missing. The poor girl became worried that you might be taking too much because of your friend's death. What happened to those two bottles, Mr. Igerinos? How did they disappear in just three days?"

I tried to swallow my nonexistent saliva. Water, I was desperate for some water …

"I'm sure there is some mistake. It's true that I occasionally suffer from insomnia, and I use a tranquilizer that I buy in Germany, as recommended by a doctor in Baden-Baden. But I haven't used it for some time, and I can't say how much of it I have left. Georgia must have gotten confused—"

He lifted his hand condescendingly.

"Don't bother, Mr. Igerinos. I'll tell you what happened. It's true that Kandartzis regularly went out around ten o'clock and returned after midnight. And perhaps he used to take those excursions on foot, as you declared. But recently he had been walking far less. Whenever he could and as far as he could, he would take the tram. After all, you know exactly where he was going. He visited Sofia Nikolesku, a former prostitute, who lives in the district of Pláka. The girl's previous profession and his position as a schoolteacher forced him to keep their affair a secret. But he had another reason for hiding, didn't he, Mr. Igerinos? He was hiding from you. Sofia Nikolesku was your mistress before she became his. Or am I wrong?"

"No! You're not wrong. But we had broken up a long—"

"Yet when I asked if you knew anyone else who was acquainted with the victim, you didn't mention Miss Nikolesku. Did you by any chance … forget?"

"It was a mistake. I should have told you right from the beginning. But Sofia has suffered a lot and—"

"I know, I know. She came to Greece when she was sixteen, after the Russian Revolution broke out. The people who 'saved' her did the same for dozens of other girls. They would collect them from their villages, whose inhabitants had been decimated by the war, and they would bring them to Greece and put them to work. While they were still fresh, they placed them in high-class brothels intended for the rich. When they grew older, they would transfer them to 'houses' servicing bourgeois family men and restless youths. The end of their 'careers' is always the same: in the brothels of the harbor, for sailors on their night ashore and for dockworkers. Those few who escape venereal disease or the knife of some drunken client end up being servants of the lowest order. You met Miss Nikolesku when she was still in the first stage of such a predetermined career. You had the means to buy a mistress for your exclusive use. As it happens, we've discovered that ever since you were a young man, you have shown a preference for 'professional' women. You purchased Nikolesku's freedom by paying a heavy price to her 'protectors.' You ensured that she had a roof over her head and a small monthly income. Your actions seem, and may even be, admirable. But the girl was not satisfied with the comparatively comfortable life that you guaranteed her. She began to take sewing lessons from a seamstress, and a few months ago started to take in work in her own right. She charged low prices, treated her customers well, and her business grew. When the circle of her customers reached a certain level, she no longer needed you and your money. That's why she left you."

I felt anger choking me. I started to protest loudly.

"You do me an injustice! And you're badly misinformed! It was I who advised her to take up lessons in sewing. I paid the seamstress to take her as an apprentice. I provided her with her first customers. I saved a girl from ruin, and you make my actions look dirty and selfish. Perhaps you don't know that it was I who broke up with Sofia, not her with me!"

My shouting left him unmoved.

"This is what she told us, too. She described you in the best terms, as her guardian angel, a knight in shining armor. And she said that as soon as you realized she no longer desired you, you had the sensitivity to withdraw. She herself would never have deserted her benefactor."

"Then what is the point of this whole story? Why are you—"

"You're not a bad man, actually. When you found out that Miss Nikolesku was interested in another man, you imagined it was a young man of her age. The aristocrat in you decided to allow her to make a better life for herself and get married. But what made you furious was the discovery that your ex-girlfriend was not in love with a boy her own age, but with your friend. They even planned to get married. When Kandartzis told you of his plans to marry your former mistress, you flew into a rage. During your quarrel, you shouted, 'You have no right to do this. I won't let you do this!' And indeed, you didn't let him.

"You left your friend's house at nine and returned home. At half-past eleven you put on clean shoes, because the ones you had been wearing were muddy, and you went back to Kandartzis' house, knowing he would be away. A neighbor who was awake saw you, as did a passerby. Both of them recognized you from a photograph we showed them. You went into his room and emptied two bottles of tranquilizers in his jug of water. You weren't in his room for more than five minutes."

"You're wrong! It was not like that! You're mixing together real events with speculation, and you are twisting the facts around. I *wanted* Sofia to marry Stefanos."

"Your actions reveal nothing of the sort, Mr. Igerinos. And there is one more thing. During the Balkan Wars, your 'friend,' as you call him, had a brief affair with your ex-wife. Women have a strange habit of leaving you for Kandartzis. I can understand you in one respect. It's hard for a man to accept such a thing, especially if it happens twice. I have with me an arrest warrant. It's better for you if you confess. The facts are undeniable. You killed Stefanos Kandartzis, enraged that a girl whom you considered your possession chose your friend instead. The fact that she chose someone as old as you, and on top of that someone much poorer than you, insulted your vanity in a deadly way. You had forgiven him earlier for his affair with your ex-wife. But you could not stand it when the same thing happened a second time with your former mistress. All the facts and the evidence indicate that you are the murderer."

Surprised at myself, I felt a strange peace come over me. I didn't even recognize my own voice as I said simply: "I suppose I ought to inform my lawyer."

Fourteen

I entrusted my defense to the criminal advocate Nikos Alexandrou. He was the most expensive lawyer in Athens, well-known for his ability to handle difficult cases and win hopeless ones. But even he was unable to avert a guilty verdict in my first trial.

Officer Antoniou had done a very good job. He had managed to assemble the few pieces of evidence he had in order to create a fully coherent case against me. Whereas I had claimed that on the night of the murder I had gone out only once, Martha testified that I went out again later that same night. When she realized that her testimony could be used against me, she tried to retract it and fell into contradictions, and the only thing she managed to do was to convince the judges that something suspicious had taken place. My assertion that on the day of Stefanos' death he and I had been playing chess was shown to be untrue by his neighbor's confirmation that the chessboard had been left behind at her house. And the court was persuaded that Stefanos and I had indeed quarreled that night, and that this was something I had tried to conceal.

In addition to the evidence of the insomniac neighbor, who testified that I had gone into the house again late that night, Dionysis was summoned to testify. During my brief encounter with Hourdakoglou a few days after Stefanos' death, he told me that Dionysis had seen me enter the yard. He tried to squeeze money out of me in exchange for his silence. When I turned him down, he decided to sell his services to Antoniou and have his minion testify against me. It was not uncommon for criminals to barter their testimony for some favor from the police. In my case, the pimp had an additional motive for "nailing" me: he hated me because, according to the way he thought, I had "gotten the better of him."

My naïve attempt to conceal Stefanos' relationship with Sofia was also held against me. The prosecutor described it as "tantamount to a confession of guilt." The old story with Anna played a decisive role as well. "First his wife, then his mistress abandoned the accused," he said in his closing speech. "This could perhaps count as a mitigating factor for his actions. But primarily it proves that Igerinos had a strong motive for carrying out his abhorrent deed."

And so, after a trial that attracted intense public interest and provided newspapers with plenty of material, the court found me guilty. Alexandrou filed an appeal, assuring me that we would definitely win that. In the meantime, I was locked up in prison.

One day, about a year after my conviction, the guard announced that I had a visitor. I was surprised, as it was not the day my lawyer usually visited me, and Martha had already come the day before. I prayed it would not be her again; her devotion and love were touching, but her constant self-recriminations were beginning to wear me down. The same scene would unfold at her every visit. She would cry and beat her breast, blaming herself for "the harm she had done me," while I, the one behind bars, tried to console her. She could not forgive herself for her *faux pas* in mentioning to the police my second excursion on the night of the murder. Moreover, as an old-fashioned housekeeper, she held herself personally responsible for the actions of the staff under her. This meant that, quite apart from her own testimony, her conscience was burdened by the evidence given by the chambermaid about the second pair of muddy shoes and the missing bottles of sleeping pills.

I walked up to the visitors' room wondering who it might be. The heavy iron door opened, and I saw her. She was standing in front of a chair, looking pale, her large, expressive eyes red from crying. She was plainly trying hard not to lose her self-control, but as a result she looked as if she might collapse at any moment. It was Sofia.

We had only managed to exchange a few words at Stefanos' funeral. The next time I saw her, I was sitting in the dock. Her testimony was impeccable. She spoke of me with the highest praise. She related in detail how much I had done for her and spoke warmly about my friendship with Stefanos. She described my relationship with her and assured the court that it was only after we had broken up, on my initiative, that she and Stefanos had decided to marry. She denied fiercely that any of this could have had anything to do with his murder. She finished her testimony stating firmly that she was convinced I was innocent.

But I, who knew well how to read her eyes—I who had seen in them fear and despair in the old days—this time, I read doubt in them as she walked past the dock. Having sensed that doubt, I never expected her to visit me in prison.

For a few minutes we just looked at each other without speaking.

"I'm leaving, Michael," she said suddenly, without any introduction.

I looked at her questioningly.

"After Stefanos …"

She stopped, looking for the right word.

"After Stefanos passed away and you went to prison, Hourdakoglou's men started following me. Up until now, they've kept their distance, but I see them everywhere: one having a coffee in the café opposite my house, another waiting at the tram stop beside me, as if by chance. The other day, as I was coming out of the house of one of my lady customers, I saw Dionysis, the one who gave me the marks on my feet, standing on the pavement across the way. He stared at me with an evil grin. The only solution left for me is to disappear from Athens for good. I know a young man my age who lives in Volos. He's a refugee from Asia Minor. A neighbor of mine has arranged the marriage. She says he's a good man, quiet, hardworking. He has a steady job at the Matsangos Tobacco warehouse. He has a small house with two bedrooms in the refugee quarter of the town. It shouldn't be hard for me to find work as a seamstress there …"

I smiled. "Yes, go, my dear Sofia. The way things have turned out … you are right, it's the best solution."

"I also wanted to say …" She hesitated, then gathered strength and continued: "I don't know if you're guilty or innocent. Everything within me says you couldn't have killed him. But then, after all those things were said, I was confused. In any event, as far as I'm concerned, you have always been my guardian angel. This will never change, no matter what may have happened. In my thoughts, in my prayers, in my dreams, you will always be the man who gave me back my life."

I went up to her shyly. She offered her forehead, and I planted a fatherly kiss on it.

"Don't worry about me," I told her. "I'll get through this. Just be happy ..."

I went hastily to the door. I knocked, and the guard opened it immediately.

Sofia's visit had unsettled me. It brought back memories, images, anxieties. I turned to my usual comfort. Martha regularly brought to my prison cell all my correspondence, which now consisted almost entirely of the various journals that I subscribed to. I opened one at random and flicked through it. One of the articles caught my attention: "On the Squaring of the Circle: A Final Assessment." I laughed bitterly.

Plutarch mentions somewhere that while Anaxagoras was in prison, he devoted himself to the problem of squaring the circle. Anaxagoras! That strange rich young man from Ionia, who neglected his estates in order to devote himself to the search for truth. An immigrant from Asia Minor, he was the first to carry the flame of philosophy to Athens, first to explain solar and lunar eclipses, and he wrote the first treatise on perspective. Because he was a friend of Pericles, the Athenians sent him to prison, making him the object for all the hostility they felt toward his friend and patron. He was sentenced for alleged impiety because he had dared to claim that the Moon takes its light from elsewhere.

While in prison, he tried to solve the problem of squaring of the circle. He was probably the first to study this problem. A few years earlier, Oenopides had laid down the rules for geometric constructions: constructions had to be achieved using only a straightedge and a compass. Anaxagoras set himself the task of constructing a square (with a straightedge and compass) that would have the same area as a given circle. No matter how hard he tried, he could not do it. Others followed, approaching the problem from different angles. They devised revolutionary techniques, such as Antiphon's method of exhaustion, which Archimedes applied so ingeniously to many problems, and from which Newton and Leibniz developed integral calculus many centuries later. They all constructed complicated curves—Dinostratus the quadratrix, Archimedes the spiral curve. They managed to calculate the area and the circumference of a circle incredibly accurately. But no one was able to square it using a straightedge and compass.

In the seventeenth century, Descartes took an important step forward. He unified geometry and algebra by devising the system of coordinates that were subsequently named "Cartesian." Algebra's power to calculate was harnessed in the service of geometry, while geometry's power to create images helped mathematicians to visualize algebraic ideas. Problems in geometry took on an algebraic formulation. Interest in the squaring of the circle was rekindled. And yet, the longed-for solution continued to evade mathematicians.

Ever so slowly, the first suspicions began to be voiced that perhaps the problem could not be solved with the use of only a straightedge and compass. This was the view expressed by Gauss, although he never offered any proof for it. The pioneering work of Abel and Galois (on the solution of equations using roots) paved the way for expressing in clear algebraic language a test to determine which constructions were possible with the use of a straightedge and compass and which were not. This test was the invention of Pierre Wantzel, an otherwise obscure assistant professor at the École Polytechnique in Paris. Wantzel was a child prodigy at school, earning top grades in all subjects. In his brief life (he was only thirty-four when he died), he studied engineering and worked for large public enterprises, he taught physics and mathematics at various schools and universities, and he dabbled in music. But the work for which he became widely known was the test that decides whether or not a construction is possible using a straightedge and compass. For the squaring of the circle, the prerequisite was that *pi* (the ratio of a circle's circumference to its diameter) should be the solution of a second degree algebraic equation.

The way forward for a solution to the mystery had been opened. In 1873, French mathematician Charles Hermite proved that the constant *e* (the basis of natural logarithms) is transcendental—that is, it's not the solution of any algebraic equation. Finally, in 1882, Lindemann proved (through the use of Hermite's method) that *pi* is also transcendental. And that was that. After twenty-three hundred years of trying, mathematicians had proven, in the usual, incontrovertible way of mathematics, that the squaring of the circle is not feasible using a straightedge and compass. A few years earlier, Wantzel's criterion had also helped to prove that it's impossible to construct a cube with twice the volume of a given cube with the use of a straightedge and compass, and also that it's impossible to trisect an angle.

"This whole saga leads us to one overall conclusion," the writer of the article summed up. "A mathematical problem might conceal much more than is suspected by the person who first formulates it. Squaring the circle was a problem connected with Euclidean plane geometry. And yet, in order for it to be solved (even if negatively) it required other, more advanced theories: Descartes' analytical geometry and Galois' theory of equations. We shouldn't be surprised that there are mathematical problems that are formulated within the framework of one theory but which cannot be solved by that theory. This is simply further evidence of the wonder, the the challenge, and the frustration of mathematics. No one will ever be able to fully lift the veil that covers this science, no one will ever describe its entire scope. Occasionally, lucky mathematicians manage to make a small hole in the veil and glimpse through it a tiny part of this transcendental truth. But the price paid for such a magnificent experience can be extremely heavy. The case of Galois is but one such example."

The medicine had done its job. I don't know how Anaxagoras felt each time he studied geometry, but recalling the odyssey of the attempts to square the circle helped me get over the anxiety that Sofia's visit had caused me. In the days that followed, a number of events took place that were much more concrete and practical, and that helped to change my mood completely.

The date of the hearing of my appeal was fixed. Alexandrou handled the matter superbly. Of course, he could not get rid of the evidence that Officer Antoniou had gathered and coordinated so skillfully. But he was able to cast doubt about the value of on each piece of evidence in turn. His strongest card was the lack of motive. He demonstrated in all sorts of ways that the engagement of my friend to my former mistress, although unpleasant for me, nevertheless could not be sufficient motive for premeditated murder. As for the brief affair in Thessaloniki between my friend and my ex-wife, he correctly described it as trivial and irrelevant. He also correctly pointed out that I'm not the type who would commit a crime of passion.

Alexandrou said to the court that he was appalled by the fact that the victim's best friend was in prison, while the human traffickers who had taken advantage of Sofia, those who had a real interest in Stefanos' death, had been elevated to witnesses for the prosecution. Hourdakoglou had not even been troubled to go through the mere formality of an interview, while the testimony of Dionysis, a crook embroiled in the underworld, had been accepted unquestioningly. How was it possible, the lawyer asked, that a member of a gang of sex-slave traders "just happened" to be standing outside the victim's house, at exactly the right moment, so that he could be in a position to incriminate a respectable member of society (this was me) against whom the gang had an old grudge because he had snatched an innocent victim from their claws? *"Reus reum non faciet!"* ("A guilty man's evidence cannot prove another man's guilt!") his voice rising to a high pitch. Indeed, because Antoniou had been convinced right from the start that I was guilty, he had not bothered to check the movements of Hourdakoglou and his gang, not even as a formality. As a detective he was justified in proceeding like that, but in legal terms, he had made a monumental error. This omission of his became a powerful weapon in Alexandrou's hands at the appellate court, because it proved that the police were prejudiced against me.

And so it came about that on May 16, 1932, at ten o'clock exactly, Nikos Alexandrou came to see me in prison, his face beaming with joy. "Michael, we've done it," he announced. "The appellate court issued its decision this morning at half-past eight. You have been found innocent due to insufficient evidence. You're a free man. Pack your things, and let's go."

Although the decision had been more or less expected—Alexandrou was sure of it—I was overwhelmed with relief. My money and social standing had ensured that I had enjoyed many privileges while in prison: I had a cell to myself, almost limitless visiting hours, excellent food, books, newspapers, and anything else I wanted. However, prison is still prison.

At half-past ten we stepped through the main gate of the Averoff Prison and onto Alexandra Avenue. I hungrily breathed in the spring air, which carried the perfume of the orange blossoms and flowers from the area of Ambelokipi ("the Vine Gardens"). To our left, the refugee settlements were bursting with life. The people who had fled Asia Minor were fighting for survival with every means at their disposal. Groups of little boys were running around playing among the whitewashed cottages. Opposite us was the Panathinaikos soccer stadium. Whenever there was a game on, the shouts and cheers had reached my cell. Before my imprisonment, I had no interest in soccer. But now I wanted to join the crowds who had kept me company with their chants and cheers during all those long Sundays in prison. I wanted to see in the flesh the heroes of folk legend whom I had not known before—Angelos Messaris, Antonis Tsolinas, and all the others, whose names had been on the lips of thousands, piercing the unbearable silence of my cell.

I had given away most of my belongings to my fellow inmates. My books I gave to the political prisoners charged under Venizelos' special law against subversive activities, while my clothes, shoes, and shaving things had gone to criminal prisoners. In my small case, therefore, I had only my toothbrush, the last edition of Hilbert's *Foundations of Geometry* (which was of no interest to the other prisoners) and some lectures published by Poincaré on *Analysis Situs,* the new branch of mathematics that he had founded. I had given another of Poincaré's books, *Science and Hypothesis* (the one Princet had been studying and explaining to Picasso's gang), to

Manolis, a philosophy student who was serving a two-year sentence for taking part in a demonstration.

Alexandrou had come to collect me in his own car, but after two years of being locked up, I was eager to walk. I passed my suitcase to the lawyer and asked him to deliver it to Martha and tell her I would be home in a couple of hours. I stood and watched the Daimler disappear. Then I crossed to the other side of the road, walked behind the stadium, and climbed up to one of the footpaths that led up to the hill of Lycabettus. I walked among the blue statice and the spiny broom and reached the little church of St. George at the top, out of breath. The slopes of the hill were covered with a lush green carpet embroidered with wildflowers—humble chamomile, arrogant poppies, bright yellow daisies. My thoughts turned to the excursions my fellow students used to make with our professors at Göttingen some thirty years ago. Though the hills around the medieval university town had a different look about them, for a moment I felt like I was there. I thought I could hear Hilbert's voice talking to Klein about the paper he was going to give the following August in Paris. I dismissed such thoughts. If I allowed myself to reminisce about Paris, I would ....

I stopped to gaze down over Athens, spread out beneath my feet. The air was especially clear. It had rained the day before, and the dust which usually hovered over Pindar's "violet-crowned city" had settled. Opposite where I stood, the Acropolis glittered, drenched in light. I looked at the Parthenon, wondering how many secrets were built into its structure. I had believed that the striking beauty of this classical building was due exclusively to the use of mathematics in its construction. But standing there, I wondered whether the aesthetic power of the golden section was really as great as was generally believed.

I could see the masts of the ships in Faliro Bay. And down the whole length of Syngrou Avenue and on either side of it, beyond the Fix beer factory, the areas where refugees had settled could be made out. I had the impression that in the twenty-plus months that my imprisonment had lasted, the city had changed radically. New settlements had sprouted up to meet the housing needs created not only by the 1922 exodus from Asia Minor but also by the increasing number of Greeks seeking their fortune in the city. It's true that all this had already begun before I went to prison, but in my cell I had seen in my mind the pictures of my childhood, so that the city before me looked brand-new. New as my own life would be from now on.

I made up my mind. I would stay in Athens for a few days to put my affairs in order, and then I would go abroad. Probably to Germany; a few days in Baden-Baden wouldn't do me any harm. Or, instead, I would go on a long voyage—ships left every week for Ellis Island in New York, the gateway to the New World.

I stood there for a while longer and then, deliberately avoiding the district of Neapolis, I descended toward Kolonaki, went as far as the top of Academy Street, and from there headed home.

Martha welcomed me with tears in her eyes. My walking home had given her time to prepare my favorite meal: vine-leaf dolmas and feta cheese grilled over charcoal with tomato, lots of oregano, and pepper. I ate with relish. My three-hour-long walk had given me an appetite. After lunch I opened a bottle of Bisquit VSOP, my favorite cognac, to celebrate my release. My eyelids became heavy. The walk, the meal, and the cognac had done their job.

"I'm going to lie down for a bit," I called out.

After a few minutes, Martha knocked on my door.

"Your journals arrived the other day," she said.

The journals could wait, but I realized that she wanted to have a look at me again, to make sure I had really come back and that it was not just a dream.

"Thank you, Martha, my dear," I said.

"Welcome home," she said. "And pardon me."

"Are you going to start again? I've told you many times. That awful man Antoniou is to blame for confusing you. And I'm to blame too, for being so stupid as not to mention right from the start that I had gone out a second time that night. But anyway—it's all over."

She stood looking at me for a while, with eyes red from crying, and then she slipped away. I gently closed the door.

The journals were the latest mathematical issues from France and Germany. In memory of my student days, I started to flick through a German periodical. I still knew enough mathematics to be able to grasp the general content of most of the articles, although some technical details escaped me.

I was reading, without paying much attention, about the developments regarding the Riemann hypothesis and the sequencing of prime numbers. I look at an item about a new definition of dimension, and I skimmed through a few other articles. Then suddenly I saw it. I felt my feet go cold and the blood drain from my head. I realized that my hands were shaking. I tried to calm down. I took a piece of paper and a pencil, sat at the small desk in my room, and began to work feverishly. My sleepiness had vanished.

Two hours later, any doubt I may have had was gone. Everything was crystal clear. And I knew exactly what I had to do. It was the only thing left for me to do …

... being the first to reveal publicly ...
he perished at sea

All the members of the school, both the initiated and the apprentices, were gathered near the fountain in front of the main building. Prominent on its façade was the emblem of the school, a regular pentagon inscribed within a circle, with its five diagonals forming the legendary pentagram, which the Pythagoreans called Hygeia, "Health." The golden section, the pinnacle of Pythagorean geometry—the divine proportion, as it was later to be called—was apparent everywhere. It was a tragic irony: the number phi, *which represented the divine proportion, was, according to Pythagorean arithmetic, not a number at all!*

Lysippos, the fourth to become head of the school of Pythagoras, began to speak.

"A few months ago," he said in a tired voice, "the council of the school was forced to permanently exclude one of the members of the brotherhood. The repeated violations of the rules by Hippasus—the fact that he taught geometry to the uninitiated, his profane discussions about the most holy secrets of the school, and primarily the fact that he dared to doubt the Master's teaching that all is number, falsely claiming that there is no number that can express the ratio between the diagonal and the side of a square—all this forced the school to come to a preordained decision. We had no choice. According to the

rules about expelled members, we gave Hippasus twice as many gifts as he had brought to the school when he was first admitted, and we ordered him to leave. The transgressor embarked on a ship that the school itself had paid for and placed at his disposal, and he set sail for the Peloponnese. This morning I received a message." He paused, took a deep breath, and continued: "It seems that the gods have decided to punish the impiety in their own way. Hippasus' ship sank in open waters and he himself was drowned."

Fifteen

At exactly half-past eight, as he did every day, Agesilaos Kondogeorgos, the public prosecutor of the Supreme Court, arrived at his office. His assistant was waiting for him in the lobby.

"Sir, this was delivered addressed to you."

Kondogeorgos took the large envelope from his subordinate's hands without a word. He didn't talk much to his assistant and generally avoided contact with the entire staff at the prosecutor's office. There was no need for him to order his coffee. According to his instructions, the coffee had to be on his desk in exactly three minutes' time.

Before entering his office, he stood in the doorway and surveyed the room with self-satisfaction. He admired the leather armchair, the oak bookcase, the big window. He went in. He had won all this by himself, by working hard but also by making all the right moves. He had supported, with moderation, each party that came to power, whether royalist or democratic or a dictatorship. He had served discreetly whoever happened to be his superior of the day until an opportunity arose to undermine him and take his place. He had taken care not to make any enemies and at the same time he developed many connections. Each successive authority would believe that they gained more by keeping him on their payroll than by dismissing him. He not only knew the law well, but he also knew ways of getting around it whenever he judged such a course to be in his interest. Above all, he kept everyone at a distance, which gave him an air of being incorruptible.

He sat at his desk, taking up his silver letter opener at the moment the girl opened the door and brought in his coffee. He waited until she left, closed the door behind her, then opened the letter and began to read.

"Georgos," he called after a while.

"Yes, sir," replied his assistant, half opening the door.

"Come in. Sit down."

The assistant obeyed, with some surprise. Kondogeorgos rarely shared his thoughts with him. Gerogos looked questioningly at his superior, who passed the letter to him.

"Read it. I've been a member of the judiciary for thirty-two years, but have never come across a thing like this. Once you've read it, tell Officer Antoniou I want to speak with him as soon as possible. The things one sees ..."

The assistant began to read.

Athens, May 16, 1932
To the Public Prosecutor of the Supreme Court

Sir,

With this letter I wish to confess to the murder of Stefanos Kandartzis. My action, killing an innocent and unsuspecting man, was not only abhorrent. It was also, as I will explain below, naïve and useless.

First, the facts:

On Thursday, January 24, 1929, I visited my close friend Stefanos Kandartzis at his house in the district of Neapolis. We sat together from five in the afternoon until nine, as we usually did. I left at five minutes past nine, knowing that my friend would go for a walk as he did every evening. I knew he would be gone for a long time. When he was lost in thought over some mathematical problem, he had the habit of taking to the streets and walking around for hours.

I got back to my house around half-past nine. I asked my housekeeper to make me a hot drink, and around half-past ten I told her I was going to bed. After a while, she did the same. At half-past eleven, thinking that she was fast asleep, I went out as quietly as I could.

This was my first mistake. I should have known that ever since she was my nanny, Martha has developed a kind of selective hearing that was attuned to my slightest movement. She heard me go out and was surprised by this, then worried. But because I got back an hour later, she didn't think it necessary to say anything to me. Officer Antoniou carried out his examination skillfully and managed to trap her. Not realizing I was under suspicion, Martha mentioned this incident, imagining she was simply confirming my own testimony regarding a minor detail of the case. She never forgave herself for this *faux pas* and to this day refuses to accept that she did nothing more than her duty.

But I digress. Taking two bottles of sleeping pills with me, I went back to my friend's house, knowing he would not yet have returned. It was already midnight when I got there. And then I made my second mistake. I failed to notice the light in one of the windows nearby and didn't anticipate the likelihood that a neighbor might see me. I was so blinded by the certainty that what I was doing was both necessary and urgent that I don't believe I would have hesitated even if I had noticed the light. I went into my friend's room and emptied the bottles of tranquilizers into the jug of water. I knew that he usually drank at least three glasses of water before he went to bed. Since the room had no tap, he was bound to drink from the jug. So I was as certain that I was murdering him as if I had plunged a dagger into his heart. And yet, because of the conversation that we had had that afternoon, I was convinced that what I was doing was right. I did feel a deep sadness, because Stefanos was the only person I loved. But neither my love for him nor my dread of the loneliness I would face living without him could prevent me from doing what I stupidly considered to be my duty.

I left Stefanos' room believing (mistakenly, as it turned out) that no one had seen me. From what I gather, I was seen coming out by Dionysis, a henchman of Iordanis Hourdakoglou's, the pimp who had brought Sofia Nikolesku over to Greece. Hourdakoglou had heard that Sofia was in a relationship with Stefanos, and he hoped to extract some money from him. This is why he had his underlings to follow Stefanos routinely. Later, when news of Stefanos' murder became known, Hourdakoglou tried to blackmail me, threatening to reveal that I had been present at the scene of the crime. I ignored his threats, which turned out to be the right tactic, since my lawyer completely destroyed his testimony in the appellate court and led the court to suspect him instead, thereby increasing the doubts surrounding my own guilt.

I returned home at half-past twelve without realizing that Martha, who had heard me go out, was listening for me to come back in.

My third mistake was that I didn't replace the tranquilizers the next day. So when Officer Antoniou astutely went fishing for information from my maid, she told him that a large quantity of the drug was indeed missing from the medicine cabinet in the house.

The rest of the story is well known. The testimony of Stefanos' neighbor, and of Dionysis, Martha, and my maid convinced the court of my guilt, and I was found guilty. My lawyer, Mr. Nikos Alexandrou, appealed, assuring me that I would be found innocent on retrial. And sure enough, the atmosphere of the second trial was entirely different. The prosecutor himself urged my release due to the uncertainty of the evidence, describing what was produced by the police as arguably a chain of coincidences. I don't know to what degree the court was swayed by the rhetorical skills of my lawyer, or what part his his hidden connections played. The fact is that this morning an order was issued for my release and I was set free, to the great frustration (I assume) of Officer Antoniou, who had played such a leading role in my arrest and original conviction.

The only thing the Antoniou failed to find was a motive for the murder; this became the strongest argument in my defense. Delving into my past, he managed to discover that I had had an affair with Sofia Nikolesku and that she had more recently formed a liaison with Stefanos. It was easy for him to build on this piece of information a case of the classic crime of passion inspired by jealousy. Easy, but completely mistaken.

It's true that I had met Sofia and helped her escape from the grasp of the gang of criminals who had been exploiting her. We had a brief affair, but neither of us was really in love. What kept her faithful to me was gratitude. On my part, I was living out a childish role of the knight in shining armor. To be honest, the only thing that stopped me from ending the relationship was the fear that if Sofia were left unprotected she would fall into the gang's clutches once again, despite the large sum of money I had secretly paid them to leave her alone. When I discovered my friend's genuine feelings for her and saw that they were mutual, I immediately (and with relief) opened the way for them by breaking up with Sofia.

It was therefore not jealousy that led me to kill Stefanos. The fact that three years after my divorce from Anna Dellaportas he had had a brief affair with her was presented as an additional motive. This was absurd. My marriage to Anna was one of convenience, and our divorce was a welcomed release for both of us. My motive was something entirely different.

I met Stefanos in August 1900 when we both attended the Second International Congress of Mathematicians in Paris. Like everyone present, we were particularly struck by the talk given by David Hilbert, in which he outlined the twenty-three problems that he believed were going to be at the very core of mathematical research during the twentieth century. Hilbert's twenty-three problems and the developments around them subsequently became a perennial topic of discussion between Stefanos and me.

Stefanos was very intrigued by the second problem: a proof of the completeness and non-contradictory nature of the axioms of arithmetic. And he believed that the solution of this problem had to form part of a wider assessment of axiomatic theory. Hilbert himself had hinted at something like this in his talk:

> When we are engaged in investigating the foundations of a science, we must set up a system of axioms which contains an exact and complete description of the relations subsisting between the elementary ideas of that science. The axioms so set up are at the same time the definitions of those elementary ideas, and no statement within the realm of the science whose foundation we are testing is held to be correct unless it can be derived from those axioms by means of a finite number of logical steps. Upon closer consideration, the question arises: Whether, in any way, certain statements of single axioms depend upon one another, and whether the axioms may not therefore contain certain parts in common, which must be isolated

> if one wishes to arrive at a system of axioms that shall be altogether independent of one another.
>
> But above all, I wish to designate the following as the most important among the numerous questions which can be asked with regard to the axioms: To prove that they are not contradictory, that is, that a definite number of logical steps based upon them can never lead to contradictory results.

During our discussions, Stefanos had repeatedly expressed the belief that there must be some mechanism, some algorithm that, after following a finite number of logical steps, could test any axiomatic system and determine whether or not it was complete and non-contradictory. As far as I was concerned, such an idea was impossible. And it annoyed me intensely to think that the consistency of mathematics could become the object of a mechanical algorithm that some mindless machine would be able to carry out. I thought that if such an algorithm did exist and someone discovered it, this would mean the end of mathematics as a creative force.

As I mentioned above, that fateful Thursday I visited Stefanos at five in the afternoon. He greeted me bursting with enthusiasm. "I've done it, Michael!" he said. "I've proven it!" He showed me fifteen pages covered in writing and explained that he had devised a method that could test any axiomatic system and decide whether or not the system was complete and non-contradictory. As a first application of his method, he had proven that Peano's system of axioms regarding the sequence of natural numbers is both consistent and complete.

He spent an hour going through his method for me. To my immense dismay, I realized that he was right. Stefanos would become famous as the man who had solved Hilbert's second problem. From that point forward, the doors of all foreign universities would be wide open for him. And if he chose to remain in Greece, the cliques within the University of Athens would be obliged to welcome him, albeit with their tails between their legs, and would start bickering among themselves over who would get him first.

But the price to be paid by the queen of sciences would be heavy. Stefanos' personal triumph would mean the end of creative mathematics. Dozens of untalented, mediocre scholars would be assured of a career devising arbitrary sets of axioms whose consistency they could test mechanically using his method. Instead of the quintessence of reason, mathematics would become a routinely mechanical game.

It was in vain that I tried to persuade him to destroy his work, to forget it ever existed. I begged and I threatened. That was the meaning of my words, "You have no right to do this; I won't let you do this," which Officer Antoniou so skillfully used against me at the trial. I even invoked ancient Greek tragedy, saying that for someone to try to prove *a priori* the non-contradictory nature of a theory is a kind of hubris.

Needless to say, Stefanos would not budge. He felt that his discovery was his life's work, a decisive step that would herald a new era for mathematics. And he tried to explain that even if he agreed not to publish his method, sooner or later someone else would discover it since Hilbert's talk had drawn so much attention to the problem. Today, all this seems obvious. But at the time I was either unable or unwilling to grasp it.

Be that as it may. History, which I've studied at length, ought to have taught me that scientific truth cannot be hidden and progress cannot be stopped by the use of trickery. Two-and-a-half thousand years ago, it was discovered at the school of Pythagoras that the ratio of a square's diagonal to its side is an irrational number. This discovery shook the whole Pythagorean philosophical edifice to its very foundations. Sure enough, if we take the side of a square as the number 1, the diagonal will be equal to the square root of 2—which can be expressed neither as a whole number nor as a fraction. The simplest of shapes had within it the elements that were enough to overturn the whole Pythagorean creed. There were naïve people at that time, like me today, who panicked and feared that the end of science had come, so they tried to impose the rule of silence on scientific truth. Tradition says that Hippasus of Metapontum, the man who dared to expose this dreadful secret of irrational numbers, was murdered. It was the first Pythagorean crime in history.

That crime didn't prevent the secret from leaking out, or the crisis it caused from erupting, or mathematics from progressing. The crisis was first resolved in the tenth book of Euclid's *Elements,* which in fact bears the general title *On Asymmetries*. And the final solution was given in the last century by Dedekind, who constructed a complete presentation of all real numbers. Mathematics came out stronger from this crisis, which, despite the Pythagoreans' attempts to avert it, was inevitable, since it was based on the disclosure of a critical error in the Pythagorean theory of numbers and measures.

However, none of this occurred to me on that fateful night. As Stefanos and I talked, and I realized it was impossible to change his mind, a mad thought began to take over me. I had to stop the disclosure of his method at all costs. We kept on talking. The cold, paranoid decision I had made calmed me down. Stefanos certainly thought he had convinced me. It's true, we didn't play chess that night. Mr. Antoniou was correct about that point, too. It was late when we finished talking. I left, having already made my plan, certain that by murdering Stefanos I would be carrying out a painful but necessary duty.

As I mentioned earlier, I got back at twelve, emptied the bottles of sleeping pills into the jug of water and returned, taking with me the manuscript of the article, which Stefanos had put away in the only drawer of his battered old desk. Before going to bed, I burned the papers, making sure that even the last bits had turned to ash. Since then I've felt no remorse for my act, until today. Pain, yes. Deep pain, because Stefanos was my only real friend, the only man whose company truly fulfilled me. But not remorse, because I was deeply convinced that I had saved from certain destruction the science that I believe to be the bedrock of human civilization. Inside, I somehow felt I was both perpetrator and victim. *Quem Deus vult perdere, prius dementat.* Whom God wishes to destroy, he first makes insane.

With my conscience clear, I planned my defense. I hired the famous criminal lawyer Mr. Nikos Alexandrou, who worked out a brilliant strategy. He never asked whether I was guilty or innocent. After all, Mr. Alexandrou doesn't distinguish between guilty and innocent men—simply between his clients and everyone else. He made sure I would not take back anything I had said in my statement; otherwise, he worked on his own. And exactly as he had predicted (or rather planned), after my first conviction, the appellate court declared me innocent, and I was set free this morning.

I deemed my release to be right because, at least up until midday today, I believed that I had not really committed any crime, but had only acted as the agent of a scientific divine justice, so to speak. But everything changed this afternoon. On my arrival home, I looked through my latest correspondence. Among the other mail that was waiting for me were the latest issues of various mathematical journals to which I subscribe. Leafing through them, I spotted an article with the title "On Formally Undecidable Propositions in *Principia Mathematica* and Related Systems." It was signed by a young Austrian mathematician named Kurt Gödel, about whom I had heard nothing until today. In the biographical note, I saw that he was born in 1906, six years after the conference in Paris, and that he's currently teaching at the University of Vienna. The reference to the *Principia Mathematica* by Whitehead and Russell drew my attention. The work of these two British mathematician-philosophers is the most serious attempt to date to establish the foundations of mathematics. Since I had, in a way, found myself in jail because of matters connected with the foundation of mathematics, you will appreciate that I had every reason to turn to this article with particular interest. In fact, I feared that Stefanos' prediction might have come true, and that someone else had discovered his method, which I had managed to keep secret in such a despicable manner.

After studying the article, I realized that matters were much worse. Having read each line and checked each step described by the writer, I felt the world collapse around me. Young Gödel had proven that no axiomatic theory rich enough to encompass classical arithmetic can be complete. He showed that as a matter of logical certainty, there will always exist propositions that—while being formulated within the framework of a theory—can be neither proved nor disproved within the theory. Even if such propositions (which take the form of axioms) are linked to an existing, established theory, that won't change, because every new axiom gives rise to newly "undecidable" propositions, meaning propositions that can be neither proved nor disproved. He also demonstrated that the non-contradictory nature of an axiomatic system is itself equivalent to one such unanswerable proposition within the framework of that very system. In other words, the algorithm that had cost Stefanos his life cannot possibly exist. Somewhere, at some point in his proof, my unfortunate friend must have made a mistake; where, exactly, we will never know, since I destroyed the only manuscript. But it's certain that the mistake was made by Stefanos, not by Gödel. The latter's article is published in one of the most prestigious international periodicals, which means that it has been thoroughly checked by top mathematicians. The fact that I've found no fault in it is of little importance, since neither did I find one in Stefanos' manuscript, being then in a hurry and in a rage. If I had allowed

Stefanos to send it for publication, the reviewers would no doubt have discovered the mistake that had escaped both his scrutiny and mine. By killing him, I have at least spared him the humiliation. Small consolation …

So my crime was Pythagorean, just as senseless and unnecessary as the one which cost Hippasus his life. I'm not, as my paranoia had led me to believe, the hand of some god who prevented hubris from being committed. The hubris was mine alone. I'm a common criminal. Even worse, I'm a stupid criminal. And I deserve the fate of criminals. At this moment, I have in my possession two more bottles of the drug that killed Stefanos. When you read these lines, I will have already meted out justice.

Michael Igerinos

Postscript

The Boundaries of Poetic License

Pythagorean Crimes is a work of fiction, purely a creation of the imagination. It does not tell a true story, in part or as a whole. Its characters—the families of Mavroleon, Igerinos, Dellaportas, and Manousakas, as well as Kandartzis, Hourdakoglou and his gang, the policemen, and the lawyers—are all imaginary; their names have been picked at random.

However, the story unfolds within an actual historical context, that of Europe and Greece in the period from 1900 to 1931. All the historical, geographical, scientific, and technological details are accurate, at least insofar as the bibliographical sources consulted are accurate. The imaginary characters of the novel meet and interact with real personalities of the past. All information connected with such figures is based on reliable sources, with one or two exceptions, referred to below.

It is not certain whether all of the leading mathematicians mentioned in Chapter Two really took part in the Second International Congress for Mathematicians in Paris, in the way one would expect at such a conference today. However, they were all alive at the time, and all references to their work and activities are accurate. Hilbert was certainly the main speaker at the conference, and the extracts quoted from his talk are faithful to the original. The controversy between him and Peano's team did take place in reality.

I had to place Picasso in Paris a couple of months too early (in reality, he first visited Paris in the autumn of 1900). Otherwise, the references to him, his friends, the places he frequented, and his habits are all accurate.

Also accurate are all references to Carathéodory, Jakobides and Hatzidakis.

Among those mentioned in the *Prelude* and *Interlude*, Hippasus is an historical figure; his story is more or less accurate, according to tradition. The other characters are creations invented to serve the needs of the story.

Finally, some information about events that took place outside the period covered by the novel:

Fermat's last theorem regarding the equation $x^n + y^n = z^n$ was proved by Andrew Wiles in 1995, whereas the Kepler conjecture ("the greengrocer's problem") regarding the stacking of spheres was proved in 1998 with the aid of computers. The Riemann hypothesis and the twin prime conjecture remain unsolved to this day.

Euler's solution of the problem of the bridges at Königsberg formed the basis of modern graph theory, which is used in the planning of networks as well as many other applications that are part of daily life.

Alice Géry-Princet-Derain remained married to Derain until his death in 1954. It seems that Picasso made the right choice of companion for his former mistress.

After his divorce, Princet fell out with "Picasso's gang" and began to frequent other artistic circles, still playing the role of instructor to artists on mathematical matters. His main sources were always the easily accessible books of Henri Poincaré, which inspired the discussions contained in this book.

Glossary

1830 Uprising, a.k.a. the Cadet Revolution, Warsaw Uprising (November 29, 1830). A revolt that took place in Warsaw when the rule of the Russian Empire was challenged in Poland and Lithuania. It began when a number of non-commissioned officers from the Russian Army's military academy attacked the Palace of **Grand Duke Constantine**, who escaped, unharmed, in women's clothing. They were soon joined by a large segment of the Polish society and were successful with a few of the local uprisings. The Ivan Paskevich–led Russian Army stopped and crushed the revolts, ending in a Russian victory.

1912, beginning of the Balkan Wars. The Ottoman Empire was driven out of the Balkans by Greece, Serbia, Bulgaria, and Montenegro, who were looking for expansion into the Macedonian territory, specifically the part belonging to Ottoman Turkey. Serbia and Bulgaria signed a treaty on March 12, 1912, allowing the annexation of Macedonian land as well as the removal of the Russian Tsar. Greece and Montenegro joined this treaty, and the new Balkan allies declared war on Turkey, leading to the First Balkan War.

1922, exodus from Asia Minor, Smyrna (September, 1922). Marked the end of Hellenic presence in Asia Minor, comprising most of modern day Turkey. During the Greco-Turkish War, refugees of Greek descent were forced out of Asia Minor and back to Greece, a place most had never known. The Turks overtook Smyrna, burning it entirely and practically erasing it from history. This disaster had a lasting effect on Greece, one that Athens still suffers from today.

a cappella (Italian for "at chapel"). Singing performance unaccompanied by musical instruments.

Abel, Niels Henrik. Mathematician who published a proof in 1824 known as Abel's impossibility theorem (also known as the Abel–Ruffini theorem), which states that, in general, polynomial equations higher than the fourth degree are incapable of algebraic solution in terms of a finite number of additions, subtractions, multiplications, divisions, and root extractions.

accession of the coast of Asia Minor (1920). The Allies had enticed Greece to enter World War I in 1917 by promising lands Greece greatly desired. The Greeks themselves had hoped to conquer Constantinople and Smyrna, and the Allies' added offering of Cyprus sealed the deal for the Greeks. The next year, as the Ottoman Empire fell, Greece didn't hesitate to claim the lands they now thought to be rightfully theirs. Based upon prior negotiations with France and Britain, the Treaty of Sevres was signed in 1920, and Greece was given rule in eastern **Thrace** and western Anatolia (Asia Minor). This acquisition of Anatolia put Greece in an extremely powerful position; overnight Greece ran and occupied the coast of Asia Minor.

acousmatic (from the Greek verb "to hear"). At the **Pythagorean** school, probationers were called "acousmatic" ("listeners") because they were required to listen to teachers in complete silence from behind a veil.

Acropolis (Greek for "city at the top"). The rocky, flat-topped hill in Athens rising 400 feet above sea level that is home to the ancient Athenian citadel containing the famous **Parthenon** temple and other important cultural and religious buildings. Chosen as a venue for the city's most significant institutions due to its defensibility, it was mainly constructed between 460 and 430 BCE under the leadership of **Pericles** during Athen's Golden Age.

algebra (from Arabic "al-jabr," meaning "reunion of broken parts"). Branch of mathematics concerned with the study of structure, relation, and quantity, in which letters and other general symbols are used to represent numbers and quantities in formulae and equations.

Analysis Situs. Influential mathematical paper published by **Henri Poincaré** in 1895 in which he gave the first systematic treatment of topology and effectively revolutionized the subject. The term itself is an obsolete synonym for "topology," a branch of mathematics that deals with continuous transformations, such as translations and enlargements.

Anaxagoras (499–428 BCE). Greek mathematician and Pre-socratic philosopher, known for his cosmology and for his discovery of the true cause of eclipses. He was imprisoned for claiming that the Sun was not a god and that the Moon reflected the Sun's light.

Antichthon, or "Counter-Earth." The **Pythagorean** model of the universe consisted of ten spheres revolving about a central fire. The external sphere contained the stars. The Earth, the Moon, the Sun, and the five known planets (Mercury, Venus, Mars, Jupiter, and Saturn) occupied eight more spheres. On the remaining sphere revolved a hypothetical planet, not visible from Earth, called Antichthon.

Antiphon's method of exhaustion. A method of calculating the area of a curvilinear shape—a shape contained by or consisting of a curved line or lines—using successive approximations by rectilinear shapes (mainly triangles).

Apollinaire, Guillaume (1880–1918). French poet, writer, and art critic who took part in many avant-garde movements in French literary and artistic circles at the beginning of the twentieth century. He is best known for his status as a literary critic, for coining the term "surrealism," and for writing one of the earliest surrealist works, *Les mamelles de Tirésias*.

Arc de Triomphe. Famed and easily recognizable arch-shaped monument at the western edge of the **Champs-Élysées** in Paris, commemorating French military dominance during the Napoleonic Wars. It was commissioned by Napoleon I at the height of his power in 1806, to be designed in the grand tradition of ancient Roman architecture, and finished in 1836. Engraved sculptures on its sides represent French nationalistic folklore, and the insides and edges are engraved with the names of generals and important military victories. On November 11, 1920, an unknown soldier was buried underneath the arch, as a tribute to soldiers' sacrifices throughout the country's history.

Archimedes (287–212 BCE). Mathematician, astronomer, and inventor of ancient Greece, who resided in Syracuse, Sicily (now in Italy). He revolutionized geometry with his contributions, including Archimedes' principle, the Archimedes screw, and the discovery of the relation between the surface and volume of a sphere and its circumscribing cylinder.

Aristotle (384–322 BCE). Ancient Greek philosopher, logician, and scientist who was a student of **Plato** and a teacher of Alexander the Great. He founded the Peripatetic school in 335 BCE at the Lyceum, a gymnasium located outside the walls of Athens, and was the author of a philosophical and scientific system that became the framework and vehicle for both Christian Scholasticism and medieval Islamic philosophy. Some of his most important treatises include *Physics*, *Metaphysics*, *Nicomachean Ethics*, *Politics*, *De anima (On the Soul)*, and *Poetics*. Aristotle single-handedly founded the sciences of Logic, Biology and Psychology, and his system of thought is arguably the most influential ever put together by a single mind.

Avenue des Champs Élysées. Avenue in northwestern Paris leading from the Place de la Concorde to the **Arc de Triomphe**. Known as the most visually appealing and prestigious street in the city, construction began under Louis XIV and was completed by Louis XV. The avenue is currently one of the most expensive strips of real estate in the world and is an important French cultural landmark.

axiomatic system. A set of propositions or postulates that are accepted without proof, which serve as the basis for a branch of a science and provide a starting point for deducing and inferring other (theory dependent) truths. For example, the axioms of arithmetic were axioms posited by **Giuseppe Peano** as the foundation of arithmetic. One such axiom he proposed was that each whole number has a successor.

Babbage, Charles (1791–1871). English mathematician, philosopher, inventor, and mechanical engineer who by 1834 had invented the principle of the analytical engine, the forerunner of the modern digital computer.

Barcelona's Barrio Chino. Located in the southern half of El Raval, a medieval, densely populated city quarter of Barcelona, Spain. Known by reputation as a slum untouched by modern development, the neighborhood nevertheless houses many high-class brothels for rich clientele as well as more modest arrangements for poorer vice-seekers. The area has no significant affiliation with those of Chinese descent (Barrio Chino translates as Chinatown), the label was applied by journalist Francesc Madrid after viewing a film about the vice industry of San Francisco's Chinatown.

Beltrami, Eugenio (1835–1900). Italian mathematician known for his examination of how the gravitational potential as given by **Newton** would have to be modified in a space of negative curvature. His work in differential geometry on curves and surfaces removed doubts about the validity of **non-Euclidean geometry**.

Benakis, Emmanuel (1843–1929). Wealthy Egyptian merchant and former mayor and former minister of the city of Athens as well as a national Greek benefactor. Benakis is also a major donator to and co-founder of the Athens College and the father of Penelope Delta, a famous Greek author of children's books.

Bernhardt, Sarah (1844–1923). French stage actress popular in both Europe and the United States who was known for her dramatic roles and for sleeping in a coffin. She was a pioneering silent movie actress, debuting in the film *Le duel d'Hamlet* and appearing later in eight motion pictures and two biographical films. She continued to perform even after the loss of her leg in 1914 due to gangrene.

Bismarck, Otto Eduard Leopold von (1815–1898). Prussian and German statesman who oversaw the unification of Germany while minister-president of Prussia (1862–1890). When the second German Empire was formed in 1871, he became its first Chancellor; it was during this post that he was nicknamed the "Iron Chancellor." Bismarck had a great and lasting influence on German policy. One of his main objectives was to minimize the power of the Catholic Church in Germany—he introduced an "anti-Catholic" movement called *Kulturkampf*.

Bois de Boulogne. Large public park (2.5 times larger than Central Park in New York City) in west Paris around the sixteenth arrondissement. Originally an ancient oak forest, the lands were used to house several monasteries in early French history. Converted into royal hunting grounds in 1256, the lands remained under control of the monarchy until Napoleon III converted them into a park in 1852. The park went through various forms and restructurings before being annexed by Paris in 1929 in its present form.

Bolyai, János (1802–1860). Hungarian mathematician, known for his work in **non-Euclidean geometry**. He was the son of a well-known mathematician, Farkas Bolyai. While studying at the Royal Engineering College in Vienna from 1818 to 1822, János became obsessed with **Euclid**'s parallel postulate (the fifth). He reached the conclusion that the postulate is independent of the other axioms of geometry and that different consistent geometries can be constructed on its negation. He devised a complete system of non-Euclidean geometry, publishing his work in 1832 as an appendix to a textbook of mathematics written by his father. Years later, Bolyai discovered that **Lobachevsky** had published a similar piece of work in 1829. From what we know, Lobachevsky published his work a few years earlier than Bolyai, but it contained only **hyperbolic geometry**. Bolyai and Lobachevsky didn't know each other or each other's works. Nevertheless, hyperbolic geometry is now often referred to as "Bolyai-Lobachevskian geometry."

bouzouki clubs. Typical Greek hang-outs where bouzouki music can be enjoyed. A bouzouki is a plucked string instrument with a pear-shaped body and a very long neck that produces sharp metallic sounds (similar to a guitar or mandolin). It is the cornerstone instrument of modern Greek music.

Bricard, Raoul (1870–1920). French mathematician who discovered self-intersecting flexible surfaces that are now known as Bricard's octahedra.

Bruant, Aristide (1851–1925). French cabaret singer who developed a singing and comedy act. Bruant appeared at *Le Chat Noir* club and later opened his own Montmartre club called *Le Mirliton*. Henri de **Toulouse-Lautrec**'s posters depicting Bruant wearing a red scarf and black cape are how he is most famously remembered.

café chantant. A type of outdoor café where usually small groups of performers played popular music for patrons. The cafés, associated with the belle époque of France—a time of economic prosperity and social peace between the late 1880s and World War I—were traditionally seen as lighthearted and bawdy establishments, with few of the political or territorial undertones typical of cabarets of the era.

calculus (Latin for "small pebble" used for counting). Branch of mathematics that includes the study of limits, derivatives, integrals, and infinite series. Historically, it was sometimes referred to as "infinitesimal calculus" or "the calculus of infinitesimals," but that usage is seldom seen today. Most basically, calculus is the study of change, in the same way that geometry is the study of space.

cancan. Dance that first appeared in the ballrooms of Montparnasse in Paris during the nineteenth century. The cancan is a physically demanding dance that is characterized by women wearing suggestive costumes and dancing provocatively with high kicks that lift their skirts up. Many famous composers, such as Jacques Offenbach, have written music for the cancan.

Carathéodory, Constantin (1873–1950). Greek mathematician who became a professor at the University of Göttingen. Carathéodory made many contributions to the calculus of variations, the theory of the functions of several variables, and the theory of point-set measure. He also developed the theory of boundary correspondence. His contributions to thermodynamics helped to develop Einstein's special theory of relativity.

Casagemas, Carles (1880–1901). Catalan painter and friend of **Picasso**. His friendship and suicide by a bullet to the head inspired a number of Picasso paintings, most famously *The Burial of Casagemas* and *La vie.*

Cauchy, Augustin Louis (1789–1857). French mathematician who wrote numerous treatises and made 789 contributions to scientific journals. Some of his research topics included convergence and divergence of infinite series, differential equations, determinants, probability, and mathematical physics. His most substantial contributions were the theory of numbers and complex quantities to the theory of series, the theory of permutation groups, and the co-founding of modern analysis with Karl Weierstrass.

Cayley, Arthur (1821–1895). English mathematician who formalized the theory of matrices. He also made contributions to the algebraic theory of curves and surfaces, linear algebra, graph theory, group theory, combinatorics, and elliptic functions. He is credited as being the first to develop a modern definition regarding the concept of a group.

Cézanne, Paul (1839–1906). French artist and Post-Impressionist painter whose works influenced the aesthetic development of twentieth-century art movements, most notably Cubism. Cézanne has been called the father of modern painting.

Charles I (1600–1649). King of England, Scotland, and Ireland from 1625 until his execution for treason in 1649; second son of James I and Anne of Denmark. He is best known for reigning during the English Civil War, a struggle for power against Puritans who rebelled against the religious policies Charles was attempting to impose on the Scots. He was succeeded by Louis-Philippe.

Columbus, Christopher (1451–1506). Spanish navigator, colonizer, and explorer of Italian origin who unintentionally encountered the Americas while searching for a direct sea route from Europe to Asia. Though not the first to reach the Americas (he was preceded some five hundred years by Leif Ericson, and possibly by others), Columbus initiated widespread contact between Europeans and indigenous Americans. The term "pre-Columbian" is sometimes used to refer to the peoples and cultures of the Americas before the arrival of Columbus and his European successors.

Constantine I, King of the Hellenes (1868–1923). Son of **George I** of Greece and Grand Duchess **Olga Constantinovna** of Russia, he reigned as king of Greece twice and also served as commander-in-chief of the Hellenic Army. He fought and commanded Greek troops in both the Balkan Wars and the Greco-Turkish War. Throughout his life he was entangled in political disagreements, the most important being his skirmish with **Eleftherios Venizelos**, which would ultimately cause the "National Schism" over whether Greece should enter World War I.

Copernicus, Nicolaus (1473–1543). Polish astronomer who is best known for his heliocentric ("the sun as the center") astronomical theory in which the earth makes a complete spin on its axis once daily and revolves annually around the sun. This treatise was famously published in *De hypothesibus motuum coelestium a se constitutis commentariolus* ("little commentary on the hypotheses formulated by himself for the heavenly bodies"), which some historians say marked the beginning of the Scientific Revolution.

Cossacks. Group of martial people who are geographically situated in the southern regions of Eastern European Russia and parts of Asia. The term Cossack comes from the Turkic *kazak,* meaning "adventurer" or "free man."

Crito (fl. late fifth century BCE). Wealthy Athenian philosopher who was a close friend of **Socrates** and is featured in *Crito,* one of **Plato**'s dialogues. It is in this dialogue that Socrates has been condemned to death and now waits in jail for the day of his execution. A visit from his close friends and followers, including Crito, leads to a conversation and debate regarding an escape Socrates' friends have devised for him. Socrates refuses the plan and prefers to accept his sentence, explaining that he will not break the laws of his city or "retaliate evil for evil."

D'Alembert, Jean Le Rond (1717–1783). French mathematician, philosopher, and writer who published *Traité de dynamique,* an important treatise on dynamics. The treatise contained the famous "d'Alembert's principle." D'Alembert was also a pioneer in the research on differential equations and their use in physics.

da Gama, Dom Vasco (1460 or 1469–1524). Portuguese explorer and one of the most successful in the European Age of Discovery and the commander of the first ships to sail directly from Europe to India. His title was 1st Count of Vidigueira, Portugal.

Daguerre, Louis-Jacques-Mandé (1787–1851). French artist and chemist, recognized for his invention of the daguerreotype process of photography. In 1829 he began collaborating on improved photographic processes with **Joseph Niépce**, and together they developed the physautotype, a process that used lavender oil.

De la Vallée-Poussin, Charles (1866–1962). French mathematician who is best known for his work *Cours d'analyse* and his contribution to the proof of the prime number theorem that was contained in two papers on the **Riemann** zeta function.

Dedekind, Richard (1831–1916). German mathematician who formulated a redefinition of irrational numbers in terms of arithmetic concepts that he called Dedekind cuts, which consisted in separating all the real numbers in a series into two parts, such that each real number in one part is less than every real number in the other.

Degas, Edgar (1834–1917). French artist, painter, and sculptor considered one of the founders of Impressionism. He is most celebrated for his depiction of Parisian life and for bridging the gap between traditional academic art and the radical movements of the early twentieth century.

Dehn, Max (1878–1952). German mathematician and student of **Hilbert** who showed that a tetrahedron and a cube with the same volume cannot be divided up into identical piles of pieces. This helped to solve Hilbert's third problem, posed at the Second International Congress of Mathematicians in 1900.

Deligiannis government. Administrations of Theodoros Deligiannis (1820–1905), Greek statesman and leader of the conservative and expansionist Nationalist Party from 1882 to 1905. Taking advantage of the nationalistic fervor and warmongering to fuel his popularity, Deligiannis was elected prime minister several times during the late nineteenth century, yet his ambitions often exceeded his means, resulting in several dismissals and electoral defeats. Deligiannis was stabbed to death by a professional gambler for implementing strict measures against gambling houses. Today he is remembered as somewhat of a national hero who catered to the wishes of his contemporary countrymen.

Demotic Greek. The modern vernacular ("domestic," "native") form of Greek developed from ancient Greek, it first became the standard language of secondary and university education in 1976. Today in Greece, a mix of both the Demotic and the archaic Katharevousa forms of Greek are used together and referred to as Standard Modern Greek.

Derain, André (1880–1954). French painter best known as a founding father of Fauvism, along with **Matisse**, for his use of vivid and unnatural colors. He also supplied the illustrations for **Apollinaire**'s first book of poetry, *L'enchanteur pourissant,* in 1909.

Descartes, René (1596–1650). French philosopher, scientist, and mathematician who also made major contributions to mathematics with his work *La géométrie*, which included the formulation for the Cartesian coordinate system. He is perhaps more famously known for his formulation of the first modern version of mind-body dualism and the expression *"Cogito, ergo sum"* ("I think, therefore I am"). Descartes has also been called the father of modern philosophy.

Dinostratus (390–320 BCE). Greek geometer who was the first to use a curve called a quadratrix to find a square equal in area to a given circle, thus solving the problem of squaring the circle.

Dirichlet, Johann Peter Gustav Lejeune (1805–1859). German mathematician who was the first person to integrate the hydrodynamic equations exactly. He is considered the founder of the theory of Fourier series and is best known for the modern definition of a "function."

Doirani, battle of (September 18–19, 1918). Fought on the southern shore of Dojran Lake, on the border between Greece and Macedonia, during World War I, setting the stage for a devastating defeat of the Greek and British armies by the Bulgarians. In the short span of only two days, the Allies were forced to retreat, having suffered huge losses; the Bulgarians claimed victory with an impressively small number of casualties.

Dreyfus, Alfred (1859–1935). A French artillery officer of Jewish origin who was falsely accused of selling military secrets to Germany, convicted of treason, and sentenced to life imprisonment on Devil's Island in French Guyana. Novelist **Émile Zola**'s famous article *"J'accuse"* divulged the scandalous cover-up by the French army in Dreyfus's case. Dreyfus was pardoned in 1906 by President **Émile Loubet**. The Dreyfus Affair is considered the catalyst for the French Radical party's 1905 victory in successfully passing legislation separating church and state.

du Bois-Reymond, Emile (1818–1896). German physician and physiologist who was the first person to give an example of a continuous function whose **Fourier** series diverges at a point in his very important work *Eine neue Theorie der Convergenz und Divergenz von Reihen mit positiven Gliedern* ("A New Theory of Convergence and Divergence of Series with Positive Terms"). His work led to a better understanding of the whole concept of a function.

Dumas, Alexandre *fils* (1824–1895). Son and namesake of famous author Alexandre Dumas. Illegitimate and from a family of mixed descent (French white noblemen and Haitian), he was picked on as a child. His father legally recognized him in 1831, and at the same time acquired the right to take Alexandre *fils* from his mother, causing her great sadness. Her suffering and Alexandre *fils*' own clearly influenced him; his torment comes through in the works he later authored. His most famous work is *La dame aux camélias* (1852), which was adapted to become the English play *Camille*.

***e*.** A mathematical constant defined as the base of a natural logarithm. The number *e* is transcendental, that is, it cannot form the solution of any algebraic equation. It is approximately equal to 2.718, with infinitely many decimal digits.

Edison, Thomas (1847–1931). American inventor who is famous for inventing the electric light bulb, starting the first electrical power distribution company, and founding the first modern research laboratory. Altogether, he held over a thousand patents in the United States, United Kingdom, France, and Germany. He was also the founder of General Electric.

Eiffel Tower. Wrought-iron landmark built in 1889 for the Centennial Exposition, designed by engineer **Gustave Eiffel** (1823–1923). The 986-foot structure represented innovative and ingenious knowledge of metal design and was a precursor to a new chapter in civil engineering and architecture. The Eiffel Tower was the world's tallest building until the completion of the Chrysler Building in New York City in 1930.

Eiffel, Gustave (1832–1923). French structural engineer and architect who designed the wrought-iron skeleton for the Statue of Liberty and supervised it being raised. He is best known for building the **Eiffel Tower** to commemorate the 100th anniversary of the French Revolution at the Centennial Exposition of 1889.

elliptic geometry. Another name for **Riemann's geometry**.

Ephesus. Ancient Greek city located in contemporary western Turkey, it was the leading seaport of the region and one of the great Ionian cities. Ephesus was the site of the great temple of Artemis (or Artemision, referred to by Romans as the temple of Diana) and was considered the world capital of slave trade from roughly 100 BCE to 100 CE, but it was eventually abandoned around 431 CE as the harbor silted over. Excavations have uncovered significant remains from the eras of the Roman and Byzantine Empires.

Epirus. Ancient Greek state now occupied by northwestern Greece and southern Albania. Was occupied from Neolithic times by Epirote tribes and was known around the time of Homer as the home of the oracle of Dodona. Molded into a state by the Molossi tribe in the fourth century BCE, Epirus reached the height of independent power in the third century BCE before falling under the rule of the Roman, Byzantine, and eventually Ottoman empires. In the early nineteenth century Epirus was divided among Turkey and Albania.

Euclid of Alexandria (fl. 300 BCE). Greek mathematician who is considered the "Father of Geometry," although little is known about his life and writings. It is possible that he was a student at **Plato**'s Academy in Athens, and that he was active at the great Library of Alexandria. His work, the *Elements*, is a mathematical and geometric treatise spanning 13 books, which consists of a collection of definitions, postulates, propositions, and mathematical proofs of the propositions. The treatise became the most popular and successful textbook in the history of mathematics.

Euclid's five postulates. The five axioms posited by **Euclid** as the foundations of geometry:

1) Any two points can be joined by a straight line.

2) Any straight line segment can be extended indefinitely in a straight line.

3) Given any straight line segment, a circle can be drawn having the segment as a radius and one endpoint as a center.

4) All right angles are congruent (identical in form).

5) If two lines intersect a third in such a way that the sum of the inner angles on one side is less than two right angles, then the two lines inevitably must intersect each other on that side if extended far enough.

Euclidean geometry. Geometry based on **Euclid**'s postulates. Until the nineteenth century and the publication of the geometries of **Riemann** and **Bolyai-Lobachevsky**, it was thought to be the only existing geometry.

Euler, Leonhard (1707–1783). Swiss mathematician and physicist who contributed greatly to analytic geometry, geometry, calculus, and number theory. He is considered one of the founders of pure mathematics. He also developed methods for solving problems in observational astronomy.

Ex oriente lux. Light from the Orient. An early Christian aphorism that means that enlightenment comes from the east, where the sun rises.

***Exposition Universelle* (May 6–October 31, 1889).** World's Fair in Paris notable for the Machinery Hall and the unveiling of the **Eiffel Tower**, which was used as an entrance gate to the event, as well as for being held during the centennial year of the French Revolution.

Faure, Félix (1841–1899). The sixth president of the French Third Republic, he held office from 1895 to 1899. Faure opposed a new trial for the defendant in the **Dreyfus** Affair, bringing infamy to his administration. He was succeeded by **Émile Loubet**.

Fermat, Pierre de (1601 or 1607/8–1665). French lawyer at the Parliament of Toulouse, France, and mathematician credited with early developments that led to modern calculus. In particular, he is recognized for his discovery of an original method of finding the greatest and the smallest ordinates of curved lines, which is analogous to that of the then unknown differential calculus, as well as his research into the theory of numbers. He also made notable contributions to analytic geometry, probability, and optics.

Fermat's Last Theorem. The name of a statement in number theory claimed to have been proven by **Pierre de Fermat** in 1637. It says, "It is impossible to separate any power higher than the second into two like powers." More precisely: if an integer n is greater than 2, then the equation $a^n + b^n = c^n$ has no solutions in non-zero integers a, b, and c. Fermat did not publish his proof, however, and no correct proof was found until 1995, some three and a half centuries after Fermat made his claim.

Fontana, Niccolò (1499–1557). Italian mathematician and engineer who is the first known person to solve cubic equations algebraically. He also published the first Italian translations of Archimedes and **Euclid**. He is well known as the originator of the science of ballistics.

Fourier, Joseph (1768–1830). French mathematician and physicist who devised the Fourier series, which is an infinite series used to solve special types of differential equations. It consists of an infinite sum of sines and cosines, and because it is periodic—meaning its values repeat over fixed intervals—it is a useful tool in analyzing periodic functions. Though investigated by **Leonhard Euler**, among others, the idea was named for Joseph Fourier, who fully explored its consequences, including important applications in engineering, particularly in heat conduction. Fourier has also been credited with discovering the greenhouse effect.

Frege, Gottlob (1848–1925). German logician, philosopher, and mathematician considered one of the founders of modern symbolic logic. He developed a method of formally representing the logic of thoughts and inferences.

Galilei, Galileo (1564–1642). Tuscan physicist, philosopher, mathematician, and astronomer who was the first to use a refracting telescope to make important astronomical discoveries. He was also convicted of heresy for supporting **Copernicus**' heliocentric theory. He has been called the father of modern observational astronomy, physics, and science.

Galois, Évariste (1811–1832). Promising mathematician whose jail sentence led to his untimely death. While in jail, it is speculated that he had an affair with the resident physician's daughter, Stéphanie du Motel, which for unknown reasons led to a duel that resulted in his death. His work, published after his death, laid the foundations for abstract **algebra** and standard mathematics. One of his best-known works is *The Fundamental Theorem of Galois Theory,* which gave a solution to the problem of finding the roots of a quintic (fifth-degree) equation.

Garnier, Charles (1825–1898). French architect in the Beaux Arts style who designed the Paris Opéra commissioned by Emperor Napoleon III and a symbol of Second Empire taste. Garnier's neo-Baroque style became characteristic of late nineteenth-century Beaux Arts design. He also designed the casino and Opéra de Monte-Carlo, and became well known for resort-style architecture.

Gauss, Carl Friedrich (1777–1855). German mathematician who made enormous contributions to **number theory**, geometry, probability theory, geodesy, magnetism, astronomy, optics, the theory of functions, and potential theory. His work and private notes helped to influence acceptance of **non-Euclidean geometry**. He was also the teacher and doctoral advisor to **Bernhard Riemann**.

Geminus (10 BCE–60 CE). Greek astronomer, mathematician, and Stoic philosopher whose works defended the Stoic view of the universe. He also wrote the influential astronomy text *Introduction to the Phenomena,* or *Isagoge.*

Géry, Alice (1884-1975). Former wife of **Maurice Princet** and widow of **André Derain**. She was a friend and girlfriend of **Picasso** and the model for his *Jeune fille accoudeé* painting (1903).

Gill, André (1840–1885). French caricaturist who was best known for the portraits he drew for the "Man of the Day" series in *La Lune* newspaper and later for the periodical *L'éclipse*. His unique characters had large heads and dwarfed bodies.

Gödel, Kurt (1906–1978). Austrian-American mathematician, logician, and philosopher. One of the most significant logicians of all time, Gödel's work has had immense impact upon scientific and philosophical thinking in the twentieth century. He is best known for his two incompleteness theorems, published in 1931 when he was 25 years of age, one year after finishing his doctorate at the University of Vienna. Gödel's proof states that in any axiomatic mathematical system there are propositions that cannot be proved or disproved within the axioms of the system itself.

Goldbach, Christian (1690–1764). Prussian mathematician who did important work in **number theory**. He is best known for his conjecture, written in a letter to **Euler**, that states that every even integer greater that two can be represented as the sum of two primes.

golden section, a.k.a. the golden ratio. According to ancient Greek artists and geometers, the aesthetically ideal partition of a line segment into two unequal parts is that in which the bigger part is to the smaller as the whole is to the bigger. This partition (in which the ratio of bigger to smaller can be proved to be approximately 1.618) is called the golden section.

Hadamard, Jacques Salomon (1865–1963). French mathematician who made major contributions to geometry and many areas of dynamic trajectories. He is well known for proving the prime number theorem and publishing papers on determinant inequality and on properties of dynamic trajectories; the latter won the Bordin Prize of the Academy of Sciences.

Halley, Edmond (1656–1742). English astronomer, physicist, and mathematician famous for calculating the orbit of Halley's comet. Additionally, he was highly recognized for overseeing and editing Newton's *Philosophiae Naturalis Principia Mathematica,* which became one of the greatest works on celestial mechanics. He also published the first meteorological chart in 1686.

Hamel, George Karl Wilhelm (1877–1954). German mathematician who contributed to function theory, mechanics, and the foundations of mathematics. He is best known for his early use of the axiom of choice to construct a basis for the real numbers as a vector space, or linear space, over the rational numbers. He wrote a number of papers on an axiomatic theory of mechanics, and an important textbook on mechanics, *Elementare Mechanik*, published in 1912.

Hatzidakis, Nikolaos (1872-1942)). Professor at Athens University who did research in differential geometry and was the first president (1918–1925) of the Hellenic Mathematical Society, founded in 1918. His father, Ionnis Hatzidakis, was also a mathematician, and the author of a widely used textbook of geometry.

Hermite, Charles (1822–1901). French mathematician who was an important figure in the development of the theory of algebraic forms, the arithmetical theory of quadratic forms, and the theories of elliptic and Abelian functions. He was the first to prove that ***e***, the base of natural logarithms, is a transcendental number. He is most famous for his solution of the general quintic (fifth-degree) equation that was published in *Sur la résolution de l'équation du cinquième degré* in 1858.

Heron of Alexandria, a.k.a Hero (ca. 10–ca. 75 CE). Greek inventor and mathematician, mainly in the field of geometry. He is famous for his formula for the area of a triangle, found in his mathematical book, *Metrica*.

Hilbert, David (1862–1943). German mathematician who contributed to the mathematics of invariants and influenced the foundation of algebraic numbers by proving that all invariants can be expressed in terms of a finite number. He published *The Foundations of Geometry* in 1902, changing the axiomatic treatment of geometry and making him one of the greatest influences in the subject after **Euclid**. At the Second International Congress of Mathematics in 1900 he presented a set of 23 problems that set the course for much of mathematical research in the twentieth century.

Hipparchus (190–120 BCE). Greek astronomer, geographer, and mathematician who made great contributions to astronomy as a mathematical science and to the foundations of **trigonometry**. He is one of the first people known to have possessed a trigonometry table and to have used it with his solar and lunar theories, which allowed him to be one of the first to reliably predict solar eclipses.

Hippasus of Metapontum (ca. 500 BCE). Greek philosopher and disciple of **Pythagoras** credited with discovering that the square root of two, and hence the Pythagorean Theorem, is irrational. The **Pythagoreans** held that all quantities could be explained by whole numbers and their ratios, which was contrary to Hippasus' discovery. They thought that his discovery was religious heresy; legend has it that they murdered him by drowning him at sea.

hyperbolic geometry. Another name for **Bolyai-Lobachevsky** geometry.

infinite summation of infinitesimal sums. The concept accepted in modern mathematics that the sum of infinitely many infinitely small quantities will yield a finite result. For example:
$\frac{1}{2} + \frac{1}{4} + 1/8 + 1/16 + 1/32 + \ldots = 1$.

Jacob, Max (1876–1944). French author and artist, close friend and roommate of **Picasso**, and a compatriot of French Resistance leader Jean Moulin. Though born a Jew, he claimed to have had a vision of Christ and converted to the Catholic religion. His conversion was of no help to him during World War II, when he was forced into hiding during the German occupation of France. Many of his immediate family were deported and killed by the Nazis. He is seen as an integral link between symbolism and surrealism in both art and writing. He often used pseudonyms, such as Léon David or Morven le Gaëlique.

Jacobins. Members of the powerful political Jacobin Club during the French Revolution (1789–1799). The club began as a moderate political faction, but after the death of Honoré Mirabeau (1749–1791)—an important moderate who favored a constitutional monarchy—it became strongly left-winged and was the initiating source behind the Reign of Terror. The term Jacobin is still used to refer to a person or policy that is left-wing in relation to revolutionary politics.

Jakobides, Georgios (1853–1932). Greek artist who was an important contributor to the Munich style movement and founder of the National Gallery of Greece, located in Athens. He is most famous for his paintings of children and mythological scenes. He supported younger artists but was personally opposed to all the new styles of the day, such as the Impressionist movement and Expressionist movements.

Kant, Immanuel (1724–1804). German philosopher from the Prussian city of Königsberg (now Kaliningrad, Russia), regarded as one of the most influential thinkers of modern Europe and of the late Enlightenment. He is most famous for his theory of transcendental idealism. Some of his most important works are *Critique of Pure Reason* and *Critique of Practical Reason.*

Kepler, Johannes (1571–1630). German mathematician and astronomer who discovered the three laws of planetary motion and two new regular polyhedra in optics. He made great contributions to calculus by calculating the most exact astronomical table known at the time. His most influential work is the seven-volume *Epitome astronomiae,* which discussed heliocentric astronomy in a systematic way.

Khayyám, Omar (1048–1122). Persian astronomer, mathematician, philosopher, and poet who wrote the famous **algebra** book *Treatise on Demonstration of Problems of Algebra,* which had a complete classification of cubic equations with geometric solutions found by means of intersecting conic sections. He is also well known for his poetry, most notably the *Rubaiyat.*

Kilkis-Lahanas, battles of (June 19–21, 1913). A three-day battle between Greece and Bulgaria, which took place during the Second Balkan War in the small town of Kilkis, Macedonia. On the third day, the Greeks overtook the Bulgarian troops and the town, burning Kilkis to the ground.

King George (Georgios) I (1845–1913). Born Prince William, from the Danish Glücksburg dynasty, he was chosen to succeed King Otto as the ruler of Greece by the Great Powers (Britain, France, Russia) because he was not a descendant of their own heritage lines. He was King of Greece from 1863 to 1913.

Klein, Felix (1849–1925). German mathematician who established one of the best mathematical research centers in the world at the University of Göttingen in 1886. He profoundly influenced geometry and present-day thinking about mathematics with his contributions, one of the most significant being the Erlanger Program, which encompassed both **Euclid**ean and **non-Euclidean geometry**.

Kresna, clashes in the Straits of (July 8–18, 1913). During the Second Balkan War, armies led by **King Constantine**, who thought the Bulgarians were already defeated, marched further into Bulgarian land. King Constantine wanted a clear, complete victory over the Bulgarians, something **Eleftherios Venizelos** openly objected to. Constantine's stubborn march led to Kresna Gorge, where the Greeks were ambushed by the Bulgarian 1st and 2nd Army, which had set up defense camps in the area. Though the Greeks had walked right into this clash, both sides were ready for peace. The battle of Kresna Gorge was the last in the Second Balkan War, and the Bulgarian and Greek governments came to a treaty.

Kronecker, Leopold (1823–1891). German mathematician and logician whose major contributions were in elliptic functions, the theory of algebraic equations, and the theory of algebraic numbers. He argued that mathematics should work with finite numbers and with a finite number of operations. One of his best-known works is *On the Solution of the General Equation of the Fifth Degree,* which solved the quintic (fifth-degree) equation by applying group theory.

***la bande à Picasso*/Picasso's gang.** Refers to the members of **Picasso**'s circle of friends. The core members were **Guillaume Apollinaire**, **Max Jacob**, and **André Salmon**. *La bande* consisted of people who Picasso thought were the most talented on the Parisian modern art scene at the beginning of the twentieth century.

Lafayette, Marquis de (1757–1834). French aristocratic general, statesman, and hero of the American Revolution. Served in the American Revolution as a general and diplomat without compensation or the king's permission. Was a key figure in the early phases of the French Revolution, serving in the Estates General and the National Constituent Assembly. Lafayette was eventually forced out of a leading role by the Jacobins due to his efforts to establish a constitutional monarchy. He spent several years in exile before returning to France in 1800 and serving in politics until his death.

Lagrange, Joseph-Louis (1736–1813). Italian mathematician and astronomer who made great contributions to mechanics with his work *Mécanique analytique,* which transformed mechanics into a branch of mathematical analysis. He also influenced the development of mathematical physics in the nineteenth century with the first analytical mechanics based on **Newton**'s infinitesimal calculus.

Lapin Agile. One of the oldest bistros of **Montmartre**, the later name of **Le Cabaret des Assassins**, switched after roughly 20 years of being known by the original. The bistro was renamed after French caricaturist **André Gill** painted a sign for the establishment in 1875, depicting a rabbit jumping out of a saucepan. Originally reputed as a locale for pimps, beggars, and anarchists, Lapin Agile became a favored spot of struggling writers, students from the Latin Quarter, and painters such as **Picasso** and Modigliani at the turn of the twentieth century. Picasso's 1905 oil painting *At the Lapin Agile* made the locale world famous.

Laplace, Pierre-Simon (1749–1827). French mathematician and astronomer who was one of the most influential scientists ever known; sometimes called a French **Newton**. One of his most famous works is *Exposition du système du monde,* which contained his nebular thesis. He proved the stability of the Solar System and was also one of the first to say that the speed of sound in air depends on the heat capacity ratio.

Le Cabaret des Assassins. Famous cabaret of ill repute in **Montmartre**, Paris. It is rumored that a band of assassins killed the owner's son during the cabaret's early days, giving it its name. The cabaret was renamed **Lapin Agile** in 1875.

Legendre, Adrien-Marie (1752–1833). French mathematician who did pioneering work in number theory, the distribution of primes, and classical mechanics. He wrote the influential work *Éléments de géométrie* in 1794. He also provided the basic analytical tools for mathematical physics with his work on elliptic integrals.

Leibniz, Gottfried Wilhelm (1646–1716). German polymath who wrote primarily in Latin and French. His seminal contributions to mathematics and philosophy are considered equally important. He invented calculus independently of **Newton**, and also discovered the binary system, the foundation of virtually all modern computer architectures. In philosophy, he was, along with **René Descartes** and Baruch Spinoza, one of the three greatest 17th-century rationalists. His works extend to physics, technology, biology, medicine, geology, probability theory, psychology, linguistics, and information science. He also wrote on politics, law, ethics, theology, history, and philology, even occasional verse.

Les demoiselles d'Avignon. Painted by **Picasso** in 1907, the work depicts the sexual freedom of five prostitutes in a brothel. Picasso later referred to this work as his first exorcism painting. At the time of its first exhibition in 1916, the painting was deemed immoral. **André Salmon** gave it its current name; Picasso had always called it *Le bordel*.

Lindemann, Carl Louis Ferdinand von (1852–1939). German mathematician who is best known for his transcendence proof of ***pi***, which proved that *pi* is transcendental and not the root of any algebraic equation with rational coefficients.

Liouville, Joseph (1809–1882). French mathematician who contributed to astronomy, number theory, differential geometry, and topology. He is best remembered for his construction of the existence of an infinite class of transcendental numbers in 1844. He also founded the highly reputable *Journal de mathématiques pures et appliquées.*

Lobachevsky, Nikolai (1792–1856). Russian mathematician whose major contribution was the development of a form of **non-Euclidean geometry** (independently from **János Bolyai**) called hyperbolic geometry. Before him, mathematicians were trying to deduce **Euclid**'s fifth postulate from other axioms. Lobachevsky instead developed a geometry in which the fifth postulate was not true. One famous consequence is that the sum of angles in a triangle must be less than 180 degrees. Non-Euclidean geometry is now in common use in many areas of mathematics and physics, such as general relativity; and hyperbolic geometry is now often referred to as "Bolyai-Lobachevskian" geometry.

Loubet, Émile (1838–1929). French politician who was the seventh president of the French Third Republic from 1899 to 1906. He is best known for pardoning **Alfred Dreyfus**, which led to the victory of French Republican forces against those of the **Royalists**, the Roman Catholic clergy, and the army. The separation between the French state and the church was completed during his presidency.

Louis-Philippe I (1773–1850). King of the French from 1830 to 1848 in what was known as the July Monarchy. He was the last king to rule France, but his title was King of the French, not King of France.

Louvre. French national art gallery and museum located in the 1st arrondissement of Paris. Originally constructed as a fortress, prison and royal palace in 1190, the Louvre was converted into a museum during the eighteenth century and opened as the first public national gallery during the Revolution in 1793. The museum houses more than 35,000 works of art, including many historically significant ones such as the *Mona Lisa*.

Lovelace, Ada (1815–1852). Lord Byron's daughter. She produced an annotated translation of Menabrea's *Notions sur la machine analytique de Charles Babbage* in 1842. Her notes on the machine and how it could be programmed, essentially a description of a computer and software, were published in Richard Taylor's *Scientific Memoirs Vol. 3* in 1843. She is considered the first programmer of the analytical engine.

Lumière, Louis (1864–1948). French inventor and filmmaker who developed a better way to prepare photographic plates and, along with his brother Auguste, invented a camera/projector called the cinematograph. Lumiére and his brother produced thousands of short films throughout their lifetime and organized the first showing of a film to a paying audience in 1895.

Macedonia. Historical region in southeastern Greece, ruled by Alexander the Great before being overtaken by the Ottoman Empire. Upon the Ottoman defeat in the Balkan Wars, Macedonia was divided by the **Treaty of Bucharest** in 1913 among Greece, Serbia, Bulgaria and Albania. (Not to be confused with the Republic of Macedonia which was formerly a part of ex-Yugoslavia, and is independent since 1991.)

Magellan, Ferdinand (1480–1521). Spanish explorer and navigator of Portuguese origin who is best known for being the first man to circle the globe. He sailed around the tip of South America and found the westward passage that is now named the **Strait of Magellan**. He is also credited with naming the Pacific Ocean.

Matisse, Henri (1869–1954). French painter and sculptor, one of the best-known artists of the twentieth century, recognized as a leading figure in modern art. He developed an expressive, freer style of painting called Fauvism (from the French "Les Fauves" meaning "wild beasts") that used vivid and unnatural colors; the style would become the forerunner of Expressionism. Some of his most famous paintings include *Odalisque with Raised Arms, La danse, Blue Nude,* and *The Dessert: Harmony in Red.*

Méliès, George (1861–1938). French filmmaker and magician who was one of the first to incorporate the fade-in and fade-out techniques in his films and to develop real narratives. In 1898, he was the first to use double exposure in his film *La caverne Maudite* and the first to use split screen in *Homme de tête.* He was also the first to use dissolve transitions in the film *Cendrillon* in 1899.

Menelaus of Alexandria (ca. 70–140 CE). Greek mathematician and astronomer who first conceived and defined a spherical triangle: a triangle formed by three arcs of great circles on the surface of a sphere. We know of four books he wrote, only one of which, *Sphaerica*, has survived in an Arabic translation.

Messaris, Angelos (1910–1978). Famous Greek soccer player who mysteriously quit after only four very successful years to finish his studies in South Africa.

Miletus. Ancient city once located on the western coast of Turkey, at the mouth of the Maeander River. Miletus was considered the greatest Greek city in the east and was a commercial and colonial power before 500 BCE. Once home to intellectual figures such as Thales, Anaximander, and Anaximenes, by the sixth century CE, both its harbors had silted over, and the city was eventually abandoned.

Minkowski, Hermann (1864–1909). German mathematician of Jewish origin who developed the new view that space and time were coupled together in a four-dimensional space-time continuum in his works *Raum und Zeit* and *Zwei Abhandlungen über die Grundgleichungen der Elektrodynamik.* His work laid the framework for mathematical work in relativity, which was later used by Einstein when developing the general theory of relativity.

Mirliton cabaret. Cabaret in the **Montmarte** district of Paris, opened in 1885 by **Aristide Bruant**, noted singer, comedian, and nightlife personality. The cabaret became noted for Bruant's "audience abuse" style of comedy.

***Monstres sacrés* ("sacred monsters").** Term for a venerable or popular public figure who is considered above criticism or attack despite eccentricity and/or controversy.

Montmartre. Highest hill in Paris, its peak is the location of the **Sacré-Coeur** ("Sacred Heart") Basilica. Its slopes were long a traditional bohemian hangout, and artists such as Van Gogh and Pissarro painted there until the twentieth century. It was also the location of clubs such as the **Moulin Rouge**. The hill has played a significant role in local historical events, such as the **Paris Commune** of 1871. Montmartre was annexed to Paris in 1860 and now hosts a vibrant nightlife scene.

Moulin Rouge ("red windmill"). Famed Parisian cabaret in the red-light district of Pigalle, easily recognizable by the red windmill on its roof. Formally a high-class brothel, at the height of its popularity it served as an adult cancan cabaret for high French society.

Mount Lycabettus. A limestone hill 750 feet above sea level, the mountain is the highest point in the surrounding area of Athens. The nineteenth-century Chapel of St. George adorns its peak. A railway regularly shuttles tourists to the top. Mount Lycabettus appears frequently in Greek folklore; one story credits Athena with creating it when she dropped a mountain meant for the construction of the **Acropolis**.

Newton-Leibniz controversy. Calculus, the most important tool for the study of physics, was independently and almost simultaneously invented by **Newton** and **Leibniz**. This led to a grievous controversy, in which each accused the other of plagiarism.

Newton, Sir Isaac (1642–1727). English physicist, mathematician, astronomer, natural philosopher, alchemist and theologian. As mathematician he laid the foundations for differential and integral calculus. In 1687, he published one of the greatest and most influential scientific books ever written, the *Philosophiæ Naturalis Principia Mathematica*. In this work, Newton described universal gravitation and the three laws of motion, laying the groundwork for classical mechanics, which dominated the scientific view of the physical universe for the next three centuries and is the basis for modern engineering.

Niépce, Joseph Nicéphore (1765–1833). French inventor, most noted as the inventor of photography and a pioneer in the field. He is well-known for taking some of the earliest photographs, dating to the 1820s.

non-constructible solution. For some problems in mathematics it is possible to prove that they have a solution, without actually ever finding or effectively demonstrating that solution. Such "solutions" are called non-constructible.

non-Euclidean geometry. Geometry in which one or more of **Euclid**'s postulates are rejected, such as **Riemann** and **Bolyai-Lobachevsky** geometries.

number theory. A branch of mathematics dealing with the properties of numbers in general, and integers in particular, as well as the wider classes of problems that arise from their study.

Oenopides. Ancient Greek astronomer and mathematician who lived around 450 BCE. Very few concrete facts are known about his work and life, though secondary sources such as **Plato**'s *Erastae* give some evidence. He is credited with being the first to use calculations of the Great Year, the yearly path of the sun in the sky, to predict solar and lunar eclipses.

Pallarés, Manuel (1876-1974). Friend of **Picasso**, with whom he shared a studio. He took Picasso to his hometown of Horta de Ebro in 1898, where they stayed for eight months. The work that Picasso started when he returned to Horta de Ebro in 1909 marked the beginnings of Cubism. That same year, Picasso painted a portrait of his friend, believed to be the first in Picasso's series of portraits. Picasso is frequently quoted as saying, "Everything I know, I learned in Pallarés's village."

Pallis, Alexandros (1851–1935). Published a Demotic Greek translation of the New Testament in 1901. *The Acropolis,* the Athenian newspaper, published the Gospel of Matthew in the new Demotic translation, which immediately gave way to riots in the streets of Athens. The participants were mainly university students; they attacked the newspaper offices, marched and protested against the palace, and took over the University of Athens.

Pangalos, Theodore (1878–1952). Influential and ultimately disgraced Greek general and politician. He helped overthrow **King Constantine I** before seizing power and assuming dictatorial powers in 1925. Forced President Kondouriotis to resign and held a fraudulent election before being overthrown and imprisoned a few months later. Pangalos was eventually deported for attempting to plan new coups.

Paraskevopoulos, Leonidas (1860–1936). Chief of staff of the Greek armed forces in Asia Minor. He fought for the Hellenic Army in the Greco-Turkish War in 1897, the Balkan Wars, and World War I. He became commander-in-chief in 1919 and was successful in expanding Greek occupation. He did lose this position in 1920 to a **Royalist**, Anastasios Papoulas, but after the war, he pursued a political career with the **Liberal** party under **Eleftherios Venizelos**; he later became president of the Senate.

Paris Commune (March 18–May 28, 1871). Uprising of an independent government in Paris, caused mainly by worker discontent and France's humiliating defeat in the Franco-Prussian War and the ensuing collapse of the Second Empire. After the end of the war, Parisians feared the conservative-controlled National Assembly would restore the monarchy, and revolutionaries took advantage of local electoral victories to form the Commune government. Government troops quickly entered Paris after suppressing other rebellions and crushed the Communards within one week.

Parmenides (born ca. 515 BCE). Pre-Socratic philosopher from Elea, a Greek city on the southeastern coast of Italy, who founded the Eleatic school of philosophy. All that survives of his work are fragments of a poem, O*n Nature*, in which he describes two methods of knowing reality: the Way of Truth, which does not allow contradictions, and the Way of Opinion, in which opposing views and conflicting appearances co-exist. Parmenides' thought strongly influenced **Plato**, and through him, the whole of western philosophy.

Parren, Callirhoe (1859–1940). Married Ioannis Parren, a journalist from Constantinople of Anglo-French descent, and moved with him to Athens, where he founded the Athens News Agency. Influenced by her journalistic surroundings, she began the weekly publications of *Efimeris ton Kyrion* ("Ladies' Journal") in 1887. Through her writing, she helped activate and lead the women's emancipation movement in Greece. On February 19, 1911, she founded the Lyceum Club of Greek Women.

Parthenon. Sacred Greek temple to goddess Athena, located on the **Acropolis** in Athens. Built between 447 and 432 BCE and considered a masterpiece of Greek architecture, the Parthenon has served at various points in its history as a Christian church, a mosque, and a military powder magazine.

pastis. Mediterranean alcoholic beverage first developed in Provence, France, its ingredients include star anise, black and white peppercorns, cardamom, sage, nutmeg, cloves, cinnamon, licorice, and sugar.

Peano, Giuseppe (1858–1932). Italian mathematician, whose work was of exceptional philosophical value. He published over 200 books and papers and was a founder of mathematical logic and set theory. The standard axiomatization of the natural numbers is named in his honor. He spent most of his career teaching mathematics at the University of Turin. It was in his first book, *Geometrical Calculus,* that the world's first definition of a vector space appeared.

Pericles (ca. 495/93–429 BCE). Prominent Athenian orator, author, and politician who played an important role in the reformation of ancient Greek government and society. Pericles had such a profound influence on Athenian culture that Thucydides, his contemporary historian, acclaimed him as "the first citizen of Athens." Pericles turned the Delian League into an Athenian empire and led his countrymen during the first two years of the Peloponnesian War. The period during which he led Athens, roughly from 461 to 429 BCE, is sometimes known as the "Age of Pericles" or the "Golden Age." Pericles started the ambitious project that built most of the surviving structures on the **Acropolis**, including the **Parthenon**.

Persephone (Roman name is Proserpina). In Ancient mythology, the daughter of Zeus (Jupiter) and Demeter (Ceres) who was abducted by Hades (Pluto) to reign with him over the underworld. She was rescued by her mother, but because Persephone had eaten some pomegranate in the underworld, she was thereafter condemned to return there during six months of every year. While searching for her daughter, Demeter refused to let the earth produce its fruits until Persephone was restored to her. As a result Persephone's story symbolizes the return of spring and the life and growth of grain.

Phanariotes from Constantinople. Prominent Hellenized Romanians and Albanians, and Greeks that lived in Phanar (Fener), Constantinople. Phanar was the main Greek quarter in the city; it housed the Ecumenical Patriarchate, and its inhabitants were very influential in the Ottoman Empire, making up the majority of the Ottoman government.

phi. In mathematics, *phi* represents the **golden section** or **golden ratio**, which is approximately equal to 1.618 but cannot be expressed as a ratio of whole numbers. As a result it is not a number in the **Pythagorean** conception.

Philolaus of Croton (ca. 470–ca. 385 BCE). Pythagorean philosopher who wrote about the soul being separate from the body. His work, *On Nature,* is noted for possibly being the first book written by a Pythagorean. It is also the major source **Aristotle** used in his writings on Pythagorean philosophy. Philolaus argued that the "cosmos" is made up of only two things: those that limit and those which are unlimited. He said further that if a thing is real, it has a number, and numbers are the only means by which anything can be known or comprehended.

pi. A constant that represents the ratio of a circle's circumference to its diameter, approximately equal to 3.14. *Pi* is an irrational number, which means that it cannot be expressed as a fraction of whole numbers.

Picasso, Pablo Ruiz (1881–1973). Andalusian-Spanish painter and sculptor, co-founder of the Cubist movement, and one of the most famous artists of the twentieth century. He was thought to be close to genius level from an early age, but his most influential and important work was done later in his life, after his mid-twenties. He was a social recluse for much of his life and is thought to have had an overall dislike for the opposite sex, especially female artists, as he rarely treated women with respect. His dislike of women, however, did not prevent him from portraying the nude female figure in many of his artistic endeavors. Throughout his life, he created works of great skill and importance, even in his last years, when he worked more fervently than ever.

Piraeus. Port in Athens. Currently the country's largest and main hub for all sea transport to Greek islands. Piraeus was barricaded with fortified barriers in the fifth century BCE, which were destroyed by the Spartans during the Peloponnesian War. Piraeus was completely burned by the Romans in 86 CE, then rebuilt; As a city it gained importance when Athens became the capital of a united Greece in 1834.

Place Pigalle. Notorious and popular adult entertainment district in Paris; location of the famous **Moulin Rouge** nightclub. It is also the location of several art museums, notably the Espace Dalí Montmartre, showcasing works of Salvador Dalí. Well-known artists such as **Picasso**, **Toulouse-Lautrec**, and Maurice Neumont once resided in the neighborhood.

Plato (ca. 427–347 BCE). Ancient Greek philosopher, student and friend of **Socrates**, teacher of **Aristotle**. He founded the Academy in Athens, which lasted almost a thousand years (387 BCE to 529 CE), and was the first institution of higher learning in the western world. He wrote over twenty philosophical dialogues and numerous letters, all of which played and continue to play an integral role in the study of philosophy, classics and world literature.

Plutarch (ca. 46–ca. 120 CE). Greek philosopher, historian, civil servant and rhetorician. He is famous for his many histories of the lives of important Greek and Roman men and is thought to have authored over 200 works. Plutarch was a deeply religious man and was even appointed to priesthood at Delphi, where he was positioned to translate the messages of the **Pythia**. He studied at the **Plato**nic Academy but never restricted himself to pure Platonism, drawing on several different schools of thought in his own work.

Poincaré, Jules Henri (1854–1912). French mathematician who, along with Albert Einstein and Hendrik Lorentz, discovered the special theory of relativity. He made numerous contributions to several fields of science apart from mathematics, including celestial mechanics, fluid mechanics, and the philosophy of science. In 1879 he received a doctorate in mathematics from the University of Paris, having completed his thesis on differential equations. The publication of his ***Analysis Situs*** in 1895 placed him as the originator of algebraic topology. Throughout his life he continued to make important contributions to mathematics, including the introduction of the fundamental group for homotopy theory, presented in his 1894 paper, which distinguished the different categories of two-dimensional surfaces.

Poisson, Siméon-Denis (1781–1840). French mathematician, geometer, and physicist who studied differential equations, definite integrals, probability, electromagnetic theory, pendulum mechanics, resistant mediums, and the theory of sound. His most important contributions to pure mathematics were the advances he made in relation to **Fourier** analysis and his research on definite integrals.

Poncelet, Jean Victor (1788–1867). French engineer and mathematician who served most notably as the commandant general of the École Polytechnique. He was a founder of modern projective geometry along with Joseph Gergonne; both simultaneously discovered the field. His work on conics with the pole and polar lines led to the principle of duality.

Pont d'Iéna. Multiple arched bridge over the Seine River in Paris, connecting the **Eiffel Tower** district to the Trocadero district. Built upon orders from Napoleon I in 1807 to overlook the Military School and commemorate his 1806 victory at the Battle of Jena.

Posidonius (ca. 135–ca. 51 BCE). Ancient Greek and Stoic philosopher; teacher to Cicero. He was one of the most important contributors to Stoic philosophy, appending to it many of **Plato**'s previous teachings. He was also a brilliant scientist, astronomer, and historian, and is credited with continuing the histories of Polybius.

Prince and the Pauper, The. Novel by Mark Twain first published in 1881; the story of two boys who look identical but lead very different lives—one is a prince and the other a pauper. Their journeys begin when they meet and temporarily exchange roles.

Prince Nicholas, a.k.a. Nicolae Brana (after 1937) (1903–1978). Prince of Romania, son of King Ferdinand I and Queen Marie. He was stripped of his royal rank by the crown Council in 1937, thus becoming Nicolae Brana. He held the title, among many, of Holy Savior of Greece.

Princet, Maurice (1875–1973). French insurance actuary and mathematician. He was a close friend of **Picasso** and of those in Picasso's artistic circle. It was probably Princet who introduced the importance of geometry to Picasso, as he used to read and lecture to him on mathematical topics. He is widely considered to be "the mathematician of Cubism."

Procopius II (1837–1902). A tyrannical archbishop of Athens, he was considered by many to be the main cause behind the revolts of 1901 in which eight people were killed and much property was destroyed. These riots were triggered by the publication of the Demotic Greek translation of the New Testament; Procopius had acted as advocate to **Queen Olga** in her push to have the scriptures newly translated and published. The king forced the resignation of Procopius, and within two days the entire papal Cabinet resigned as well.

Prussia. A former influential country in the Germanic region of northern Europe, Prussia was a significant military and cultural power in the eighteenth century, leading to the formation of a unified German empire in 1871. Taking up more than half of contemporary Germany, Prussia was the region's most industrial and politically active center until it was formally abolished and divided in 1947 as a symbolic strike against German World War II militarism and aggressive culture.

Ptolemy's geocentric model. In his treatise *Almagest,* Ptolemy (ca. 100–164 CE) presented a model of the universe in which the Earth was immobile at the center and all other celestial bodies (including the Sun) orbited around it in a circular motion. This model was universally accepted until Copernicus, **Galileo**, Kepler, and **Newton** established the heliocentric model of the universe, in which planets orbit around the Sun.

Pythagoras of Samos (ca. 575–495 BCE). Pre-Socratic philosopher, mathematician, cosmologist, and revered by followers as a sage. He left Samos during Polycrates' tyranny and made his home in Croton, then Metapontum. He is one of the most important and influential historical figures, and it is due to him and his followers that mathematics had such great influence on many philosophical works.

Pythagoreans. The students and followers of **Pythagoras** and the Pythagorean School. Their belief system was dominated by mathematics, but it was also profoundly mystical. Followers had to adhere to specific rules and initiation practices, such as abstaining from eating beans and taking vows of silence. For many years, they made up an influential section of the philosophic and mathematic communities, and are considered a main inspirational source for **Plato** and Platonism.

Pythia. The priestess of the Delphic Oracle, the shrine to Apollo located at Delphi, and the religious center of the ancient Greek world. She was the prophetess of the messages she obtained directly from Apollo and was the most important oracle in ancient Greece. Her last prophecy was given in 393 CE to Emperor Theodosius I. Messages delivered by the Pythia, often ambiguous, were translated by a priest, and the Greeks lived by them; great wars, empires, and lives were lost and won because of the oracle. Engraved on the outside of the temple are the phrases: "Know thyself" and "Nothing in excess."

quadratic equation. An equation in which the variable appears raised to powers up to and including the second, for example: $3x^2 + 2x - 2 = 0$.

Queen Olga, Olga Constantinovna of Russia (1851–1926). Wife of **King George I** of Greece. They married in 1867, when she was only sixteen years old, and went on to have eight children. Olga was a direct descendant of Euphrosyne Doukaina Kamatera, the Empress of the Byzantine Empire (ca. 1155–1211 CE). It was her personal initiative to have the Bible translated into Demotic Greek rather than Koine Greek; her goal was to publish a translation of the scriptures that could be more widely understood. The campaign backfired, however, resulting in riots and heavy opposition against the queen, her translator **Alexandros Pallis**, and **Archbishop Procopius II**.

raki. Traditional Turkish alcoholic beverage made in Anatolia, most commonly made from raisins and regional fruits.

Ravachol, a.k.a. François Claudius Koeningstein (1859–1892). French anarchist and terrorist. He carried out three bombings against political and judicial leaders. He was captured by means of an informant on March 30, 1892, for his bombings at the Restaurant Véry. He was condemned to life in prison at his first trial, but soon after, at a second trial regarding three murders, he was sentenced to death. Ravachol has since become a legendary figure symbolizing desperate revolt.

Renoir, Pierre-Auguste (1841–1919). French artist who became one of the most famous Impressionist painters. He had a lifelong passion for art, and even when he was unable to hold a paintbrush as an old man, he would strap a brush to his arm, forcing his arthritic limb to continue his passion. He studied art in Paris as a young man and later befriended another famous Impressionist, Claude Monet. Many of his paintings are some of the most expensive today, worth over 70 million dollars, and all of his work is held in very high esteem worldwide.

Reynaud, Charles-Émile (1844–1918). French science teacher, responsible for the first animated films. He created the Praxinoscope in 1877 and the Théâtre Optique in December 1888, and on October 28, 1892 he projected the first animated film, Pauvre Pierrot, at the Musée Grévin in Paris.

Riemann hypothesis. A complicated mathematical conjecture concerning the distribution of primes and involving complex numbers. It to this day one of the most challenging mathematical problems. The Clay Mathematical Institute offers $1,000,000 to anyone who comes up with its solution. Detailed information on the problem can be found in Marcus du Sautoy's *The Music of the Primes* (2003) and John Derbyshire's *Prime Obsession* (2003).

Riemann, Georg Friedrich Bernhard (1826–1866). German mathematician who made important contributions to analysis and differential geometry, some of them paving the way for the later development of general relativity. In 1854 he gave a presentation at Göttingen with the title *Über die Hypothesen welche der Geometrie zu Grunde liegen* ("On the hypotheses which underlie geometry"), which was published in 1868. His revolutionary ideas generalized the geometry of surfaces, which had been studied earlier by **Gauss**, **Bolyai** and **Lobachevsky**.

Riemann's geometry. Riemann proposed a geometric model in which there is no concept of parallels. Imagine a universe limited to the surface of a sphere. The lines would be the circles and would always intersect. The model was proven to be non-contradictory and was used by Einstein in his general relativity theory.

Rousseau, Théodore (1812–1867). French painter famous for his landscape renderings. He became successful at the early age of nineteen, when his work was accepted for the first time by the Paris Salon. He later became a close friend of Jules Dupré, another landscape artist, who had a great deal of influence on him. Though Rousseau enjoyed success throughout his artistic career, he was at the same time one of the most highly criticized artists of his day.

Royalists/Liberals. Ultra-partisan factions during the time of the National Schism in early twentieth Greek history, mainly revolving around the tensions created by the monarchy—supported by the Royalists—being questioned in its decision making and power by more liberal, democratically inclined statesmen supported by the Liberals.

Russell, Bertrand (1872–1970). British philosopher, historian, logician, mathematician, advocate for social reform, and pacifist. He won the Nobel Prize for literature in 1950. He was schooled at Cambridge, where he acquired a First Class degree with distinction in philosophy and was elected as a fellow of his college in 1895. While attending the 1900 International Congress of Mathematicians in Paris, he became highly interested in the mathematical field. He researched the works of **Peano**, who had made a considerable impression upon him at the conference, and by 1903 he had written his first major book, *The Principles of Mathematics*, co-authored by **Alfred North Whitehead**. He continued to write a number of important works throughout his life on mathematics, philosophy, and politics.

Russell, John Lord (1792–1878). Prime minister of Great Britain and grandfather to **Bertrand Russell**. He was very active in his political career, initiating many bills and reforms, including the bill for the repeal of the Test and Corporation Acts, which prohibited Catholics and Protestant non-conformists from holding office, and the Catholic Relief Bill, which later resulted in Catholic Emancipation. Lord Russell also enacted other reforms that greatly improved civil documentation and civil liberties.

Russian Revolution (1917). The Russian Revolution consisted of a series of revolutions and events that caused the historic, dynamic change in Russian society and government, ultimately leading to the replacement of the old Tsarist autocracy with the Soviet Union.

Sacré Coeur Basilica (Church of the "Sacred Heart"). Roman Catholic church and popular tourist destination in Paris. Located at the summit of **Montmartre**, the highest point in Paris, it is known for its perpetual adoration of the Blessed Sacrament on display there as well as its patriotic significance.

Sainte-Pélagie prison. Prison in Paris, operational from 1790 to 1895. Famous inmates included the Marquis de Sade and **Évariste Galois**.

Salmon, André (1881–1969). French writer and art critic who was a major defender of Cubism through all its stages. He embraced the bohemian lifestyle, living in the Bateau-Lavoir along with **Picasso**, **Max Jacob**, and **Guillaume Apollinaire** and forming the unprecedented artistic group of the Parisian Bohemia. He took on his journalism career full force around 1909 and went on to pen numerous reviews, poems, and literary pieces. In 1964, the French Academy presented him with the Grand Prix award for poetry.

Sardou's *Tosca*. 1887 drama by semi-successful French playwright Victorien Sardou (1831–1908) written for the actress **Sarah Bernhardt**. His most famous work, the play is set in Rome in mid-1800, and it deals with contemporary issues of the politically charged time.

Schinas, Alexandros (1870s–1913). Greek anarchist and assassin of **King George I** of Greece. Schinas shot King George I from behind, only two feet away, while the king was walking in Thessaloniki; the king was dead before reaching the hospital. Schinas was imprisoned and tortured, whereupon he admitted to being a Turkish agent. He fell to his death from a police station window six weeks later. The assassination outraged the Greek government and her allies in the Balkan League, and they immediately declared war on Turkey.

Schulze, Franz Eilhard (1687–1744). German professor and anatomist who was the first to discover that certain silver salts had adverse reactions when in the presence of light. This discovery, when partnered with the camera obscura, would ultimately lead to the process of capturing an image and fixing it.

Siegfried. The mythical hero in the German *Nibelungenlied* and Wagner's operas *Siegfried* and *Götterdämmerung*. The character came from Norse mythology, in which he is named Sigurd, and it is from him that the Norwegian royal family claims its descent. The Siegfried line is also the name given to the 400-mile defense system built and used by the Germans in World War I and World War II.

Socrates (469–399 BCE). Ancient Greek philosopher considered one of the founders of Western philosophy. He strongly influenced **Plato**, who was his student, and **Aristotle**, whom Plato taught. His most important contributions were to the field of ethics, but he also lent his name to the concepts of Socratic irony and the Socratic Method, or elenchus. He was famously accused and found guilty of corrupting the minds of the Athenian youth, and, although given opportunity to go into exile, he preferred to stay in the city, which sentenced him to death by drinking hemlock. An account of his trial is given in Plato's dialogue, *Apology*.

Sophia, Princess of Prussia (1870–1932), marriage to Constantine I. Constantine and Sophia, actually third cousins by descent, were married October 27, 1889. Sophia caused turmoil in 1890 when she announced her decision to convert to Greek Orthodoxy. She was thrown out of Germany, barred from entering the country, and promised by her former family and faith that she had condemned herself to eternal damnation. The couple was noted not only for their political affiliations, but also for the strange and sometimes bizarre events that seemed to constantly surround them.

Sorbonne. College of the University of Paris, located in the Latin Quarter. The institution was created in 1253 by Robert de Sorbon, the chaplain of Louis IX, as an intellectual center of Roman Catholic religious thought. It became purely secular near the end of the nineteenth century.

squaring of the circle. Probably one of the oldest problems in mathematics: given a circle, construct a square with exactly the same area.

Theodosius of Bithynia (ca. 160 BCE–ca. 100 BCE). Greek astronomer and mathematician who wrote the *Sphaerics*, a book on the geometry of the sphere which provided the mathematics for spherical astronomy.

Theotokis, Georgios, resignation as Prime Minister (1844–1916). Known for his high morals and calm demeanor, Theotokis represented the New Party, serving as Prime Minister of Greece four times. Nevertheless, his support for the teaching of Demotic Greek in standard education and his involvement in the Gospel Riots forced his resignation in 1901.

Thesion. District in Athens named after the Doric temple Hephaestion (or "Thesion") located at the northwest side of the Agora, built at the same time as the **Parthenon**. In Greek mythology, Hephaestus, the son of Hera and Zeus, was a semi-comic figure who created weapons and other magical contrivances at huge furnaces operated by Cyclopes (he was the patron god of metalworkers). Remains of metal working factories and potter shops have been found around the temple, which was jointly dedicated to Athena Ergane, the patron goddess of pottery and crafts.

Thessaloniki, march of the Greek army into (October 26, 1912). One of the events that eventually led to the Second Balkan War and hostilities between Bulgaria and Greece. When the Greek army entered the city of Thessaloniki before the Bulgarian army, the Bulgarians requested that they be allowed a battalion to enter as well. However, the Bulgarians sent a brigade instead, giving cause for alarm to the Greek forces, who took this act of trickery as a plot to gain power.

Thiers, Government of. Administration of Louis Adolphe Thiers (1797–1877), French statesman, journalist, and historian. Following the overthrow of the Second Empire, Thiers came to prominence for leading the suppression of the **Paris Commune**. He served from 1871 to 1873 as provisional president before resigning due to a vote of no confidence in the National Assembly. He was noted for efficient economic policies, negotiating the Peace of Versailles with **Bismarck**, and the quick repayment of war debt to Germany. His insistence on a conservative republic alienated him in the political arena, however, and led to his dismissal.

Thrace. An ancient southeastern European country on the eastern part of the Balkan Peninsula, encompassing modern-day Turkey, north-eastern Greece and southern Bulgaria. In Greek mythology, Ares, the god of war, was said to reside in Thrace; his son Thrax was the Thracians' mythical ancestor. Homer also mentions Thrace in the *Iliad*. From 1300 to 600 BCE, the Thracians controlled a large area of the Balkan lands, before being reined in and conquered by various forces, including the Macedonians, Bulgarians, and Ottoman Turks. The area eventually set its modern-day borders around the World War I era.

Toulouse-Lautrec, Henri de (1864–1901). French post-Impressionist artist of many mediums born into an aristocratic family. He was born with a genetic disorder and broke both legs in his early teens, which never healed properly nor continued to grow after the fractures. Because of this, as a grown man Toulouse-Lautrec stood at only five feet and one inch tall. His exclusion from society drove him to immerse himself in his art, and the suffering and forced separation he endured influenced his art and life dramatically. As an adult, he spent his time in brothels and seedy venues in the company of bohemian artists, cabaret dancers, and prostitutes. His art depicted the flaws of society and of individuals with emphatic lines and color, personifying the grotesque reality he endured.

Treaty of Bucharest. Treaty signed in 1913 by Bulgaria, Romania, Serbia, Montenegro, and Greece signaling the end of the Second Balkan War.

tricolore ("three-colored"). French flag consisting of the three national colors red, white, and blue.

trigonometry (from the Greek words for "three," "angle," and "to measure"). Branch of mathematics that deals with triangles, and with the relationships between the sides and the angles of triangles, as well as with the trigonometric functions, which describe those relationships.

twin prime conjecture. Two prime numbers that differ by 2, for example, 3 and 5, 5 and 7, 11 and 13, 17 and 19, etc. There is an open debate as to whether there is an infinite number of such pairs.

Utrillo, Maurice (1883–1955). French painter born in **Montmartre**, Paris. He was encouraged to take up painting by his mother when he was diagnosed with a mental illness at the age of twenty-one. He specialized in cityscapes and was highly regarded by the time he was in his thirties.

van Gogh, Vincent Willem (1853–1890). Dutch post-Impressionist artist who pioneered the Expressionist form in art. He moved to Paris in 1886 to join his brother Theo, who became his main benefactor, and eventually met Camille Pissarro, Claude Monet, and Paul Gauguin. These master artists had a great impact on Van Gogh and led him to develop his colorful style for which he is now famous. Van Gogh produced over 2,000 works of art, but he is also well-known for cutting off his left ear after an argument with Gauguin. Van Gogh suffered from mental illness and depression after this episode and within two years he committed suicide.

Venizelos, Eleftherios (1864–1936). Greek politician who revolutionized many aspects of Greek affairs and served as prime minister of Greece numerous times. He is widely regarded as the "father of modern Greece." His reorganization of Greek society and the military greatly aided the Greeks and profoundly affected the outcome of both the Balkan Wars and World War I. Nevertheless, his policies caused a standing conflict between the **Royalists** and his own supporters, the Venizelists. His defeat in the 1920 elections led Greece to defeat in the Greco-Turkish War. He would later regain his position and help in the restoration of Greek foreign affairs, but his retirement led, once again, to the decline of the republic.

Venizelos' party. Followers of active Greek statesman and revolutionary **Eleftherios Venizelos**. Party members were rivals of the **Royalists** during Greece's National Schism in the 1910s over the extent of the monarchy's power in national affairs. Venizelos gained popularity by making constitutional, military, and financial reforms and by strengthening the Greek union through several epochal wars. His party relied on anti-Royalist, anti-conservative platforms, taking after idealized Western democratic theories. The party began to factionalize and revamp after significant electoral defeats in the 1920 elections, due mainly to war-weariness on the part of the general public.

Verne, Jules (1828–1905). French scientist and author who pioneered the science fiction genre in literature. He is most famous for the novels *Journey to the Center of the Earth* (1864), *Twenty Thousand Leagues Under the Sea* (1870), and *Around the World in Eighty Days* (1873). He became close friends with **Alexandre Dumas**, *père,* and gained writing advice from him as well as from Victor Hugo.

War of '97, a.k.a. The Thirty Days' War. The war of 1897 was fought between Greece and the Ottoman Empire regarding Ottoman rule in Crete. The Greeks ultimately lost the war, but the Turkish government was forced by European powers to release its conquests from the short war.

Weber, Louise (1866–1929). French cancan dancing sensation with the stage name La Goulue. She was known for her captivating and audacious dance routines. She became famous as one of the highest paid entertainers of her day when she headlined at **Le Moulin Rouge** nightclub for six years.

Whitehead, Alfred North (1861–1947). English mathematician who became a philosopher. He wrote on algebra, logic, mathematics, philosophy of science, physics, metaphysics, and education. He co-authored *Principia Mathematica* with his former pupil, **Bertrand Russell**, a seminal 3-volume work on the foundations of mathematics.

Wiles, Andrew (1953–). British mathematician who proved **Fermat's Last Theorem** in 1995.

Zeno of Elea (ca. 490–ca. 430 BCE). Pre-Socratic Greek philosopher who was a member of **Parmenides**' Eleatic School and famous for his paradoxes. Zeno, Parmenides, and Melissus of Samos are usually referred to as the Eleatic philosophers and they set a new standard for philosophical argument. Of Zeno's paradoxes, the most well known are the stories of Achilles and the tortoise, the arrow paradox, and the stadium paradox, which are all used to argue the impossibility of motion and/or plurality.

Zola, Émile (1840–1902). French author, journalist, and political activist. He is considered a fundamental leader of the naturalistic school of literature. While working as a political journalist he openly criticized Napoleon III. He played a key role in the exoneration of **Alfred Dreyfus**, which resulted in him being sentenced to jail for libel and removed from the Legion of Honor. He died at the age of 62 from carbon monoxide poisoning caused by a stopped chimney. His death has been attributed to his enemies, but there is no proven evidence to fortify the accusation.

Zut. French curse of general use and minimal offensive meaning; likened to the English "darn it" or "damn it/damn." It was also the name of the infamous hang-out of artists like **Toulouse-Lautrec**, **Picasso**, **Max Jacob**, and others in Picasso's gang.

Also Available from
ParmenidesFiction™

◆◆◆

THE ARISTOTLE QUEST:
A Dana McCarter Trilogy
by Sharon Kaye